THE END OF THE OCEAN

Also by Maja Lunde:

The History of Bees

MAJA LUNDE

THE END OF THE OCEAN

SCRIBNER

LONDON NEW YORK SYDNEY TORONTO NEW DELHI

Originally published in Norwegian as Blå by Aschehoug, Oslo, 2017

First published in Great Britain by Scribner, an imprint of Simon & Schuster UK Ltd, 2019
A CBS COMPANY

Published by arrangement with Aschehough Forlag

SCRIBNER and design are registered trademarks of The Gale Group, Inc.,
used under licence by Simon & Schuster Inc.

1 3 5 7 9 10 8 6 4 2

Simon & Schuster UK Ltd
1st Floor
222 Gray's Inn Road
London WC1X 8HB

Simon & Schuster Australia, Sydney
Simon & Schuster India, New Delhi

www.simonandschuster.co.uk
www.simonandschuster.com.au
www.simonandschuster.co.in

A CIP catalogue record for this book is available from the British Library

HB ISBN: 978-1-4711-7551-0
TPB ISBN: 978-1-4711-7552-7
EBOOK ISBN: 978-1-4711-7553-4
AUDIO ISBN: 978-1-4711-7555-8

Typeset by M Rules
Printed and bound by CPI Group (UK) Ltd, Croydon CR0 4YY

To Jesper, Jens, and Linus

SIGNE

Ringfjorden, Sogn og Fjordane, Norway, 2017

Nothing stopped the water. You could follow it from the mountain to the fjord, from the snow that fell from the clouds and settled on the peaks, to the mist that rose above the ocean and again became clouds.

The glacier grew every single winter; it accumulated snow, every winter it grew as it should and every summer it melted, releasing drops, drops that became streams, flowing downwards, driven by gravity, and the streams joined other streams, becoming waterfalls, rivers.

We were two villages that shared a mountain and a glacier and we'd had them for as long as we could remember. One side of the mountain was a vertical wall, where the Sister Falls descended; they crashed straight down for 711 meters towards Lake Eide, a deep green body of water after which the village Eidesdalen was named and which provided fertile growing conditions there for animals and human beings.

Eidesdalen, Magnus's village.

They couldn't see the fjord in Eidesdalen; they weren't accustomed to having the taste of salt on their lips, the salt was not carried by the wind and they could not smell the ocean, but they had their water, the water without taste, the water that made everything grow, and later Magnus said that he had never missed the ocean.

On the other side of the mountain it was milder, less harsh. Here the water accumulated in the River Breio, the salmon river, the water ouzel's river, the freshwater mussels' river. It forced its way through a crevasse in the landscape, forming this chasm with millions of drops every single second, in waterfalls, in streams and in calm, smooth stretches. When the sun shone, it became a luminous ribbon.

The River Breio continued all the way to Ringfjorden, and there, in the village at sea level, the river met with salt water. There the water from the glacier became one with the ocean.

Ringfjorden, my village.

And then they were together, the water from the glacier and the water from the ocean, until the sun absorbed the drops once more, drew them up into the air as mist, to the clouds where they escaped the force of gravity.

I'm back now. Blåfonna, the glacier that once was ours, has forced me to return. There is no wind when I reach Ringfjorden, I am obliged to use the engine to travel the final stretch, and the clattering sound drowns out everything else. *Blue* glides through the water and leaves only small ripples in its wake.

I can never forget this landscape. It has created you, Signe, Magnus once said. He meant it had imprinted itself in me, the way I walk with my legs slightly bent, as if I am always confronting a hill. Nonetheless I am surprised now when I see it again: the summits, the falls, the vertical meeting with the horizontal.

People travel here from far away to see this landscape and find the sight to be "beautiful, fantastic, amazing." They stand on ship decks as large as football fields while enormous diesel engines spew out exhaust fumes, stand there and point and gaze at the clear blue water, the bluish-green hillsides where fragile houses cling tightly to forty-five-degree-angle slopes, and more than one thousand meters above them are the mountains, the earth's stripped, sharp edges, breaking

love, "wow, it's snow," whether it's winter or summer.

But the tourists don't see the Sister Falls or Sønstebø's summer farms on the mountain, they have long since disappeared; they can't see the River Breio, which was the very first to go, before the ships arrived, long before the Americans and Japanese came with their telephones and cameras and telephoto lenses. The pipes are hidden underground and the damage inflicted on the wildlife by the excavation work has slowly been concealed by vegetation.

I stand there with the tiller in my hand, moving slowly as I approach the village. I pass the power plant, a huge concrete building all by itself down by the water; it is heavy and dark—a monument to the dead river and waterfall, from there the cables stretch out in all directions, some of them cross over the fjord. They have even received permission for that.

The engine drowns out everything, but I remember the sound of the power lines, the soft humming in wet weather, water against electricity, a crackling. It has always given me goose bumps, especially in darkness, when you can see how it sparks.

All four of the moorings for visitors at the wharf are vacant; it's too early for tourists and the moorings are used only in the summertime, so I can take my pick. I choose the spot furthest out, mooring the craft astern and at the bow, and put out a spring line to be on the safe side; the wind from the west could blow up without any warning. As I pull the throttle control completely astern, I can hear the reluctant gasps of the engine shutting down. I close the hatch to the saloon and place the bunch of keys in the breast pocket of my parka. Attached to the key ring is a big cork ball that ensures it will float and makes a small bulge over my stomach.

The bus stop is where it has always been, outside the consumer co-op. I sit and wait; the bus comes only once an hour. That's how it is here: nothing much happens and everything must be planned. I have just forgotten this after all these years.

Finally it appears. I am accompanied by a group of adolescents. They come from the high school that was built in the early 1980s—the new one, the nice one, one of the many things the village could afford. As they talk and talk about tests and homework assignments, I can't help but notice their smooth foreheads, soft cheeks; they are astoundingly young, without any marks whatsoever, without the traces of a life lived.

They don't even bother to glance at me. I understand them well. For them I am just an aging woman, a little shabby and unkempt in a worn-out parka, with gray locks of hair sticking out from beneath a knitted hat.

They have new, almost identical hats, with the same logo in the middle of the brow. I hasten to take off my own and put it in my lap. It is full of fuzz balls. I start picking them off one by one and my hand fills up with lint. But there's no point, there are too many of them to remove and now I don't know what to do with them, so I end up sitting there holding a soft mound in my hand. Finally, I drop it onto the floor. The wool floats weightlessly down the aisle, but the adolescents don't pay it any mind, and why should they look at a clump of gray lint?

Sometimes I forget how I look. After a while you stop caring about your appearance when you live on board a boat, but once in a great while when I see myself in a mirror on land, when the lighting is good, I am startled. Who is she, the person in there, who in the world is that skinny old biddy?

It is strange—no, surreal, surreal is the word—that I'm one of them, the old people, when I am still so completely myself through and through, the same person I have always been; whether I am fifteen, thirty-five or fifty, I am a constant, unchanged mass, like the person I am in a dream, like a stone, like one-thousand-year-old ice. My age is disconnected from me, only when I move does its presence become perceptible—then it makes itself known through all its pains, the aching knees, the stiff neck, the grumbling hip.

But the young people don't think about my being old, because they don't even see me. That's how it is, nobody sees old ladies. It has been many years since somebody looked at me. They just laugh youthfully and openly and talk about a history quiz they've just taken, the Cold War, the Berlin Wall, but not about the subject matter, just about what grades they got. And nobody mentions the ice, not a word about the ice, about the glacier, even though it should be what everyone is talking about here at home.

Here at home ... do I really still call it home? I can't fathom it, after having been away for almost forty years, no, soon fifty years. I came home only to clean up after a death in the family, to grieve the compulsory five days after the funerals—first my mother's, then my father's. A total of ten days is all the time I have spent here during all these years. I have two brothers here, half-brothers, but I hardly ever speak with them. They are my mother's boys.

I lean my head against the bus window, look at the changes. The area is more built-up, the buildings closer together, a new construction project consisting of white prefabricated houses with small windowpanes clings tenaciously to the hillside. The bus passes the indoor swimming pool; it has a new roof and there is a big blue sign at the entrance: Ringfjord Water Fun. Everything sounds better in English.

The bus climbs upwards, inland. A couple of the young people get off at the construction site at the top, but most of them remain seated. We ascend, the road changes, narrows, becomes full of potholes, at almost the exact same time as we drive into the neighboring municipality. This is where most of the young people get off. Apparently they still don't have a high school out here, still don't have an indoor swimming pool, here in the town of Eidesdalen, the little brother, the loser.

I get off with the last of the young people, stroll slowly through the center of the village. It is even smaller than I remembered. The general store has been shut down. While Ringfjorden has grown, Eide is a fraction of its original size … but it's not for Eide's sake that I have come today, I can't cry for Eidesdalen anymore—that battle is over, it ended many, many years ago. It is now the ice that has brought me here, Blåfonna, and I take the dirt road leading to the mountain.

Even the national newspapers write about it, I have read the articles again and again, and can hardly believe the words. They are extracting ice from the glacier—pure, white ice from Norway—and marketing it as the most exclusive ingredient, to be put in a drink, a floating mini-iceberg, surrounded by golden liquor, but not for Norwegian customers, no, for those who have really deep pockets; the ice is to be shipped to desert nations, the homes of oil sheiks, and there it will be sold as if it were gold, white gold, to the wealthiest of the wealthy.

It starts snowing, winter's final spasm, April's way of thumbing its nose, as I climb towards the mountain. There are little pools of frozen water on the road, rimmed with crystals. I put my foot down against the thin surface ice covering a small puddle, shatter it, hear it break, but it's no fun any longer, not the way it once was.

I grow short of breath. It's steep and further than I remembered.

But I finally reach it, finally I see the glacier. Dear, dear Blåfonna.

All glaciers melt, I know that, but nonetheless it's something else witnessing it. I stop, just breathe; the ice is still there, but not where it used to be. When I was a little girl, I walked from the edge of the glacier almost all the way to the mountain cliff where the waterfalls disappeared below, where the glacier and the waterfalls were connected. But now the glacier is located high up on the mountainside. It's a long way, a hundred meters perhaps, between the cliff and the blue tongue. The glacier has moved, as if trying to escape, get away from humans.

I continue climbing through the heather. I have to feel it, have to walk on it, touch it again.

Finally I have ice under my feet; every step makes noise, a

slight crunching sound. I keep going, and now I can see the extraction area, the gouges in the grayish-white glacier, and deep gashes in the blue interior where the ice has been cut away. Beside it there are four large white bags that are full, ready for pick-up. They use chainsaws, I've read, chainsaws that are not lubricated, so the pieces of ice won't be sullied by oil.

Nothing should surprise me anymore, all the things human beings do. But this, this nonetheless tears something open inside of me, because Magnus must have sat at a board meeting and smilingly approved this, maybe even applauded it.

I walk closer. I have to climb to come right up against it, as the gouges were made where the glacier is the steepest. I take off one mitten, place my hand against the ice; it is alive beneath my fingers—my glacier, a huge, calm animal that sleeps—but it is a wounded animal, and it can't roar, it is being drained minute by minute, second by second, it is already dying.

Too old to cry, too old for these tears, but nonetheless my cheeks are damp.

Our ice, Magnus, our ice.

Have you forgotten about it, or did you perhaps not even notice it, that the first time we met, it was with melting ice from Blåfonna in our hands?

I was seven, you were eight, do you remember? It was my birthday and I was given a present of water, frozen water.

*

All of life is water, all of life was water, everywhere I turned there was water. It gushed from the sky as rain or snow, it filled the small lakes in the mountains, lay in the form of ice in the glacier, it flowed down the steep mountainsides in thousands of small streams, accumulated into the River Breio, formed a flat surface in front of the village in the fjord, the fjord which became the ocean when you followed it west. My whole world was water. The ground, the mountains, the pastures were just teeny tiny islands in that which actually was the world and I called my world Earth, but thought that it should actually be named Water.

The summer was so hot, as if we lived somewhere else entirely, the heat didn't belong here and the English tourists staying at our hotel, how they sweated, sitting outside in the big garden under the fruit trees, fanning themselves with old newspapers. They said that they never imagined that it could be so hot here up north.

When I awoke, the bed was empty, Mommy and Daddy were already up. I used to sleep between them; during the night I tiptoed into their room and lay down in the middle of the double bed. They asked if I'd been dreaming, but that wasn't why.

"I don't want to be alone," I said. "I want to be with somebody."

They must certainly understand that; they slept here with somebody every single night, but regardless of how many times I came in, they didn't understand. Every single evening when I went to bed, they reminded me that I had to sleep in my own bed, all night, not just half the night. I said that I would, because I understood that was what they wanted me to say, but then I woke up anyway. Every night I sat up and felt how empty the bed was, how empty the room was, and then I tiptoed in, no, I didn't tiptoe, young children are no good at tiptoeing and especially not me. I just walked, without thinking about how I was making noise, without worrying about waking them. I walked across the cold floorboards, into their room where I always climbed in from the foot of the bed, because then I could push my way down in between them without having to crawl across either of their big bodies. I never needed a duvet, because their bodies, on either side of my own, were warm enough.

But on precisely this morning I was lying in bed alone, they were up, but because it was my birthday, I couldn't get up to join them. I knew I had to lie there quietly, I remembered it from last year, that on your birthday you're supposed to lie still and wait for them to come, and the itchiness, I can still remember the itchiness, how it erupted in my arms and feet, the unbearable waiting, that it was almost not to be borne, that perhaps it would even have been better *not* to have a birthday at all.

"Are you coming soon?" I said cautiously.

But nobody answered.

"Hello?!"

I was suddenly afraid they wouldn't come, that they had gotten the day wrong.

"MOMMY AND DADDY?!"

Or that they'd forgotten all about my birthday.

"HELLO, MOMMY AND DADDY!!!"

But then they appeared, carrying a cake and singing. They stood on opposite sides of the bed and sang in their high and low voices, in perfect unison, and then all of a sudden it was too much, all of it. I had to pull the duvet up over my head and stay in bed even longer, even though I really wanted to get up.

When the song was over, I received presents—a shiny ball and a doll from Mommy, with a mouth that smiled a terribly broad smile.

"It's creepy," I said.

"No, it's not," Daddy said.

"Yes, it is," I said.

"I thought it was so cute when I saw it in the store and it was the biggest doll they had," Mommy said.

"They didn't need to make it with a smile like that," I said.

"You have to say thank you," Daddy said. "You have to say thank you to Mommy."

"Thank you," I said. "For the doll. That's creepy."

I always spoke my mind, said what I thought, and maybe they were irritated but never enough to try to make me change my behavior. Or maybe it wasn't all that simple to change it.

I remember the doll and the rest of the presents I received. I am pretty sure that I got all these things on this day: two books about flowers from Daddy; a herbarium, also from him; and a globe that lit up from both of them. I thanked them for everything. So many presents. I was aware that nobody I knew received as many, but nobody I knew had a mother who owned an entire hotel with almost a hundred rooms either. There were eighty-four, but we always said *almost a hundred,* and we also had our own private wing, we just called it the wing, with three living rooms and four bedrooms and a kitchen and even a maid's room.

She had inherited all of it from my grandfather, who died before I was born. There were pictures of him hanging everywhere, of old Hauger. Everyone called him that, even I did. Mommy had also inherited his name—Hauger, a boring name, but in spite of that, she kept it. She never took Daddy's surname, Daddy's Oslo name, because you can't just rid yourself of a name like Hauger, Mommy said. Then they would also have to change the name of our hotel, Hauger Hotel, and she couldn't do that, because our history was in the walls, all the way back to the year it was built, which was written above the entrance in numbers carved out of wood: 1882.

I was given cake, both in the morning and the rest of the day, so much cake that my stomach couldn't contain all the sweetness. I also remember that feeling, that I was seven years old and so full of cake that it felt like my chest would burst, but I kept eating all the same. Family members came by and they all sat together at a table in the garden—Mommy's entire family, Grandmother, the aunts, the two uncles by marriage, cousin Birgit and my three boy cousins.

The guests talked and carried on noisily, but I made the most noise because I couldn't sit still, not then, not later, and I had a loud voice that Daddy said could carry all the way to Galdhøpiggen. He always smiled when he said this, all the way to Galdhøpiggen, Norway's highest mountain, and he was happy that I shouted so much, he said, proud of it, but Mommy was of another opinion, she said that my voice cut right through to the bone.

I made so much noise that I didn't hear the truck. It was only when Mommy asked me to come to the courtyard that I realized that something was up. She took my hand and led me around the corner, while she waved at the guests and said that they had to come, too. She laughed in their direction, at me, and there was something unusual about her laughter— she laughed the way I usually laughed, wildly and a little too loudly, and I laughed as well, because I felt that I had to.

I turned around and looked for Daddy. I found him, way in the back of the crowd of guests, alone. I wanted to hold his hand instead, but Mommy was pulling too hard.

Then we turned the corner and I jumped, didn't understand what I saw. The entire courtyard was white; the light reflecting off it sparkled, making me squint.

"Ice," Mommy said. "Snow, winter—look, Signe, it's winter!"

"Snow?" I said.

She stood beside me and I could tell that something about this was important to Mommy, something about the snow, which was actually ice, but I didn't understand what and now Daddy had also come over to stand beside her and he wasn't smiling.

"What's this?" Daddy said to Mommy.

"Do you remember," Mommy said to me, "that you said you wished your birthday was in the winter?"

"No," I said.

"That you cried when Birgit had her birthday and it snowed?" Mommy continued. "And you wanted a snowman, do you remember?"

"Have you driven it all the way down from the mountain?" Daddy said to Mommy, and his voice was hard.

"Sønstebø brought it for me, he was going to pick some up for the fish-landing station anyway," she answered.

I turned around and noticed Sønstebø, the farmer from Eidesdalen, standing beside the truck, looking at me and smiling. I understood that he was waiting for something, waiting for me, and behind him stood his son, Magnus.

There you were, Magnus. I knew who you were before, because your father sometimes came with ice on his truck and then it happened that you were with him, but nonetheless, I think of that moment as the first time I saw you. You stood there, barefoot, your feet brown from the sun and dirt, and you were waiting for something—like all the others, you were waiting for me. You reminded me of a squirrel, with round, brown eyes that noticed everything. You were just eight years old, but you noticed that something was at stake, I believe, something that wasn't said, that somebody needed you, or would come to need you. That's how you were. That's how he was.

"So Sønstebø had to make an extra trip?" Daddy said softly. "All the way from the mountain?"

I hoped that he would put his arm around Mommy, the way he did sometimes, put it around her and squeeze her against him, but he didn't move.

"It's Signe's birthday, she wished for this," Mommy said.

"And what does Sønstebø get in return?"

"He thought it was fun. He loved that I wanted to do it, he loved the idea."

"Everyone loves your ideas."

Then Mommy turned to face me. "You can make a snowman, Signe. Wouldn't you like to do that? We can make a snowman, all of us!"

I didn't want to make a snowman, but nonetheless, I said yes.

I slipped in my good shoes and almost fell, my balance was off on the white surface she called snow, but Mommy grabbed hold of me and kept me on my feet.

The moisture and the cold penetrated the soles of my shoes, hard granules of ice spilled across my feet and melted against my thin knee socks.

I bent down, took a fistful of snow in my hands and tried to make a snowball, but it was like pearl sugar, it just disintegrated.

I looked up and everyone was watching me, all the party

guests were watching. Magnus stood completely still; only his eyes moved, his gaze went from the snow to me and back again. He had never received snow for his birthday, it was probably only hotel daughters who received that and I wished he wasn't here to see this.

But Mommy smiled, smiled as broadly as the doll, the largest in the store, and again I tried to make a snowball. I had to manage it, there had to be a snowball, I had to make a huge snowman, because I didn't remember that I'd wished for a winter birthday, I couldn't remember that I had ever spoken with Mommy about this, or that I had cried on Birgit's birthday. But I had, and now Daddy was angry with Mommy. Maybe I had said that I wanted a doll, too, and forgotten about it. It was my fault, all of this, that I was standing here and that my feet were so exceedingly cold, with ice water dribbling through my fingers, that everyone was standing here and behaving oddly around me, that the dry courtyard was turning muddy and vile, that Daddy looked at Mommy with a gaze that I didn't understand, and that he put his hands down into the pockets of his trousers in a way that made his shoulders narrow, and that Magnus was here. I wished with all my pounding, seven-year-old heart that he hadn't seen me like this.

That's why I lied. For the first time in my life I lied. Some children can lie, they do it without thinking twice. It's easy for them to say that they didn't take the cookies from the jar or that they lost their workbook on the way home. But

I wasn't that kind of child, just like I was never a child who liked to imagine things; make-believe games and pretend worlds were not for me, and maybe for that reason, neither was lying. I had so far in my life not been in situations where I needed to lie, and I had also never considered the idea that it was actually possible, that a lie could solve something.

But now I did it, the lie pushed its way forward, because it was my fault, all of this, I thought, with cold toes and wet knee socks, with my chest full of cake rising towards my throat, my mouth, and I had to stop the look in Daddy's eyes, that's why I lied, I had to get him to take his hands out of his pockets and reach for Mommy.

I thought through the lie in a flash, made it up in my mind before I presented it. In a quiet voice I hoped sounded genuine, I said, "Yes, I remember it, Mommy. I wished for a birthday in the winter. I remember it."

And to make it really respectable, to make the lie fully plausible, I filled my hands with rotten pearl sugar snow and held them out to Mommy, to Daddy.

"Thank you. Thank you for the ice."

Now, I thought, now everything will certainly be fine. But nothing happened. One of the guests cleared his throat, softly. My cousin tugged at my aunt's skirt, peered up at her, but all the adults just looked at me and waited, as if something more was supposed to happen.

That was when he came, Magnus, his feet moving quickly against the ground from the truck, over to me.

"I'll help you," he said.

He bent down; the hair on his young boy's neck was close-cropped and his skin tanned. He took some ice between his hands and made a snowball that was much nicer than mine.

Those bare feet of his on the ice, it had to be freezing cold, but he didn't seem to care, because now we were making a snowman together, out of the rotting, melting snow, and I no longer noticed all the others around us, all those still standing there watching.

"We need a nose," he said.

"You mean a carrot," I said.

"Yes, a nose."

"But it's actually a carrot," I said.

And he laughed.

DAVID

Timbaut, Bordeaux, France, 2041

T he heat trembled above the road in front of us. It shim-
mered on the hilltop, like water, but disappeared as we
approached.

We still didn't see any sign of the camp.

Above us the sky was blue. Not a single cloud. Blue, always
blue. I'd started to hate that color.

Lou slept against my arm, rocking gently as the truck drove
over bumps in the asphalt. It had been a long time since anyone had done any road maintenance. The houses we passed
were abandoned, the fields dry and scorched brown by the sun.

I turned my face towards Lou, sniffed at her head. Her soft,
little-girl hair smelled of acrid smoke. The sour smell of fire
was in our clothes, too, even though it had been many days
since we left Argelès. Since we became half a family.

Twenty-two days—no, twenty-four. Already twenty-four
days had passed. I had lost count. *Wanted* perhaps to lose
count. Twenty-four days since we ran out of Argelès. Me with
Lou in my arms. She cried. I ran until we could no longer hear

the fire. Ran until the smoke was just a haze in the distance. Only then did we stop, turn towards the city and ...

Stop, David. Stop. We are going to find them now. They are here. Anna and August will be in the camp. Because this was where Anna wanted to go. She had spoken about the place for a long time. It was supposed to be decent. There was food here and electricity from solar panels. And, not least, there was water. Clean, cold water from a faucet.

And from this camp it was supposed to be possible to continue north.

The driver put on the brakes. He drove onto the side of the road and stopped. Lou woke up.

"There," he pointed.

In front of us was a military-green tarpaulin fence.

Anna. August.

The driver let us out. He mumbled "good luck" and drove away in a cloud of dust.

The air hit us like a hot wall. Lou blinked towards the sun, clinging to my hand.

The fireball in the sky sucked every drop of moisture out of me. The asphalt was burning. It was so hot it had to be on the verge of melting.

My phone was broken. My wristwatch had been bartered away. I didn't know what time it was. But the fence before me still cast a short shadow, so it couldn't be more than three.

I walked quickly. Now we would find them again. They had no doubt arrived here before us.

We reached the entrance. Two guards wearing military uniforms sat by a table.

They looked at us without seeing us.

"Papers?" one of them said.

"I'm looking for someone," I said.

"Papers first," the guard said.

"But—"

"Don't you want to go inside?"

I placed our passports in front of him, but left Anna's and August's passports in the bag. The guard didn't need to see that we had them. He would certainly only start asking questions.

He leafed quickly through the pages in my passport, stopped at the photograph. I was startled every time I saw it. The guy in the picture, was that me? Such round cheeks, almost chubby. Had the camera distorted my face?

No, that was just how I was at the time. Stout, not fat, merely in good health.

Or maybe normal, actually. Maybe that was how we all looked before.

He picked up Lou's, it was newer, but Lou grew so fast. The child in the passport could have been anyone. Four years old when the photograph was taken. Smiling. Not as serious as she is now.

I had braided her hair this morning. I was good at it. Brushed it and divided it into two identical halves, with a sharp parting in between. Then I quickly made two tight braids that hung down her back. Maybe it was because of the braids we had finally been picked up by a driver. Now I hoped they distracted people, so they wouldn't notice how dirty she was, and thin. So they wouldn't notice her seriousness—she seldom smiled, my child. Before, she was the kind of child who was always jumping, running, skipping. But now the braids just hung down her back, completely still.

The guard continued looking at me. Clearly he was comparing me with the photo in the passport.

"It's five years old," I said. "I was only twenty."

"Do you have anything else? Other papers that can confirm your identity?"

I shook my head.

"This was all I managed to take with me."

He looked at the picture one more time, as if it could provide him with answers. Then he took out a stapler and two light-green slips of paper. With practiced movements he stapled them on random pages in the passports.

"Fill this out."

He held it out to me.

"Where?"

"Here. On the form."

"I mean … where? Do you have a table?"

"No."

I took the passports. He had left mine open at the page with the green form.

"Do you have a pen, then?"

I tried to smile. But the guard just shook his head in resignation. His eyes did not meet mine.

"I've lost mine," I said.

That wasn't completely true. It wasn't lost, the ink was used up. Lou had been crying so much the other night on the road, sobbing softly with her face hidden in her hands. I let her draw. She drew thick blue lines of ink on the back of an old envelope we found on the side of the road. Drew pictures of girls in dresses and colored in the skirts. She pressed the pen down so hard that it made holes in the paper.

The guard rummaged through a box on the ground. He pulled out a battered blue ballpoint pen with a broken plastic casing. "I want it back."

I had to fill out the form standing up. I had nothing to lean the passport against. My handwriting came out wobbly and strange.

I tried to hurry. My hand shook. Occupation. Last place of work. Last place of residence. Where we had come from. Where we were headed. Where were we headed?

"The water countries, David," Anna used to say to me. "That's where we have to go."

The drier our own country became, the more she talked about the countries in the north, where the rain didn't just come once in a great while during the cold months, but also in the spring and summer. Where long-term drought didn't exist. But where instead the opposite was true: the rain was an affliction, arriving in storms. Where rivers flooded over and dams burst, abruptly and brutally.

"What are they crying about?" Anna said. "They have all the water in the world!"

Where we lived we had only the salty sea, which was rising. That and the drought. That was *our* flood. Relentless.

First it was called the two-year drought, then the four-year. This was the fifth year. The summer seemed to be without end.

People had started leaving Argelès back in the autumn of last year, but we stayed put. I had a job to attend to; I couldn't leave it, the run-down old desalination plant that converted the sea into fresh water.

But the power came and went, the stores were emptied of food staples and the city became emptier, quieter. And hotter. Because the drier the earth became, the hotter the air was. Previously the sun had applied its forces to evaporation. When there was no longer any moisture on the earth, we became the sun's target.

Every day Anna talked about how we should leave. First straight up north, while it was still possible, before everyone closed their borders. Then she talked about different camps. Pamiers, Gimont, Castres. This one near Timbaut was the last.

As she talked, the temperature rose. Refugees from even further south passed through our city, stayed a few days, traveled on. But we stayed.

I stood there with the pen in my hand. Where were we headed?

I couldn't answer this by myself. I had to find Anna and August first.

The man behind us in the line bumped into us, but didn't seem to notice. He was tiny and shriveled, like he didn't fill out his own flesh. There was a dirty bandage around one of his hands.

The guard quickly stapled the green form into his passport. The man accepted it without another word. He already had a pen in his hand and stepped aside to write.

It was my turn again. I gave the guard the passports and the forms with the ten pieces of information that were supposed to be everything he needed to know about Lou and me.

The guard pointed at the item at the bottom.

"And here?"

"We haven't decided yet. I have to speak with my wife first."

"Where is she?"

"We were supposed to meet here."

"Supposed to?"

"Will. We have agreed to meet here."

"We've been asked to ensure that something is written in all the fields."

"I have to speak with my wife first. I'm looking for her. I said so."

"Then I'll put England."

England, smack in the middle between south and north, still habitable.

"But there's no guarantee it will be England where we ..."

Anna didn't like England. Didn't like the food. Or the language.

"You have to put something," the guard said.

"So we won't be committed to it?"

He laughed a curt laugh.

"If you should be lucky enough to be granted residency, you must take whatever country you get."

He leaned over the form and wrote quickly: "Great Britain."

Then he gave me back my passport.

"That's everything. At night you must stay here, but during the day you can come and go as you please, both inside and outside the camp."

"Understood," I said.

I tried to smile again. I wished he would smile back. I could have used a smile.

"You'll be assigned a spot in Hall Four," he said.

"But where can I ask about my wife? And my son? He's just a baby. His name is August."

The guard raised his head. Finally he looked at me.

"The Red Cross," he said. "You'll see them as soon as you enter."

I wanted to give him a hug, but instead just mumbled, "Thanks."

"Next please," he said.

We walked quickly through the gate. I pulled Lou behind me. As soon as we were inside, I became aware of a sound.

Crickets. They were sitting in a tree above us, rubbing their wings together feverishly. There was no water, but nonetheless they kept at it, as energetically as hell, staying the course. That was perhaps how one should approach this. I tried breathing more calmly.

The camp consisted of some huge old warehouses spread out across a flat field. Big trees cast shadows. They still had leaves; the roots must go deep. A sign on the wall informed us that the place had once been an awning factory. "Sunshades for all your needs," it read. No doubt they'd done good business.

We continued walking through the camp. Between the buildings were a dozen or so military tents and just as many barracks. They were set up in straight lines and all of them had solar panels on the roof. There was no trash anywhere. People sat here and there, resting in the heat. Everyone was clean and wore clean clothes.

Anna had been right. This was a good place.

"There," I said, and pointed at a flag that was flapping on the roof of a barracks a short distance away.

"What country is that from?" Lou asked.

"It's not a country. It's the Red Cross," I said. "They know where Mommy and August are."

"Do they?" Lou said.

"Yes," I said.

Lou held my hand, with her dirty, sticky child's hand. Anna used to nag her about washing her hands. The same ritual took place before every single meal. *Remember to wash your hands, remember the germs.* If she could see Lou now.

We turned a corner, and Lou came to an abrupt halt.

"A line," she said softly.

Damn.

"We're good at that," I said, and tried to make my voice sound cheerful.

During the past year everything was rationed. We stood in lines for a gallon of milk. For a cut of meat. For a bag of apples, every other kind of fruit. The lines for fruits and vegetables were the longest. There were so few bees, so few insects. They had disappeared gradually, but when the drought came, the extinction rate accelerated. No insects, no fruit. I missed tomatoes. Melons. Pears, plums. Digging my teeth into a juicy plum. Cold from the refrigerator . . .

Lou couldn't remember a life without lines. And she was the one who had come up with the idea that we could *sit* in line, instead of *standing* in line.

The first time she sat down, it was from sheer exhaustion. She was whining. On the verge of tears. But when I sat down beside her and said we were on a picnic, she laughed.

Sitting in line had now become routine for us. The lines were a place for games. Outings in the country. School. Dinner parties. There were especially a lot of the latter. Lou loved games about eating.

I gave Lou a cookie, the last one I had in my bag. She crunched on it and smiled.

"There's like a yellow cream inside," she said, and showed me the dry, grainy cookie.

We kept playing through the first course, the main course, dessert and cheese. For a few moments I managed to think only about the game.

But mostly I looked for Anna. Waited. She could appear at any moment. Walk towards me with August in her arms. He would smile with his mouth open, showing his four teeth. And she would hold him out to me so I could take him, hold him while she hugged me, and Lou would also join in. All four of us would stand like that, together.

Then the door to the barracks opened and it was our turn.

The floor was clean; it was the first thing I noticed. A hard, wooden floor, without a speck of dust. There were several cables coiling across it. And it was cooler in here. A fan on the wall droned loudly.

A woman who was half hidden behind the monitor of a desktop computer smiled.

"Have a seat, both of you."

She pointed at two chairs in front of the desk.

I quickly explained our case: that the family had been split up when we left the south, but that we had agreed to meet here.

"It was my wife's suggestion," I said. "She wanted us to come here."

The woman started typing on the computer. She asked for the names and birth dates of both Anna and August, asked what they looked like.

"Look like?"

"Do they have any special characteristics?"

"... No ... Anna has brown hair. She's quite short." It suddenly sounded like I thought there was something wrong with her. "I mean ... relatively short. Five foot two, I think. And pretty," I hastened to add.

The woman smiled.

"She has brown hair that gets blonder in the summertime. Brown eyes," I said.

"And the child?"

"He's ... an ordinary baby. He has four teeth and still doesn't have much hair. Perhaps he has a few more teeth now, actually. He was cranky the last few days. I believe his gums were itchy."

What more should I say? That he had a tummy I liked to bury my face in? That he laughed loudly and shrilly? That he howled like a foghorn when he was hungry?

"When did you last see them?" the lady asked.

"When we left," I said. "The day we left Argelès, July 15th."

"The time of day?"

"Midday. Lunchtime."

Lou had stopped looking at me now. Instead she pulled her legs up beneath her, leaning her head towards her knees.

"What happened?" the woman said.

"What happened?" I repeated.

"Yes?"

Suddenly I didn't like her prying.

"What has happened to many people," I said. "We had to flee, were some of the last people to leave the city. And we got separated."

"Was that it?"

"Yes."

"And you haven't heard from her since?"

"How could I? The network is down. Telephones don't work. But I've tried. Otherwise I wouldn't be sitting here now!"

I drew a breath. I had to calm down, couldn't start screaming. Be positive. Show that I'm a good guy.

Besides, I liked the woman. In her fifties, a narrow face. She looked tired, working hard for others all day, that kind of tiredness.

"We agreed," I said as clearly and calmly as I could. "We agreed to come here. That was our plan."

She looked at the computer again and wrote something else.

"Unfortunately I can't find them registered here," she said slowly. "They're not here. And neither have they been here."

I looked at Lou—had she heard anything? Maybe not. She was sitting with her forehead against her knees, making it impossible to see her face.

"Can you check one more time?" I said to the woman.

"There's no need," she said flatly.

"Yes, there is," I said.

"David, listen—"

"What's your name?" I said.

"...Jeanette."

"OK, Jeanette. You probably have a family of your own. Imagine if we were talking about your people?"

"My people?"

"Your family. Your loved ones."

"I have lost somebody too," she said.

She had lost somebody too.

Of course she had lost somebody as well. Somebody she searched for, somebody she would maybe never see again.

"I'm sorry," I said. "What I mean is that you are the one with access to the records." I pointed at the computers. "Isn't that what you do? Find people?"

Find people. It sounded childish. I was a child for her, no doubt, a child with a child. I straightened up. Ruffled Lou's hair, tried to look paternal.

"We have to find Anna. She's her mother," I said. "And her brother," I hastened to add. She mustn't think that I'd forgotten about August.

"I'm sorry, but you've been separated for twenty-four days," she said. "Anything could have happened."

"Twenty-four days isn't that long," I said.

"Maybe they've ended up in another camp," she said, and now there was something comforting in her voice.

"Yes," I said quickly. "That must be what happened."

"I can put in a missing persons notice," Jeanette said.

She smiled again, really trying to be pleasant. And I responded, just as pleasantly: thank you, that was kind of you. I wanted to show her that I could do this too. I sat stiffly, holding my arms tightly against my body. I hid my elbows from her, hid the rings of sweat on my T-shirt. I looked at Lou again.

I still couldn't see her face. She was sitting just as stiffly as I was, with her face pressed against her knees.

Afterwards she had marks from her knees on her forehead where the fabric of her trousers had created a faint grid pattern on her smooth skin.

I didn't take her hand. I wanted to run. Scream. But I forced myself to walk calmly.

The crickets. They stay the course. They can take this.

I am a cricket.

SIGNE

I should fix something that needs fixing. On a boat there is always something to be taken care of, to be oiled, coiled, sealed, cleaned or secured. On a boat you never have time off. Or I should pay a visit to the hotel, say hello to my half-brothers. I should, I've hardly seen them since they took over the hotel. But all I do is sit here in the saloon drinking tea, unable to move. I have been home, here in Ringfjorden, for a full twenty-four hours now, and all I do is sit here listening.

The *rat-a-tat-tat* of the helicopters—the sound has been there since this morning, back and forth over the mountain, from the glacier to the defunct fish-landing station and back. The station has been reopened for this new business: there the ice is chopped and packaged before being shipped out.

The *rat-a-tat-tat* sound rises and falls, no longer a sound, something more physical, something lodged inside me. The vibrations shake the water of the fjord, the deck, and send shivers down my spine.

Maybe people in the village complain about this, maybe they write to the local newspaper, whining letters to the editor. Because they must have something to say, they must have some kind of opinion? I haven't spoken to anyone yet, haven't asked, but now I get up and go to the store.

I nod to the woman at the cash register, who doesn't appear to recognize me. And I don't remember her face either. I am one of the few people who left the village, one of the few who chose another life. Signe Hauger, the journalist, the author, the professional activist—people here have perhaps not read anything *by* me, but they have certainly heard *about* me. At least they've heard the gossip, even though that was many years ago, when I chained myself to a barricade in protest and was put in jail.

But she doesn't recognize me, no, because she nods back indifferently. I should ask her what she thinks about Blåfonna, about the helicopters. Most people like sharing their personal opinions. Perhaps I can engage her in some idle chatter; it's a strange expression *idle chatter*, as if small talk required no effort whatsoever. I don't have the strength for this kind of social banter, whether I know the other person or not. But today I'm going to ask about something specific, so that's different. All the same, I can't bring myself to walk straight up to her; that would seem strange, unnatural. I decide instead to wait until I pay for my groceries.

I start picking out the things I need: bread, juice, dishwashing liquid, canned goods, tea. As I'm doing so, the bell above the door jingles faintly. The door opens and two elderly women enter.

They engage in some chatter, though it's more zealous than

idle. They carry on as if they were being paid for it, but they're not talking about the helicopters or about the ice, apparently nobody is talking about Blåfonna. It takes me a while to realize who the women are; their voices give them away. We went to school together and they sound astonishingly similar to how they were when they were girls, the rising and falling intonations, the laughter.

I step out from behind the shelf—not saying hello would be foolish and maybe they know something about the glacier, maybe they actually care—but a word, a name, a flood of words causes me to stop.

Magnus.

They've started talking about him, and one of them turns out to be his sister-in-law. He has moved to France, she says with obvious envy, he only comes home for board meetings, is apparently not planning to step down as chairman of the Ringfallene Company yet. He loves that job, but is otherwise enjoying his retirement down there, playing golf and attending wine-tasting events. It is apparently wonderful, she actually uses that word, *wonderful*, and I stay put behind the shelf.

Wonderful. Yes indeed, I can imagine. I saw him once a few years back, from across the street in Bergen, he was on his way to a meeting, no doubt, he was wearing a suit, carrying a briefcase and an all-weather jacket, the standard uniform of Norwegian, adult businessmen. He didn't see me, but I had time to study him. A life of plenty had made a visible impact on him—the largest part of his body was his stomach. He had turned out like many others from our generation. An upholstered body in an upholstered existence, in our wonderful new world.

I wait until they have finished chatting, wonder whether they will say anything more about him, but now they seem to be talking about their own grandchildren, trying subtly to outdo one another with stories of these young people's achievements and the closeness of their bond, how often they see them and not least how much their adult children rely on them, the grandmothers, to keep the wheels of daily life turning smoothly. And they don't stop—one can apparently talk about grandchildren indefinitely. I sneak away from my basket, towards the door and open it carefully so the bell won't make too much noise.

I know that I love you, I used to say.

I love you, Magnus used to reply.

"Is the word love an absolute or does it have degrees?" I asked once.

We were lying close together in bed, as our heartbeats slowly calmed. I think we were at his place, we usually were.

"What do you mean?" he said.

"Are there degrees of love or is the word itself so strong that it's always absolute, always one hundred per cent?"

"You are at any rate the only person who can turn language's most emotional word into something theoretical," he smiled, stroking my arm.

"But if there are degrees," I said, "wouldn't the verb *know* make it stronger? Isn't my sentence actually stronger than yours, when I say that I know?"

"You mean that you love me more than I love you?"

"Yes. I think maybe that's true," I said, and snuggled up against him even closer.

"I don't believe that."

"*Know*. It adds a certainty to the expression that makes it stronger."

"You want me to take this seriously?"

"I want you to take everything I say seriously."

"Fine. Then I may as well say that it opens up room for doubt. The words *I know* allow for the possibility that a time, a period, a moment may arrive when you actually no longer know. And you also imply the opposite ... that the state of *I don't know* exists. And the downgraded *I believe*. While my version, on the other hand ..."

"Yes, let's hear about your version, my *beloved* Magnus."

"Three simple words, Signe. Three words that are a cliché. But also the truest, because I am not looking forward, or backwards or towards anything else but us."

"But you."

"What?"

"Anything else but you. You are not referring to anything but your own feelings," I said.

"Fine," he said.

"So you're saying that I'm qualifying my feelings?"

"I'm saying that I love you."

"Is that different from *thinking it*? You *think* you love me."

"Right now I *think* you wear me out."

"Words. Are. Important."

"Words. Are. Important. For. You."

"I am going to be a journalist," I said, and smiled. "So you'll have to learn how to live with it."

"You weren't planning to become a journalist when I chose you."

"It was in the cards, though."

"Maybe it was."

"And by the way, were you the one who chose me? Does the man choose the woman? The positive force choosing the negative? I always thought I was the one who chose you."

"Dear de Beauvoir. I give up. You chose me."

"Yes. I chose you."

"Can we go to sleep now?"

"Yes. Good night," I said.

"I love you," he said.

When I get back from the store, the helicopters are silent, but another sound has taken over. The sound of loading. A guy wearing overalls is driving a forklift back and forth from the fish-landing station to a small cargo ship in the harbor. Containers of ice are stacked on European pallets, and he lowers them on board. The forklift moves with careless, sharp movements; a solid banging sound can be heard

THE END OF THE OCEAN

when they strike the inside of the ship and disappear into the cargo hold.

Then there is silence, the forklift is parked beside the wall by the fish-landing station, everyone leaves the harbor and tomorrow the skipper will come, start the engine, take the ice, my ice, our ice, transport it south, to other countries, to people who have never seen a glacier, never held snow between their hands, and there it will melt in glasses, in drinks, there it will be destroyed.

Magnus doesn't need ice, he has his swimming pool and his plump wife Trine. She was already around when they were engineering students, I remember. I wonder if he fell for her already there and then, maybe even before we broke up. No doubt he has grandchildren who come to visit. He doesn't need ice cubes, probably only drinks red wine, Bordeaux, burgundy, Beaujolais, succulent drops with a fruity hint of plum. But nonetheless, he has signed off on this.

The cargo ship bobs in the water. The ice lies within; tomorrow it will be shipped away, tomorrow it will disappear.

Magnus is behind it; he doesn't have to be, yet he is, he is behind it and nobody cares.

I'm the only one who cares.

The cargo ship is right over there, no one is guarding it.

Magnus is responsible and I am alone in this—but I am the only one who can destroy it.

I am nearly invisible—a small, gray woman wearing a

knitted cap covered with fuzz balls, I am old, old as stone, like Blåfonna.

I can't destroy everything, but I can destroy this.

I can't shout about everything, but I can shout about this.

I can dump the ice in the ocean and disappear.

DAVID

Lou clung to me tightly as we walked from the Red Cross to Hall 4. Her sticky little hand did not let go of me. It felt like she had not let go of me since we left home. She never objected to anything, did everything I said and didn't let go.

Being alone with a child is like being a person and a half. It is completely different from being alone with a girlfriend. A girlfriend is just as old as you are, or almost anyway. She can satisfy her hunger pangs on her own. Make sure she's hydrated. Change her underwear. She can hold you, hold you tightly, support you. She can carry half the burden. When you're alone with a child you are always the one doing the holding.

The hall was located right behind the sanitary facilities. A huge, run-down factory, divided up into long corridors and small cubicles by old awning cloth that had been hung from the ceiling. Striped yellow, blue and red fabrics, cheerful colors.

There were beds in all the cubicles. Most of them were empty. The floor was clean and the doors were open; a refreshing draft cooled off the hall.

"Look," I said. "Number thirty-two. That's ours."

Our own little nook, with two military-green cots, a metal cupboard and a plastic box for storage. There were sheets on the beds and a bottle of antibacterial handwash for both of us. Maybe there wasn't enough water for hand washing.

"The walls are made of cloth," Lou said, and touched the striped awning cloth with her hand.

"Isn't it nice? Like a theatre," I said.

"No. Like a tent. It's like we're on a camping trip," Lou said, and finally let go of me.

"This can be our camping table," she said, and pulled the plastic box out between the beds. "And this is the tablecloth." She pulled her dirty handkerchief out of her pocket and placed it on top.

I tossed our bag into the cupboard. It occupied only half the space.

Everything we owned, in half a cupboard. I used to own an apartment, a small, flat-screen television, a cell phone, easily fifteen T-shirts, at least seven pairs of pants, eight pairs of shoes, a heap of socks that were never matched and folded in pairs, a table, four chairs, a couch, curtains, cutlery, two good knives, a cutting board, a bed, two children's beds, an entire shelf of books, a calfskin wallet, two potted plants that Anna took care of, three flower vases, bedding for four, a solid heap of towels, most of them faded from the wash, two warm jackets, three scarves, four hats, five caps, two half-empty bottles of sunblock, shampoo, dishwashing liquid, a dishwashing brush, a toilet-paper rack, cleaning bucket, mop, seven washrags, a changing table, diapers, moist towelettes, two floor mats, a poster with a picture of Manhattan before the last rounds of spring flooding, a wife, two children ...

I pushed the door to the cupboard shut.

In the cubicle opposite ours I caught a glimpse of the old man from the line. He was lying down with his face to the wall.

I started making up the beds. The mattresses were thin and wrapped in sticky plastic that smelled of disinfectant. One sheet underneath, one on top. No pillow. Lou could continue using her sweater for a pillow. She had done so during the days we were on the road. She liked rolling something up to put under her head when she slept.

At that moment the man in bed moaned. I could hear him writhing in pain. The bed emitted a metallic squeak. And he wailed. A soft whine of suffering.

I went out into the hallway between the cubicles. The man didn't notice me. Again he writhed in pain and turned his bandaged hand over.

I ventured into his cubicle. He didn't react as I drew close to him. The bandage was brown with filth and on one side of it there were yellow stains where puss had oozed out.

He smelled bad. Rancid and a little rotten. All of him or perhaps just from the hand.

He moaned again and opened his eyes, stared straight at me.

"Sorry," I said. "Didn't mean to disturb you."

He sat up. His movements were stiff, his eyes glassy with pain.

"Do you have any ..." he asked in French and held up his hand. "Something or other. Just so I can get some sleep?"

I shook my head and pointed at the bandage. "How long has it been since you had that changed?"

At first he didn't reply. He looked down at the filthy dressing.

"My daughter dressed it."

"Your daughter?"

"She's a nurse."

"But was that long ago?"

"I don't remember."

"It has to be changed."

Fortunately the man didn't object and let himself be led. I held Lou by one hand, and with the other I guided the man gently forward.

I asked where he came from. What his name was.

Francis, he mumbled in reply. He'd made his way here from Perpignan.

That made me happy.

"We're almost neighbors," I said. "We're from Argelès."

He didn't reply, perhaps didn't think it was very close, and he would be right about that.

Then we reached the first-aid barracks.

No line here. We were admitted immediately and welcomed by a nurse in a bleached white uniform. She smelled of soap.

The room was cool. The air dry. A box on the wall emitted a low humming sound; there was air conditioning in here as well.

Francis sank down into the chair she pulled out for him and placed his hand on her lap. We stood right behind him.

The nurse carefully loosened the bandage and he whimpered. There were tears in his eyes and his face twisted.

As the bandage was slowly unwound, the odor intensified, the stench.

"Go sit over there," I said to Lou.

For my own part, I couldn't refrain from watching.

The wound was deep and festering, more yellow than red, a long gash in his flesh. The color of the skin around it was a sickly color, grayish.

"Wait a minute," the nurse said, and left the room.

A little time passed. I tried talking to Francis, about Lou and me, about how we were supposed to meet my wife here.

He nodded in response, but said nothing about himself.

Finally the nurse returned with a doctor. They had clearly already conferred, because the doctor sat down with the man immediately, took his hand in his lap and studied the wound.

"How did you get this?" she asked softly.

The man looked away.

"I cut myself . . . on a saw."

"A saw?"

"I was going to saw some wood. Didn't have an axe."

"This is not a cut from a saw," the doctor said. "It will be easier for me to know what to do if you tell the truth."

He raised his head and gave her a look of defiance but suddenly relented. "A knife. Three weeks ago yesterday," he said loudly. "Three weeks and one day."

"You were lucky," the doctor said. "Had the cut been an inch or so higher up, it would have hit the aorta."

"Lucky?" Francis said, and I could hear him swallow. "I don't know about that."

"I'm going to give you antibiotics," the doctor said after a moment. "And you must come in every other day to have the wound cleaned."

"What's the point of that?"

"The antibiotics will get rid of the infection."

"And the point of that?"

"Of what?"

"Getting rid of the infection?"

"Do you want to lose your hand?"

He said nothing more.

The doctor surrendered her seat to the nurse, who poured disinfectant over the wound with expert hands and rubbed in an ointment.

Francis was no longer concerned about hiding his pain. Now he swore energetically.

"Hush. The child!" I said.

"Sorry," he said.

"That's OK," Lou said from her corner. "Daddy says things like that too."

Francis laughed.

But then the nurse brought another bandage which she wrapped carefully around his hand.

"It's too tight," Francis said.

"How's that?" the nurse tried.

"Still too tight."

"I'm loosening it now."

"It feels like it's stopping all the blood circulation. You're going to give me gangrene."

"It must be wrapped snugly."

"It must be that damn ointment. It stings."

"When you clean a cut, it's supposed to sting," Lou said softly from her corner.

He peered up at her. All of a sudden there was something boyish about him.

"You're right," he said. "I'd forgotten about that." He stared down at his hand wrapped in the white gauze bandage that contrasted sharply with his dirty skin, and said nothing more.

"Does it feel all right?" the nurse asked.

"Yes," he said. "All right."

Then he discovered the old bandage. It was lying on a steel tray on a table beside the nurse.

"What are you going to do with it?"

The nurse looked at him, uncomprehending.

"With the bandage?"

"What do you mean? The old one?"

"Are you going to throw it out?"

"Yes, of course."

Francis didn't reply.

"Look here," the doctor said, and handed him something blue in a transparent wrapper. "You can cover the bandage with this when you bathe."

He made no move to accept it, so I reached out my hand and took it for him.

"Are you relatives?" she asked.

"No, we just live in the same hall."

"Do you know whether he has anyone?"

I shook my head.

"Keep an eye on him, would you please?"

Francis moved sluggishly on our way back to the hall. As we walked away from the barracks his pace slowed more and more, until finally he stopped walking altogether.

"I just have to ..."

He didn't say anything else, but turned towards the first-aid barracks again. Then he walked quickly back and disappeared inside.

"What's he doing?" Lou asked.

"Wait outside," I said.

She released my hand and went to stand beside the barracks. I walked over to the door and opened it a crack.

The first thing I heard was a scratching sound. The room was empty—the nurse had left, but Francis was standing in a corner.

He was busy digging through a trash can and didn't notice

me. Then he evidently found what he was searching for. The old bandage. He quickly stuck it into his pocket with a furtive movement. I ducked away from the door and hurried back to Lou.

"What did he do?" she whispered.

But at that moment he came out. His steps were lighter.

"It feels better already," he said. He turned towards Lou and suddenly he smiled. "That's a good one you've got there," he said to me.

I pulled Lou close to me and nodded.

"Yes, she's a good one."

The first night in a bed in twenty-four days. When I closed my eyes, an image of the faces of Anna and August flashed through my mind. Then I fell asleep before I could think anymore.

But then the dreams came. Worse than before, maybe because I slept so deeply.

I was falling—no, sinking through water. Towards the bottom, and I let myself sink, I didn't struggle against it.

I would soon run out of air, my chest contracted, but nonetheless I did nothing to get back to the surface again.

I couldn't breathe. Mustn't inhale, mustn't fill my lungs, mustn't drown.

The surface above me, light blue, a shimmer of bubbles where I had fallen.

That is where I am headed. That is where I have to go.

But all I did was sink.

*

I woke up with a jerk.

Drew a breath. Filled my lungs. Air.

Around me it was light. It was morning already.

I turned over and lay in bed watching Lou as my breathing calmed.

She was sleeping on her back with her arms sticking out and her legs splayed in opposite directions, like a starfish. She was in constant movement. Took up room. Demanded space. When she was sleeping, she forgot to make herself small.

We'd had her far too soon. I knew we shouldn't have started having children so early. I was only nineteen years old, and Anna had just turned twenty. We blamed it on the water crisis, on the shortages that came along with it. Because everything was in short supply. Condoms as well. I was happy about that, that Anna blamed the crisis and not me, given that I had actually promised to pull out in time.

She asked me if we should get rid of it. If I was sure. She could manage, she thought, if I didn't want to have the baby.

And I didn't want to have the baby. But I didn't want to get rid of it, either. *Get rid of it*, like it was a thing. I got angry because she used those words. We argued. Her belly grew. We argued some more. Then it was too late.

Then there she was, the little child, pink and wrinkled up like a raisin, and the life I had had before suddenly felt like it had belonged to somebody else.

Morning sounds around us in the hall. Hushed voices,

footsteps, the igniting of a cooker, a bed creaking as some-body gets up.

I let Lou sleep. Her internal clock was turned upside down, she went to bed far too late in the evening.

I had been so strict about the bedtime business before, back when there were things to show up for—work, school.

But after the school closed, we started letting Lou stay up later. There was no reason not to.

I would straighten this out now. When Anna arrived, I would enforce a clearer schedule. Set bedtimes, set meal-times. Maybe we could also practice reading a bit. Maybe there were books here. She had missed out on many months of school already.

Lou's body twisted and she rolled over on her back. Her mouth opened, she was breathing rapidly, fearfully, her eyes were moving behind her eyelids. What does one dream about when one is a little girl who doesn't know how life will turn out?

She whimpered loudly. "No ..."

She twisted and turned again, her crying grew louder. It was so defenseless, so full of pain. The tears trickled out of her sleeping eyes.

"Don't ... Stop ... "

I leaned forward quickly and shook her.

"Lou, Lou?"

She turned away from me, still in the dream.

"You have to wake up, Lou."

I took her child's body, warm with sleep, into my arms, lifted her up. She resisted, as if she wanted to stay in there.

"Lou, please."

I stroked her hair, dried the tears on her cheeks.

Finally her eyes fluttered open. She stared up at me. For a second she was far away, and then suddenly she sat up, ready to run.

"It's burning, Daddy, it's burning!"

"Lou, no," I took hold of her. "No, sweetie, it was only a dream."

"But it smells of smoke. I can smell it. We have to get out of here!"

She turned towards her clothes, snatched up her shorts, started pulling them on.

I stood in front of her, bent my knees so my face was level with her own. Gently, I took hold of her shoulders.

"It's not smoke, sweetie. There's no fire."

"But I can smell it!"

I sat down. Pulled her up onto my lap, feeling how she tensed up all her muscles.

I held her tight. Spoke softly:

"Take a whiff, what do you smell?"

She sniffed quickly.

"Smoke."

"Try again."

She sat completely still, sniffed again.

"Smoke."

"Give it one more try."

She didn't sniff anymore. She just breathed more calmly.

"... Nothing," she said finally.

"Nothing," I said.

Her body was relaxed now.

I leaned my face towards her head. Sniffed. Yes, it smelled of smoke, but it came from her hair, her clothing. The way I also stunk.

"You know what we get to do today?" I said.

"No."

"We get to take a shower."

"A shower?"

"Yes. We get to shower every Tuesday."

"Is it Tuesday today?"

"Yes. So we get to take a shower."

"We need it."

"Yes. We need it."

Lou held the towel she'd been given with both hands. Then she opened it, like it was a present, the stiff creases from the folds still in place.

She lifted it to her face.

"It smells of soap."

I felt my own towel. The stiff fabric was rough against the skin. A clean, pure scent.

"You have to go there," I said, and pointed at the "Ladies" sign.

"And what about you?"

"I'm going to the men's shower."

She nodded. I could see that she didn't want to be alone, but she didn't make a fuss about it.

"Remember to wash your hair," I said. "Use one spurt to get it wet and then work it into a lather using both hands."

I demonstrated with my fists in my own hair. "And then you have to use the next two spurts to rinse it. Get all the soap out."

"I will."

"Remember that you only have three spurts. First one. Afterwards, two."

"And get all the soap out of my hair."

The shower had no heating unit, but the water from the first spurt was lukewarm anyway. It never really got cold in this heat.

The spray hit me on the back of my head, hammering against my skull. I tried to absorb the sensation of each individual drop against my skin, taking pleasure in every single one.

Then the spurt of water abruptly came to an end. I turned towards the shower head. A little water was still trickling out, less and less, until there was no more.

One tenacious drop hung there. Finally it dripped off the shiny head and fell to the floor. Then nothing more.

There was a soap dispenser on the wall. I was almost a

little moved by it, that someone had remembered that we needed soap, too.

I pressed it. Liquid soap in the palms of my hands. I rubbed my hands together, worked up a lather.

I washed myself thoroughly and for a long time. Hair, neck, hands, feet, crotch and behind.

The lather was slippery against my skin, removing all the grease. Removing the ash.

I had never been so dirty before, so sticky, so dry, so stinking of sweat. And smoke.

For a moment I didn't think of anything else, not even of Anna, not of August, just about the soap, the water, about how it was like getting my body back, shedding a layer of skin.

I did as I had told Lou to do, using the last two spurts to rinse my body. The soapy lather lay in soft heaps on the floor by my feet.

I quickly dried myself off. The rough towel felt good against my skin and turned a light-brown color when I rubbed my arms with it, massaging away dead skin cells.

Then I took my clothes out of the bag. They were just as dirty, just as smelly. I would have to ask if we could wash them, too.

Beneath the clothes were Anna's and August's passports. I picked up Anna's and held it in my hand, as I had done so many times in the past weeks. The cover was slippery beneath my fingers. I opened it.

Anna wasn't smiling in the photograph. It was black and

white, making it difficult to recognize her. You couldn't see that her hair had a golden tint. Or that there were green flecks in her eyes. Or that she had one of those quick strides, as if she were a bit busy and cheerful, even when she was feeling the opposite.

But it was the only photograph I had.

I lifted the passport to my nose, sniffed it. It still smelled of smoke.

I was clean now. Had washed the fire off me.

I had removed the memory of her when I washed the smell of smoke off me.

Abruptly I hugged the T-shirt against me, inhaling the acrid smell of smoke. She was still there, she and August. They were still here.

SIGNE

I take a shower in the cubicle between the saloon and the forepeak cabin, listen to the pump running, taking care not to splash too much on the bulkhead, directing all the water into the tub underneath me, because there is no drain in the room. My body feels quick and agile as I wash myself, primed, as if I were twenty years old again. Afterwards I fill up the tank with water from the faucet on the dock, as it must be completely full. I have to be able to stay away from land until they stop searching. To be on the safe side, I also fill up two 20-liter jugs and stow them in the afterpeak—enough water to be out at sea for weeks while they are searching, *if* they search, if they realize that I am responsible and they will perhaps do so, people in the village have seen me, know *Blue*, know my story. They can put two and two together.

During the final hour before the sun goes down and people leave the quay, I just wait, sitting on deck having a cup of coffee, forcing myself to eat calmly, a few slices of bread with peppered mackerel. The food tastes better than anything I've eaten in a long time; I chew slowly, looking at my father's old house. He lived down here by the harbor once upon a time, but now the house is empty. When he died, I sold it for a song to someone who wanted to use it as a vacation cottage. Apparently they aren't there much. The windows are dark empty squares.

The house is just as silent as the harbor, because now everyone has left and I am alone.

I jump ashore, walk towards the cargo ship, a heavy vessel of iron with patches of rust along the seam welds. I hop lightly from the quay down onto deck, landing almost without a sound.

The door to the wheel house is locked, but otherwise all the doors are open; they haven't even thought about locking up, can't imagine that something could happen here, deep in the bowels of the fjord. Bowels, something shameful, a dark *inside*, where nobody really cares, where everything that has meant something to us has slowly been developed, exploited, where the rivers, waterfalls and grazing lands have disappeared. Nobody cares. Neither do they care about Blåfonna being destroyed. They don't want to hear, don't want to see, they are like him, all of them, his entire generation, my generation, they just want better wines, larger vacation cottages, faster internet connections.

I go down into the cargo hold. It's cold, a freezer is humming, I find a switch, blink at the bright light, at the frost vapor from my own mouth, at the containers—they haven't been properly secured, have been left out on the floor. I walk over to the closest, stroke the hard plastic. They must be expensive, cast in one piece, shiny, royal blue, hard plastic. These will not decompose for 450 years, maybe 500 years, maybe even longer, longer than a plastic bottle, longer than a disposable diaper, a pair of sunglasses, a Barbie doll, a fleece-lined jacket. Much, much longer than any human being.

I open the top one, have to tug at the lid, it has already frozen shut and inside it is the ice, vacuum packed in an extra layer of plastic, protected by a thick lining of white insulation material; for a moment I run my hand across it, feeling the cold beneath my fingers, then I put the lid back in place.

The first one is surprisingly light. I carry it up the ladder, fling it towards the iron deck, feeling the reverberation under my feet when it lands. I don't worry about trying to be quiet, take the lid off all the way, and yank the blocks of ice out of the plastic, my fingers tingling. I pull out a pair of gloves I remembered to bring along and then I hurl it over the railing, down into the fjord.

The second one also goes overboard easily, the third, the fourth, but then it becomes too difficult, I can't manage any more. There are far too many containers.

I look at the crane on the quay—maybe I can use it, but there is no key in it, so I go down into the cargo hold again, stand facing the containers, looking at them. I can't manage all of them. I step closer. My gaze slides across the broadside and I notice a joint in the woodwork aport—no, an opening, there is a hatch. Further up on the bulkhead I spot a button.

I press it and the hatch responds immediately, sliding open with a loud creak.

Now I can lift the ice directly out—the fifth, the sixth, the seventh—soon I lose count. I fling the containers onto the floor, they're not going into the water, although they will perhaps end up there anyway, to join the mountains and islands of plastic in the ocean and slowly decompose into microplastic, disappear into the digestive system of a fish, be served up on a plate to be eaten by a human being, who eats his or her own garbage, the way we all eat our own garbage every single day.

The plastic feels hard beneath my fingers when I remove the lid of yet another container, then I lift it, carry it towards the hatch, flip it over and dump the huge white blocks out into the water where they hit the surface with a gentle splash. The ice bobs on the surface—white, shiny cubes against the pitch-black water, amidst the uneven yellow reflections of light from the lampposts on the wharf. Sweat trickles down my back, but my hands are cold inside my gloves, so frozen that I have lost all feeling in them, and the sensation is painful, but satisfying. The ice blocks lie in the water like small icebergs, just the upper portion of them is visible, that's how it is with floating glaciers, more below the water than above, but these won't harm anyone, won't destroy, I am the destroyer here, because the water is warm and the ice will quickly melt. When the skipper comes to start the engine in a few hours, the blocks will already be smaller and, moreover, the salt water will have ruined them. This ice can never be used as ice cubes, it can never, ever be served on a sheik's table, in a crystal tumbler, in a drink, in Saudi Arabia or Qatar.

Ice that melts, ice that melts in salt water, I am a part of it now, a part of what is taking place at all times. I am compounding the changes. I laugh, startled by the sound of my own laughter, an unfamiliar croaking like a frog. They are dying, the frogs, being wiped out in silence, without the world caring, one third of the world's species are in danger of extinction, but nobody thinks about it, the frog, as it moves through the world's marsh landscapes, always in contact with water, slimy, modest, not disgusting enough to be hideous, not strange enough to be amusing, just odd, how it croaks, how it hops, how it flees from humans.

Finally I am almost finished. My back is aching, twenty kilos of ice in every container, so heavy, too heavy. I count rapidly, only twelve more, only 240 kilos. I am about to open yet another container but my hands are trembling, my fingers are stiff and then they stop. I'm tired, am just so tired, too old for this kind of lifting, my flesh and bones protest, far too old.

I sit down on the containers. Oh, Magnus, I am incapable of hurling the last of the blocks of ice overboard, our ice, it has been left in peace until now, until you came. But it hasn't been silent, because ice is never silent, it has its own sound, it creaks. Ice creaking is one of the world's oldest sounds and it frightens me, has always frightened me. It's the sound of something going to pieces. And the sound of a stone that fails to penetrate the ice, but gives off an echo all the same, is a sound like no other, the brief reverberation of the water below, a reminder of everything imprisoned underneath, of how solidly in place everything is.

But it has been a long time since I threw a stone at an ice-covered surface. The ice no longer forms on the lakes. In the wintertime, pollen season is already underway in January. The ice is washed away by the rain and the world is being covered by flowing water. I used to go skating, I remember, on the fjord, I skated faster than everybody. Magnus stood onshore and watched me, we were ten or eleven, we still didn't know one another but I remember that I liked that he watched me, that he knew I was the fastest. I had skates that I screwed onto my boots, with sharp blades. Nobody uses those any longer, they buy new skates every single autumn, new skates every year for the children. Black hockey skates or white for figure skating, they think that one has to have skates, but nobody uses them, because the lakes don't freeze over any longer and everything I have done has been to no avail. I have really tried, I have been fighting for my entire life, but I have been mostly alone; there are so few of us, it was futile, everything we talked about, everything we said would happen has happened, the heat has already arrived, nobody listened.

Magnus, your grandchildren will not be able to skate across the lakes. Nonetheless, you have approved this—our glacier, the ice—you have disassociated yourself to such a large extent from everything that once was ours, or perhaps you have always been like this, you have just let it happen. I can hear you, how you are thinking now, how people like you think, we're just following the development, what I have allowed to happen is happening everywhere, evil's banality, you have become like Eichmann. But nobody holds you accountable. Your Jerusalem never arrives.

I have these twelve containers, twelve containers containing ice one thousand years old. I am not going to throw them overboard, because you have to see them, Magnus, you can't just sit down there and let it happen; it's not supposed to be as easy as that, you are going to see the ice, feel it, you will personally stand next to it while it melts, you will have the chance to walk on it, step on it, it will melt beneath your feet, the way it once melted under our feet.

Again I start lugging containers. One by one I take the twelve containers of ice with me out of the cargo ship, over onto *Blue*.

DAVID

Once again my hands were immersed in soapy water. It foamed between my fingers and soaked through our clothing.

My shirt swelled like a taut balloon on the surface until the water prevailed.

As the filth released its grip on our clothes, the color of the soap and water changed from transparent to a nondescript grayish brown.

The air in the sanitary barracks was stagnant, with a strong odor of cleaning products. Familiar. Anna's head bent over the washing machine at home. August's teeny-tiny garments, clean and damp. The smell that spread through the room, covering up the aroma of food and the faint stench emanating from the trash can in the heat.

Anna and the laundry. The teeny-tiny garments.

I swallowed and tried to concentrate on what I was doing.

A few spots refused to come out, and remained in the fabric like shadows. Dried blood from a scrape on the knee that had long since turned a rusty brown color. Purple spots from unripe cherries picked one night in someone's garden. They appeased our hunger pangs for a little while, but the craving in our stomachs was replaced by a sour sensation.

It was our fourth day in the camp. Already every day was the same. Jeanette's office in the morning. Nothing new. Every day I asked if there was anything more I could do, anything else. But she shook her head. Then eat. Sweat. Listen to Lou talk, unable to pay attention. Pull myself together. Ask somebody about the time. Nothing new, no. Try to listen to Lou. Try to play. Try not to think. About Anna, about August, about the fire. Eat again. Wait for the evening, for the heat to abate. Sleep. Wait for the next morning and another visit to the Red Cross.

But today we were allowed to wash our clothes. Laundry tubs were set up on a simple work bench. Seven liters of water we had been given for this. A little treasure trove of water.

Lou was also washing her clothes. She was wearing only her underpants and scrubbing her shorts in a tub in front of her.

The door behind us opened. I turned around. It was a woman holding dirty laundry in one hand and a small water jug in the other.

I nodded and said hi.

She mumbled a reply, took one of the tubs down from the shelf, poured some laundry detergent out of a can, sprinkled it across the bottom, and filled the tub with water, doing everything quickly and expertly.

She sat down on the other side of Lou. I tried to smile, but she didn't seem to notice, was busy with her laundry.

She put a dress in the water, a floral print, it looked expensive. After that a blouse made of a thin, silk-like fabric.

"Nice," I said.

"What?"

"The blouse."

"Thank you."

She studied me for a couple of seconds before returning to her laundry.

She was in her late thirties, maybe even forty. Her skeleton seemed to be pressing through her skin. Her collarbone stuck out, but not because she didn't eat enough, more because she was like that, naturally thin.

Or maybe she was one of those who always watched her weight, exercised. There had been a lot of people like that before. I remember that dieting was something women talked about. She was pretty, I saw that now—not beautiful, but pretty. Classic. The way you look if you come from a family where rich men marry elegant women. The families just become more and more attractive with each generation, until finally everyone forgets how ordinary people look.

One seldom saw her kind in Argelès. The tourists who came to the town were a different sort. They liked the amusement park on the beach and the pedestrian street where you could buy knock-offs of famous labels. I had only seen her kind on the few occasions I had traveled further north up the coast, in Cannes and Provence.

But now she was here, among all the rest of us. The former kinds of distinctions no longer existed.

Her movements were quick. Unfriendly? Maybe she didn't like my watching her.

"Been here long?" I asked, sort of to explain my staring.

"A while."

"Do you like it?"

"Excuse me?"

I laughed. "Sorry. Wrong question. I get it."

She didn't smile. Just kept rubbing her dress.

"Fine, fine." I held up my hands to show that I gave up, that I wouldn't bother her anymore.

She continued washing with quick movements, putting more clothing into the tub. Only women's clothing, I could see.

"Are you here alone?" I asked.

"I thought you were done talking," she said.

"We're alone, too," I said and pointed at Lou.

She stirred the contents of the tub a little. The suds foamed between her fingers. She stared at the clothes. Then she drew a breath. "You're not alone," she said. "There are two of you."

She hid her face from me, but couldn't hide her voice. It wasn't accusing. It wasn't angry and dismissive like before. She just said it, plain and simple.

Abruptly I felt ashamed. She was right, I shouldn't say that I was alone, because I had Lou. I still had Lou. Who at this moment was playing with the laundry water while talking softly to herself. Something about the ocean. The ocean at home?

The woman rinsed the soap out of her clothes with the last of the water from the jug she had brought along, wringing them out with rhythmic movements. Her hands were slender, delicate. The water gushed out of them.

Suddenly I wanted her to wring out our clothes, too, in the same way. For my own part I hadn't even made it to the rinse cycle yet.

"Would you like to eat with us?" I asked when she stood up to leave.

"You don't give up, do you?" the woman said.

How should I reply? That I felt bad for her? That was why I asked. Or that I liked her hands? You don't say such things. Besides, I already regretted it. That I had asked. I shouldn't invite other women to dinner. I had Anna.

"We have to dry our clothes first," she said, without waiting for my answer.

Was that a yes?

"Can't we eat while they're drying?" I said.

Because there wasn't really anything wrong with our having a meal together, was there? It wasn't exactly as if I had asked her out on a date, either.

"You're new here," she said. "We have to guard them while they're drying."

"Huh?"

"They disappear."

"Oh."

I blushed; I should have realized that.

We sat there, the three of us, by the clotheslines in the shadow of the sanitary barracks, looking at our wet clothing hanging in the sun.

There was no wind, so the garments hung limply from the line, but the heat did the job. And we just sat there.

She didn't suggest taking turns, so we could watch each other's clothing in shifts. Maybe she didn't trust me. I hadn't really given her any reason to.

Or maybe she liked sitting like this. It was a way of killing time, was maybe how people lived here.

I didn't suggest it either, actually. Because it was quite nice. We had found a place in the shrinking shadow of the barracks.

Lou played again, more wildly than usual. She ran back and forth between the drying garments.

The woman was silent. I was silent as well.

It occurred to me that I'd forgotten to ask her name, but couldn't bring myself to do it. It felt private, like everything else about her.

Afterwards I learned it anyway. We were in the mess hall and had finished our meal. A casserole in dented aluminum bowls. Lukewarm.

Lou wolfed down everything she was given, as if she were

afraid the food would disappear if she wasn't quick enough. It was late in the day and she had only eaten a few dry crackers for breakfast. I had forgotten while we were waiting for the clothes to dry that the child needed food. Scatterbrain. But now her tummy was full and she was calm and she said, as simply as only she could say it: "My name is Lou. What's your name?"

"Lou is a nice name," the woman said and abruptly got to her feet.

"But what is your name?" Lou asked.

The woman took a step away from the table. "Marguerite."

Marguerite. Like a daisy.

"Daddy's name is David."

The woman took one more step.

"That's nice. Thanks for the company."

"Where are you going?" I asked. "We could eat together later, too?"

"Yes," Lou said. "We could."

"Maybe," Marguerite said.

But it didn't look like she meant it.

"Fine," I said.

Makes no difference to me, I wanted to say. But I didn't say anything. And she had already turned to leave. Was headed away.

I thought she needed us. But she didn't, I could see that now. A woman like her didn't need people like us.

I was just a child, dragging another child with me. We

came straight from the sandbox, both Lou and I. We were dirty, even though we were clean. Completely unlike her. Nonetheless, I didn't want her to walk away, with that bony back of hers, so slender and erect.

"I was just trying to be nice," I said to her back.

"Me too," she said, without turning around.

And then she disappeared.

For some reason or other my eyes were stinging. But crying didn't help, I knew that.

Besides, it was so hot, so hellishly hot. The mess hall tent was hot. The sun beat down on the roof. The walls were folded up to let the air in, but it didn't help, because not even the faintest breeze could be felt. Only dry, sweltering heat.

Around us people sat on the benches, sweating. Red in the face, their skin shiny. Everyone looked the same. I didn't know any of them.

I emptied the water out of my cup. It was as warm as piss and tasted like rubber.

Waiting and waiting.

I stood up suddenly.

"Come on," I said to Lou.

"I haven't finished eating."

"Finish up, then."

She pushed in the last spoonful.

"Come on," I said. "Hurry."

"Where are we going?" Lou said.

"Out," I said.

"Why?"

"They said we could go wherever we wanted. During the daytime we can go wherever we want."

I took her by the hand and pulled her out of the tent.

We hurried through the camp. The sweaty faces were everywhere. Strangers, only strangers.

I had been surrounded by so many people.

A wife. Two children. Parents, in-laws. A sister.

My big sister and I, God, how we had argued when we were little. About everything. Alice never let me win. For a time I thought that she should have. She had the option. As the oldest, she had the power. The oldest always has the power. And the responsibility.

But letting me win would perhaps have meant breaking the rules of the game between us. Because we were supposed to argue, in a strange way I think we almost wanted to, that siblings *want* to argue. It's so easy, much easier than being good to one another.

She was always older than me. Much older. After I had children, the age difference was sort of obliterated for some reason or other. It was strange that she still lived the life of a young person, while I changed diapers and heated nursing bottles. But now, after the past few months, I started thinking of her as my big sister again. Not older, but *big*.

Alice, my big sister … I didn't know where she was, either. That clever sister of mine, clever with words, clever with numbers, clever with her hands. She built things, all the time.

No, not built, constructed, but she never had the chance to become an engineer as she had planned. The crisis overwhelmed her. She created so many things: a windmill in the garden, a solar-cell-powered dollhouse, won an inventor's contest at school. Where was she now?

My family. Alice, Mom, my aunts. Grandmother and Grandfather. Eduard, the only one of my friends with whom I had cried. Where was he? Where were they?

And Dad ... my elderly father. That feeble body of his, the unsteady gait, where was he? He was tougher than I'd thought; people like him usually didn't survive the summers. Hundreds of thousands of elderly people had passed away in recent years because of the heat. The nights in particular took their toll, the extreme heat, the aging bodies never found rest. But Dad lived. The heat didn't get to him, like it did with the rest of us, it didn't have any effect on him.

I had been angry with him for so many years. Angry with him for having had children far too late in life. So late that he couldn't bring himself to be a father. Couldn't bring himself to do the things a daddy does, what the other daddies did. Toss me into the air over his head, wrestle with me, raise his voice when I did something I wasn't supposed to do.

Alice had been enough for him, a careful girl, well behaved, seldom dirty. I was simply far too much. With Dad I felt like I was all elbows, clumsy. Hard and sinewy. Far too loud, my movements uncontrolled. He never said it, but I was still young when I started noticing how he would leave the room when I came in. His sighs. How he lifted his book—always some book or other—protectively up against his face, using the book as a shield.

He didn't even manage to follow up on my schooling, didn't understand my impatience, my confusion over the letters of the alphabet. He had never been like that himself. I used to think that he'd always been old. And I was madder than hell with him for precisely that.

But still. Now I couldn't imagine the world without that failing old body of his, without his sighs and his thousand-yard stare. My diminished old father. I had given up on him too soon. I could have tried to approach him. I should have. While there was still time.

I should have understood that he survived for a reason, that I was fortunate.

But they just left, he and Mom. One day in October of last year they closed up the house, covered the furniture with sheets and locked the door. They wanted to take the train to Paris, she had a cousin there. Alice went with them, too. From there they hoped they would be able to continue further north. In May we received our last message from them. They hadn't been granted residency anywhere, but were going to try to get to Denmark on their own. After that ... nothing.

I walked quickly. We passed the halls. The sanitary barracks.

I pulled air into my lungs. Dad ... stop thinking about him, you have to stop thinking about him. About Dad. About Mom. About Alice.

Because there were too many people. Too many of them. I didn't have enough hope for so many people. Only for Anna and August. Their faces, the smell of August, his gurgling, the hollow of Anna's neck, snuggling against it, in it. Just the two of them. That would have to do. If I could have them, it would do.

"Where are we going, Daddy?"

Lou trotted alongside me, struggling to keep up. "Daddy?"

"I don't know. Out."

I took a breath. Tried to smile at her. "We'll just go for a little walk."

She didn't want to go, I could see it on her face. But she didn't protest. She just took my hand and held it tightly. Wherever I went, she followed.

I stepped briskly, adult strides.

I had to get some air. Had to stop thinking. Stop yearning. Just wait.

Anna. August.

Wait.

"You're walking so fast," Lou said.

"Sorry," I said.

And I pulled her towards the exit.

SIGNE

t's easy to find out where he lives. Some things have actually become easier and he clearly hasn't made any attempt to hide it, the address is posted on several sites on the internet.

I look through the maritime maps, I have what I need, having sailed these waters before, so I quickly undo the mooring lines, start the engine and leave Ringfjorden, gliding through silent, pitch-black water.

It's as if I can feel the ice. The helm of *Blue* seems heavier under my hand, the distribution of weight is different and it infiltrates my body, as if the locus of my own center of gravity had also shifted. It feels like the boat is lying low in the water, but that can't be right—a couple of hundred kilos is nothing compared to the boat's 3.5 tons, it can't be enough to produce this change.

Painful shocks tingle through my fingers, the warmth in them starting to return. I have put on gloves, thick knitted gloves, threadbare on the fingertips, it was Mom who knitted them, she struggled for months with these gloves; I can't remember her ever knitting anything else, they are water- and wind-resistant, wool keeps you warm even when it's wet.

I put my foot carefully on the throttle and press it slowly towards the floor, letting the engine run at the highest rotational speed I think it will withstand. I don't raise the sail. I make do with the engine, the iron sail. The night is calm, the ocean lustrous, and nonetheless I must get away, quickly, before somebody discovers what I have done.

The mountains flatten out as I approach the ocean. I remember this fjord being long, the trip out taking an eternity. It was almost meaningless to try to make it all the way to open sea, too much for one day, I remember thinking, even though that was also all I wanted, to get out.

For some people the mountains are a security blanket. They wrap themselves up in them, pull them over their heads to hold them in place. Magnus was like that, they made him feel calm, he said. I never understood how he could think like that, because they loomed over me, I could feel their presence even when I was a child—the heaviness, the weight of them.

That feeling only released its grip at higher altitudes. Daddy used to take me up into the mountains, ever since I was small, just him and me, to the glacier, to the Sister Falls, and up there, when I was with him, I could breathe.

Had it been up to me we would have gone hiking every single day, Daddy and I. He stopped all the time to show me plants, insects or animals, point out small things on the ground, or birds, no more than specks way up in the sky, which I never would have noticed without his help.

We often followed the river up to the mountain.

He loved the River Breio, that was what had brought him here. He came to Ringfjorden as a young student. He was going to write a long dissertation about the freshwater pearl mussel, *Margaritifera margaritifera*, an unassuming small species that lived partially hidden between stones and gravel at the bottom of the river. He told me that the larvae pass through a parasitic juvenile phase, maturing in the gills and fins of salmon and trout, while the adult mussel filter-feeds on microorganisms, and in this way also cleans the river for the surrounding environment.

"That tiny creature can live more than a hundred years," he said, his eyes shining. "Think about it, Signe, once it has been created, it lives longer than a human being. Irreplaceable for the entirety of its lifetime."

The first time he came to the village, he stayed at a hotel and by breakfast time on the second day he had already noticed Iris, the daughter of the hotel owner, and she noticed him. They quickly became an item. Bjørn and Iris were their names, names that went so well together, I remember thinking. *Bjørn*, meaning bear, a huge, powerful animal that lumbers heavily through the world, and Iris, a fragile, slender blossom, deeply rooted in one place. But actually, it should perhaps be the opposite; she should have had his name, he should have had hers.

It had apparently been beautiful, what they had, during the initial period, the first years, but then it grew ugly. Nothing is uglier than something that once was beautiful.

For Daddy the hate that sprang up in him lasted for the rest of his life. He never forgave her for taking the river away from him.

I think I know when it began, at least I know when it began for me, but maybe they had already been talking about the development project for a long time, during the late-night hours, in angry, whispering voices that didn't awaken me, they must have done that, but all I remember is the day she came home and told us that the development project had been approved.

I think he had a deadline, an article that he was supposed to write, because he was sitting bent over the typewriter out on the porch—he liked working out there, in the fresh air. I envied him that typewriter, what he accomplished on it—all the words, sentences that unfurled onto the paper before him, the speed of his fingers hitting the keys, the letters on the type bars knocking against the paper—and then I pushed my way onto his lap and said that I wanted to type as well.

He let me, as he so often did, but the rhythm wasn't the same when I typed, the sound didn't travel through the house, the letters didn't turn into sentences, it took such a long time. I had only just learned how to combine letters into words, so I searched and searched with my index finger.

Besides, Daddy's lap was hard and his legs restless. He had put his feet on the floor so his thighs sloped forward and I was always on the verge of sliding off. But I tensed the muscles in my body and just kept going.

"There," he said, finally. "Now you've tried. Now I have to get back to work."

"No," I said. "I want to write a story."

"That's enough for now," Daddy said.

"No," I said.

But he lifted me off the chair and gave me a quick hug, as if to apologize, and I held him tight. His beard stubble scraped against my cheek, but I still wanted the hug to last.

"Let go of me now, Signe."

"I want to write," I said.

"You must listen to me now," he said.

"BUT I WANT TO WRITE WITH YOU," I shouted, right into his ear.

"Ow! Signe!"

He took hold of me and set me firmly down on the floor.

"You can't scream into people's ears like that."

"WHY NOT?"

"You will ruin their hearing. The ear is a finely tuned organ that we have to take care of. Just *a single* loud noise can injure the ear. Your hearing will never be better than it is now. You must take care of your hearing. Both your own and that of others."

"Oh."

Daddy turned back to the typewriter and quickly found a sheet of paper and a pencil.

"Look here. Write something for me," he said. "Then we can spend some time together later."

"About what?"

"Write about what you see."

But I didn't move.

"There are titmice on the bird table," he said. "Write about them. What kinds do you see, what do they eat, how are they doing now during the spring?"

"Why?"

"Afterwards I can help you with the Latin names."

I got to work and composed several lists that day, writing down the names of small animals on the shore, seabirds in the sky, weeds in the garden, insects by the brook, but the writing of my lists went slowly and I envied Daddy his type-writer because if I had it, I thought, I could have written just as much as he did, just as fast, just as powerfully. I would collect the entirety of nature on the pages, just the way he did, and maybe one day somebody would even publish what I had written, the way his texts came back in thick journals, so everyone could read them.

He never got around to helping me with the Latin names because soon it was dinnertime and Mommy came home with big news.

She told us over dessert, delivered the news into our lives as if it were something we should eat covered with cream.

"Today it was finally approved," she said. "They're going to install a pipeline to channel the River Breio."

I didn't understand the meaning of what was said, not then, but I saw that she was smiling, that she thought this was good news. However, she didn't say anything more and I realized that she was unsure about the kind of response she would get from Daddy.

"What?" was all he said, as if he hadn't heard her words.

And he put his spoon down on his plate, even though it was still full of whipped cream and applesauce.

"It was approved," Mommy said.

"But it wasn't supposed to come up for a vote until the next city council meeting."

"We had it approved today."

"That can't be right."

"Bjørn, this is what everyone wants."

He got to his feet, the plates on the table rattled. He shouted something: ugly words, words I wasn't allowed to use.

But she spoke calmly, in the same voice she sometimes used with me. "People have been working for this since the 1920s."

"But don't they understand what they have?" he shouted. "What the river is?"

"That's exactly what they do understand. It's an incredible opportunity. A whole new start for Ringfjorden."

"A new start?"

He spit the words out, as if they nauseated him.

She spoke a bit more, in the same calm voice.

He tried to respond in a subdued tone of voice, but failed.

And now her voice rose, too. The words flew back and forth between them, faster and faster, louder and louder.

There was something strange about the whipped cream—

it was too thick, almost butter. Else, the housekeeper, must have forgotten about it, whipped it for too long. It coated the inside of my mouth and throat like a cloying membrane and I stood up without excusing myself from the table, because they wouldn't have heard it anyway, the way they were screaming.

They didn't notice that I'd left them, that I hadn't even finished my dessert.

I walked through the parlor, into the dayroom, but the sound of their voices followed me. I opened the door to the porch— out here there must be another sound that could drown them out, birds or waves on the fjord, but there was no wind and no birds were singing and I could still hear their voices.

Then I discovered the typewriter. Daddy had abandoned it. The sun was shining, and when I ran my finger over the typewriter the metal was warm.

They didn't see me out here, didn't hear me. I sat down at the table. Daddy had left a blanket there, protection from the spring wind. I wrapped it around me and turned to face the typewriter.

I lifted both index fingers and lowered them to hit the letters. The A was beside the S, the R and the T were side by side. The P was at the top on the right, as if the alphabet came to an end there.

I can write a story, I thought, a story about elves and princesses, something magnificent and beautiful that I can present at school and everyone will love it, or something I can save and keep working on, and it will bring me glory and honor while I am still very young, make me a famous author.

I wanted to write a story, but I could only ever write about what I saw, back then as now. I could only write what I heard, because the sounds from inside the house grew louder, they grated on me, like the wind, like the cold or a storm, the words thundered through the porch door and it was impossible to write anything else.

Power company, I wrote.

Guests, I wrote.

Future, I wrote.

"The freshwater mussel will die out," Daddy cried.

Die, I wrote, as quickly as I could. Die, died, have died.

"And the water ouzel, it lays its eggs by the river."

A water ouzel, the water ouzel, several water ouzels, all the water ouzels.

"It's just water," Mommy screamed. "But it can be converted into electricity, it can create jobs. It can bring life to the village."

"You're just thinking about the hotel," Daddy shouted.

"The hotel is what we live on. Have you forgotten that? Not your underpaid journal articles."

"But this is the River Breio!"

"It's just water."

Water, I wrote. One water, the water, several waters, all the waters.

No. All the water.

Nobody heard me typing, how quickly I was typing, suddenly, how adept I had become at finding the letters.

DAVID

We passed the fence. I led Lou out onto the highway. A light wind was blowing there. I wanted to walk briskly, taking huge strides. But Lou held me back. How tightly she hung on there, to one of my hands, while her other hand was neglected. She should have had someone's hand to hold there as well.

The only sound was that of her shuffling child's feet.

"Can you walk a little faster?" I asked.

"Yes."

But she walked just as slowly, dragging her feet, and did not say a word.

Before she would have protested. Howled. Screamed.

"It would be better if you said something," I said.

"Like what?"

"You think walking here is boring, don't you?"

"No, I don't."

"Yes, you do. You hate walking."

"No, I don't."

And then she really tried to walk faster. She trotted beside me.

"Take it easy," I said.

Suddenly I felt pretty lousy.

"We're just going for a little walk, right?" I said. "Just for something to do. A short walk."

"How far?"

"One minute."

She didn't know how to tell time, had no idea that if she counted slowly to sixty, the minute would have passed, that one minute is nothing at all. Sometimes I was surprised at how easy it was to fool her, which made me feel even worse. Not because I fooled her, but because of how easy it was.

I just couldn't bear to go back to that sweaty, claustrophobic camp. Here, out on the road, we were at least in motion. We could pretend we had a goal. But there was nothing to walk towards, nothing on which to focus your gaze. Just one little, forest-covered mound was sticking up in the landscape. A ridge was perhaps the word. Really it was no more than a bump amidst all the flatness.

A displaced bump.

"Has a minute passed?" Lou said after a while.

"Soon."

"I taste like salt," Lou said, and placed the tip of her tongue against her upper lip.

"Salt's good," I said.

I missed the salt. I missed the mountains and the ocean.

Here the air was dry. Earthy, almost sandy. It got into your nose. The air wasn't fresh. While at home the smell of salt water was everywhere.

Salt purifies. Preserves things. You can put food in salt and it will be preserved forever. You can pour salt water on cuts and yes, it hurts, but salt is clean, one of the cleanest things in the world.

People have even started wars over salt.

For me, salt was my job. A job I enjoyed. I had had this job since Lou was born. I had to quit school then, bring home a paycheck. No two ways about it.

I had never thought I would stay there, in Argelès. Had always thought I would move away. Ever since I was young, I had envied the tourists who came and left every single summer. They invaded the summers for those of us who were natives, taking over, eating enormous quantities of *moules-frites* and sunning themselves to a crisp on the beach. Until they took their beach towels and hats and the smell of suntan lotion with them and went away.

But in recent years the tourists hadn't come. The faucet was turned off. They disappeared. And I wanted to disappear too. From the empty restaurants, from the deserted shopping street, from the amusement park that slowly rusted away in the spray from the rising ocean, the punctured inflatable castle and the overgrown miniature golf course.

They disappeared. I stayed. With Anna, with Lou and, later, with August. In our crowded apartment by the harbor, where the salt water often forced its way into the cellar. But my job was a bright spot. The plant was located at the end of the esplanade. Before there had only been grassy dunes there, and a sun lounger rental business that had never managed to make a profit, because this was the windiest spot on the entire beach. But also the most beautiful, for those who took the time to notice and were able to ignore the wind.

I was lucky to get the job. Thomas was a friend of my father and a good boss. And my duties were fine. Noisy, but fine. We wore ear defenders to protect ourselves from the sound of the turbines. I worked with salt every day, and liked the smell. But the objective was precisely to eliminate the salt.

We monitored operations as the seawater was channeled through the turbines, separating the salt from the water, osmosis in reverse. Fresh water ran out the other end—good, clear water.

Desalination was the future, Thomas used to say. And he told us about the facilities in other places in the world, in Florida and southern Spain, where there were many. These were the facilities that irrigated the ever-expanding desert.

But with each passing day, Thomas grew more and more worried, because the machinery at the plant was constantly breaking down. Parts fell to pieces, we couldn't replace them. And we were unable to produce enough water. We were too small-scale, and it wasn't cheap enough, either. And when the desalination plants in Spain were leveled to the ground during the battles over the River Ebro, when our neighboring country became divided, he hardly slept at all any longer. He talked and talked about the EU. About the time when Europe was united. He talked about how everything was just disintegrating, every day he told me of a new conflict. Personally, I had given up paying attention a long time ago. I couldn't bear to read the news. Because people were fighting everywhere, it seemed—north against south, the water nations against the drought nations. And there was also internal strife in some countries. Like in Spain.

Those who have something to protect forget about everything else, Thomas said. To each his own. Nobody takes care of anyone except their own people.

But it didn't help that he talked, it didn't help that I tried to listen. It didn't help that we worked as hard as we could. It didn't help that France had approved the construction of three new plants.

That's how quickly things can change. One day you wake up to the sound of the alarm clock, eat breakfast, go to work, argue, laugh, make love, do the dishes, worry about your bank account being drained before the end of the month ... you don't think about how everything you have around you can disappear. Even if you hear that the world is changing. Even if you notice it on the thermometer. You don't think about it until the day when it's no longer the alarm clock that wakes you up in the morning, but the sound of screams. The flames have reached your city, your house, your bed, your loved ones. Your house is in flames, your bedclothes catch fire, your pillow starts smoking and you can't do anything but run.

"Salt is death," Thomas said. "Salt kills."

Towards the end, before we had to leave everything be-hind, I was often allowed to borrow his battered plastic boat. I would take it out on the ocean by myself, tell Anna I was going fishing, even though it was seldom possible to catch anything any longer. After docking the boat, I used to stand on the beach with my feet in the water, the water that rose slowly and relentlessly, and that was exactly what I thought. Salt is death. This ocean is death. It is rising and spreading its salt everywhere. And then I closed my eyes and prayed to a God I didn't believe in, prayed that when I opened my eyes again and stuck my hand in the water, the ocean would have become something else. That when I tasted my fingers, it would taste of nothing, the way fresh water does. Clean, clear nothing.

Sometimes I would stand there like that. For a long while. But I never tried to taste my fingers. I just clung to the thought, to the idea that the water of the rising ocean would one day be fresh.

I squeezed Lou's hand a little harder, out of a need to confirm that she was still there. We had walked quite a distance now. I turned around, could just make out the contours of the camp fence far behind us.

"Look there," I said to Lou. "It's nice here."

A shadowy lane appeared on our left, with tall trees on both sides. We continued walking down it. Beneath the trees. The temperature dropped several degrees.

Lou must have felt it, that it was pleasant walking here, because now she was walking faster.

We walked around a bend. I turned my head and could no longer see the highway behind us. Ahead of us there was another bend in the road. I liked that we were alone here. That there was no longer any trace of the refugee camp. That I could pretend that we were just an ordinary father and daughter, out for a walk on an ordinary road, in an ordinary world. Like before.

We walked for five minutes, maybe ten, passed some stone houses, a small farm. In two places I saw people. An elderly woman carried a sewing chest out to a car. An elderly man took a swing down from a tree. They were headed out, packing up, trying to make their way to the north, like everyone else. Otherwise it was deserted everywhere. Abandoned, here as well.

Only traces of the people who had lived here remained. Curtains that someone had chosen, garden furniture where someone had relaxed, chimneys from which smoke had risen, a garden rake that had drawn careful grooves in the gravel in the yard, the pétanque court where the balls had landed in the sand with a crunch.

I could have lived here, I thought, even though it was far from the ocean. Here, along this lane, in this shade, I could actually have lived, this could have been my home.

Yet another house appeared, the last on this stretch of road before the forest. The house was neither large nor fancy, but nonetheless it was a palace compared to our apartment at home.

It must have been abandoned a long time ago, or inhabited by someone who couldn't be bothered to maintain it properly. The yard was overgrown with dry weeds and the paint was peeling off the front door. There were shutters covering all the windows.

By the side of the house I spotted the lid of an old-fashioned rainwater tank. It was locked with a rusty padlock. It could be as old as the house. Was there still water in it?

Lou walked into the withering garden. It had once been overgrown, but now the apple trees were dried up and the leaves on the branches were yellow.

There was a shed with the door slightly ajar—maybe the wind had blown it open. Lou walked over and closed it. Then she turned around and pointed at something.

"What's that?"

Behind me, far inside the garden, there was something large and tall under the dark trees, covered by several green tarps. It was long and oval, with something sticking out on both sides. A kind of stand could be discerned on the ground.

Lou tugged at me. "Come on."

The tarps were dirty and worn, but securely attached, held in place by ropes in different pale, sun-bleached colors. Green, blue and grayish white, crisscrossing. Some of them were rotting. They had to be of cotton or hemp. But most of the plastic cords were still in one piece.

In some places leaves had gotten stuck between the ropes.

The leaves had become tiny pockets of soil, where seeds had landed. From which small plants were growing. Small plants which in turn dried up and died from the drought.

We walked over to it. I reached out my hand and took hold of one of the tarps, trying to make out what it was covering.

It was soft, like there was nothing behind it, but then my fingers came up against something hard—a beam? I slid my hand upwards. The first beam met another under the tarps and something was resting on them, something enormous, heavy. And then suddenly I knew.

"It's a boat," I said.

A boat on a stand, in a garden, miles away from the ocean.

It must be big.

I started from behind and paced it out.

At least ten meters long.

And tall. At least three meters from the keel to the top of the cabin.

"Can we take off the tarps?" Lou asked.

The knots were hard between my fingers. I struggled to undo one after the next. It was as if the wind and the weather had helped tighten them.

Lou helped out, too, but most of the knots were too difficult for her. We had nothing we could use to cut the ropes and, besides, I didn't want to destroy them. We were going to cover the boat again later, after we had seen it. We just needed to take a look. Nobody would notice.

I wound up the ropes carefully as I undid them, into huge coils that I laid side by side on the ground in the dry grass.

Lou moved them around, started sorting them by color. The blue ropes in one pile, the green in another. She could report that there were seven ropes in all.

My fingertips were sore and the palms of my hands raw by the time I had finally untied all the knots. The tarps hung in place by themselves. Four of them. I pulled them off and they slid across the hull with a sweeping sound as they dropped to the ground.

It was a sailboat. The mast lay on the roof of the cabin. The hull was dark blue, like the ocean in the evening, and there were four windows on each side.

It rested on a stand made of unpainted wooden beams, handmade from the looks of it, but solid.

There was a ladder lying over two crossbeams, a half-meter above the ground, as if it belonged there.

I pulled it out. Aluminum, with paint splotches, but all in one piece and lovely. I lifted it up onto one end, placed it on the grass and leaned it against the side of the boat.

"Are you going to climb up?" Lou asked.

"We have to, don't we?" I said.

"Is it allowed?"

I smiled.

"Do you see anyone we can ask?"

She looked around. "No."

"Do you think I should do it?"

"I don't know. You decide."

THE END OF THE OCEAN

"You decide, too," I said.

"Oh."

"Should I do it?"

"Yes. If you want."

I adjusted the ladder, pulling it a little further out so the approach angle was less steep. Then I stepped on the first rung.

The second.

The third.

The stand under the boat protested, creaking loudly. A tiny jerk shuddered through the entire structure. I stopped.

"Daddy?"

Maybe it wasn't as solid as it looked. Or maybe it had something to do with the structure? I tried one more step.

"Daddy, maybe you shouldn't do it after all?"

"It will be fine," I said.

But it wasn't, I could feel the impact of my steps reverberating through the stand, like I was in the process of tearing it down.

"Daddy?"

"OK, OK."

I climbed down, took hold of the ladder and leaned it against the end of the boat instead. A swim ladder was attached up there and the ladder became an extension of this, like I was climbing up from the bottom of the ocean.

I tried again; it was easier to keep my balance now, the stand didn't grumble. I climbed up a couple of rungs to make sure it would hold.

No creaking now, it felt solid and stable.

I jumped down to the ground again, reached my arms out towards Lou.

"You can climb right in front of me. I'll take care of you the whole time."

She didn't reply, looking uncertainly at the ladder.

"Come on." I nodded towards the boat. "It's like the ladder to the slide on the playground . . . at home, just a little longer. And I'm right behind you."

She drew a breath, looked up at the boat, walked over to the ladder and stepped onto the first rung.

"Good, Lou."

She climbed right in front of me, between my arms. I looked directly into her neck, which was slender and tanned and still a little dirty. I hadn't noticed that she hadn't washed everything off when she showered. She should have had somebody to help her. Sometimes I wished she had been a boy. It would perhaps have been easier.

She started climbing more quickly. I had to concentrate on keeping up with her. She took determined steps upwards, climbing like the child she was, boy or girl. First she lifted her right foot, and then her left, up to the same rung, so both feet were solidly planted on one rung before she attempted the next.

Then she reached the top. She struggled to get over the railing, but I pushed her up from her bum.

When she was finally standing on deck, she smiled.

"I was first."

"That you were."

I climbed up after her, crawling up over the railing. I stood on deck for a moment, looking around.

A bench on either side, a tiller in the middle.

An opening covered by boards, a keyhole in the board on top.

Another keyhole—for the engine, no doubt—and some instruments down along the floor, a couple of measuring devices and a lever for the gas and gears.

And a cool breeze was blowing through the air. We were just far enough above the ground to feel the effect.

The floor and bench in the cockpit were made of wood that looked dry, a gray color, blistered, as if in need of oil or stain.

Only the helm had been preserved, the lacquered finish was still shiny. The woodwork was golden.

I positioned myself in front of it, took hold with my right hand. Planting my feet on deck, I straddled my legs and shaded my eyes from the sun with my hand like I was scanning the sea.

"Ship ahoy!"

Lou laughed her one-of-a-kind laughter.

"Land in sight! Can you see land?" I asked in a skipper's voice.

"No," she said. "It's not land."

"You're right, it's not land, just the ocean, as far as I can see. And waves. Huge waves."

"A storm!" Lou said.

"Don't worry," I said. "The captain will pilot you safely through this."

"Are you the captain?"

"That I am ... and look! Do you see the pirate ship?"

We sailed. We fought off pirates. We met dolphins and a mermaid. Lou shouted, gesticulating with her arms, and took the helm. She laughed loudly.

Soon she wanted to be the captain. And I became an obedient sailor, albeit a pretty stupid one. She had to explain everything to me, while she laughed even more. Because the sailor got everything mixed up, couldn't tell the difference between right and left, port and stern, and was afraid of everything, especially the pirates.

But we made it, nonetheless. Thanks to an amazing ride on the backs of two dolphins. And especially, thanks to her.

"Thank God for your heroism and your shrewdness, Captain," I said.

"Shrewdness?"

"That means to be sly," I said. "You are a sly captain."

We played for an hour, maybe two. I breathed easily up there on deck, beneath the shadow of the trees, where there was a breeze.

But Lou kept looking at the boards that blocked off the opening.

"Can we open the door?"

"No," I said.

And she wouldn't let it go.

"We have to open it," she said a little while later and pounded on the boards. "You can break them, can't you?"

"We can't go around breaking other people's things," I said.

"Oh. OK, then," she said, her face ashamed.

Then she thought about it. "But they're not here?"

Lou didn't ask for things very often. And she didn't give up very often either.

"Fine," I said. "We can see if there is a key inside."

"Where?"

I pointed. "In the house."

"But isn't the house locked too?"

"We may have to break something, then," I said. "After all."

"We won't tell anyone," she said quietly.

I had to laugh.

We broke a window in the back and entered what turned out to be the living room.

I tiptoed through the house, but stopped when I realized what I was doing and began walking normally. I could stomp as loudly as I liked. There was nobody around who could hear us anyway.

The rooms were simple, unpretentious. Not many ornaments, just an overloaded bookshelf against the wall in the living room, and on one of the long walls a photograph of a snow-covered mountain by a fjord.

The people who had lived here must have left without

taking much with them. Maybe just clothing and the most essential items.

I suddenly felt like I was trespassing on somebody else's life and hurried through the rooms to the front of the house. I stepped out into the hallway.

There on the wall was a key cabinet. So simple. Tidy. It looked like a little bathhouse, with yellow and white stripes, the old-fashioned kind that could still be found in some places by the beach.

Anna and I always misplaced our keys. We agreed they should be put somewhere specific, but it was like we could never decide where. I had bought a couple of hooks, but never hung them up. We could never agree on where they should hang and whether we could just screw them directly into the wall or if we needed wall plugs.

We weren't very good at such things. I was quite handy—it wasn't that. It was just that there were so many decisions to be made and we had to make them together, which made it difficult. Even the simple task of putting up a few key hooks.

But here the keys hung in rows. It was easy to spot the one I was looking for. A small key at the end of a blue string, attached to a huge, round clump of cork. Of course. It was a key with a life jacket.

Lou stood beside me, a bit too close, panting eagerly into my ear as I tried to unlock the hatch, twisting and wiggling the key. I tried applying some muscle.

"Sit down on the bench," I said.

"But then I can't see."

"You can see afterwards."

I tried again, yanking away, roughly. The key turned in the lock.

I had to fiddle with it a bit before I discovered that what was above the entryway was actually a hatch that could be slid backwards and that I had to push this back before I could loosen the two boards that were the door.

The lower board was wedged stuck, as if there were a vacuum in the woodwork. But Lou was on her feet again and standing close to me, peeking into the boat.

"There are benches inside, too," she said.

"Mm."

"And a table."

I gave the board a solid kick. It gave way, loosened. And then it could be pulled up.

Lou peeked inside, clapped her hands.

"How cozy!" She spun around. "It's so cozy!"

Girls.

But she was right. It *was* cozy. Everything was compact and neat, everything fit together, could be taken apart, stacked, closed up and secured.

We explored the boat for a long time. Lou kept crowing with joy, like she was playing in a playhouse.

She took out cups and plates from a cupboard, white with blue letters.

"What's written on them?"

"*Navigare vivere est*," I read.

"What does it mean?"

"It's Latin and ... something about navigation, about being at sea, that that's life. Sailing is life, maybe ... yes, I think so. Sailing is life."

Wow. I was impressive.

"Sailing is life," she laughed.

Nothing compared to the sound of that laughter. I would do anything to hear that sound.

When she discovered that the dining-room table could be lowered to the level of the surrounding benches, she was overjoyed.

"They fit!"

And there was a mattress that could be put on the table, so the benches and table became a bed.

"I want to sleep here."

"You can't very well sleep on the table."

"Can too. And you can sleep in there."

She pointed inside the forepeak.

"Or in the bathroom," she said.

There was a compartment with a toilet inside between the saloon and the forepeak.

"You want me to sleep in the bathroom?"

"Yes!"

She was sweating from the heat, red in the face. Locks of hair had come loose from her braids and hung over her eyes, but she didn't care, just pushed them to one side.

"But there isn't room."

"You have to sit on the toilet all night."

"The captain's orders," I said.

Afterwards, when the sun was low in the sky, we sat in the cockpit, facing each other on the benches. Her feet didn't reach the floor, so they dangled freely. Lou stroked the woodwork of the bench with her hands, thinking.

"I'm patting the boat."

"I'm sure it likes that."

"Nice boat."

She kept stroking it, lovingly. But then she stopped suddenly.

"Ow!"

She held up her right hand, so I could see her little white palm. A splinter was lodged in her flesh next to her thumb.

"It hurts!"

I took her hand; the splinter was in deep.

"Take it out!" she cried.

"I don't have anything here. We need a pair of tweezers."

"Take it out!"

"We'll go back. To the first-aid barracks. They'll have what we need."

"I don't want to! Take it out now!"

"Lou, you have to go down the ladder."

"No!"

I tried to persuade her.

I coaxed, I cajoled.

Finally she started climbing down the ladder in a fashion, but she didn't want to use her right hand and tried to hang on using just her fingers, whimpering incessantly.

"It's just a little splinter," I said.

"It's huge. Huge!"

We left the boat without putting the tarps back on, walking down the road while she hollered. It was a dumb boat. She was never going back. She even hated it.

"Shitty boat."

"It's not the boat's fault," I said. "It's just that nobody's been taking care of it. We can see if we can find some oil. Then we can polish the benches and oil them. Or varnish. Maybe there's some in the shed. Then the splinters will disappear. And then it will be completely smooth."

I realized that I liked the plan. I wanted to return tomorrow, I wanted to work on the boat. But Lou didn't want to.

She kept howling, dragging her feet down the road, stopping constantly, asking me to wait, but when I waited and called "come on" in my nicest voice, she didn't come. She just stood there.

And I had to walk back to get her, leading her by her left hand, while she held her right hand up in the air demonstratively. The entire time she complained about how much it hurt, in a voice ever increasing in volume.

"You have to carry me. Carry me!"

And I was losing my patience as well. That was enough

now, enough. I drew a breath, as if air in my lungs would calm me. It didn't help.

My cheeks were hot, my heart was pounding hard and Lou wasn't quiet for a single second.

"Lou, please. You're a big girl. You have to walk by yourself."

I spoke softly, but tried to inject a kind of authority into my words. That didn't work either.

That's how I ended up putting to use all the tricks I knew.

I didn't have all that many of them.

First I begged.

"Lou, please, sweetie, please calm down and start walking."

Then I commanded.

"Lou. That will do. I can't carry you. Now you must come."

Then I threatened her.

"If you don't come now, you won't get any dinner. I will eat your dinner. I will eat everything."

She would have to go to bed hungry, I said. She would get very hungry. No dinner if she didn't pull herself together, behave like a big girl. Stop acting like a crybaby.

And finally I tried bribing her again.

"If you start walking properly now, you will have your dinner. Mine too. Along with your own."

But nothing worked. Finally, I pulled her up onto my back, just as she wanted. Her legs curled around my waist, she was far too tall.

"Here I go, carrying you," I said, "just because you have a tiny splinter in your finger."

"It's not in my finger," she fretted. "It's in my hand."

And I kept carrying her. She was a sack on my back. Heavy and shapeless. And horribly sweaty, hot and dirty. While she whimpered and whined.

The sound was killing me. No, it could drive me to commit murder.

Nasal wheezing, *uhuuhuuhuu ... uhuhu ... uhuuhu ...*

She hadn't been this way for weeks. Months. She hasn't behaved like this on a single occasion since people started fleeing from Argelès, since our city and our home had been destroyed.

Like a child.

SIGNE

Finally I can see the ocean meeting the sky. It grows lighter; the sun will soon rise behind me, above the mountains in the east. I keep on, towards open water, wait for the wind, look at the meter—the diesel tank is full, I can keep going like this for a long time and in the course of a few hours no doubt the wind will help me.

I take in the sensation of the helm against my hands, the smooth, varnished woodwork; I have to steer manually, there's not enough wind and it's too unstable for the self-steering wind vane. There are skerries astern, so I set my course for the southwest. Maybe they've discovered it by now, what has happened in the harbor, the ice bobbing in the fjord. Maybe they have discovered it and simultaneously noticed that I am gone, too. They will figure it out before long, certainly—the company, the police, Magnus—but by then it will already be too late, I will already be far out at sea.

The feeling of being underway, that's the best thing about a boat, knowing that you will get there, but not knowing when. Having a destination, but having not yet arrived.

I glance at the twelve containers of ice. I put them in the

saloon, stacked them on the red wool-upholstered couches. It's cramped but I can still reach the cooker, the instruments, and I can creep into the forepeak cabin and sleep there later, but not out here on deck, not on the open sea.

In the course of the morning the wind picks up—a light, early summer wind from the southeast. I raise the sail, the wind catches hold of it, that's how it should be, just like that, surging forward in a broad, diagonal cross. I adjust the wind vane, am so glad I have it instead of autopilot, those cheap mechanisms rust just like that. The manufacturers advertise that they will last forever, are maintenance-free, but at sea nothing is maintenance-free, salt and water will sooner or later have their way with everything, the way nature sooner or later destroys everything man-made. I drag cushions out of the cockpit's stowage space aport, lay them on the bench and settle in there, turning my face towards the sun. It is warm, prickling my skin. It has been a day and a half since I last slept; now I shut my eyes and drop off for a few minutes, awaken again, glancing around me quickly. No vessels in sight, land is already far behind me. I can glimpse only a strip of land on the horizon in the east, there is nobody here but me. I can rest a little more, because I have control over the boat, can steer it alone, like so many solitary skippers before me, like Joshua Slocum, the first man to sail around the world alone. How did he manage it, without a wind vane, without GPS, or an echo sounder, for 74,000 kilometers? He was fifty-one when he started in 1895 and his journey lasted for four years. He completed the sailing trip, but perished in the end, was lost at sea and nobody found him, maybe the *Spray* is still sailing the seven seas, maybe I will meet it out here, maybe only time and gender differentiate us, for the solitary sailor's loneliness overshadows most dissimilarities.

The skipper's nap is also something we have in common, under a blanket on the leeward cockpit bench, five minutes of rest, deep sleep, dropping straight into a dream, before I wake myself up, get onto my knees, look around me for a few seconds—still no boats, no skerries, no obstacles—the seconds I am awake scarcely exist. I sink down on the bench again and am back in the same dream.

The wind and the rushing roar of the ocean become the rumbling of a river. I am beside the River Breio, standing on the bridge, a rough construction of sun-bleached wood. I am young and an adult at the same time, I am just me, the person I have always been, whether I am fifteen, thirty-five or fifty. I am running late for something—a flight, to India, I have to catch a flight to India, I will be in Narmada for months, protesting against the dam they are building, the dam that will put villages underwater, force thousands out of their homes, protesting against the untouchables' lack of rights. That's where I'm headed, but before I leave, I have to check my suitcase, make sure I haven't forgotten anything; it's by my feet and I try to open it, but the lid is stuck, the suitcase is held together by two straps. I fiddle with them, the leather

of the straps is stiff between my fingers, I can't get them undone and I know the plane is departing soon, that there is
only this one flight and then I notice that I'm not wearing
shoes, I can't go all the way from here to the airport without
shoes on, maybe there are shoes in the suitcase I can't open. I
lift it, take it with me, walk slowly across the bridge, continue
across the site access road, it is full of sharp stones—big, hard
stones that cut the skin on the soles of my feet. I pick my way
forward, trying to find spots to put my feet, but my progress
is slow, I am walking too slowly.

I wake up, look around me, the 360-degree gaze, the coast
is clear, but I don't close my eyes to sleep again, instead I sit
up. I am here, but also still there, by the river.

I remember a walk, I was maybe nine or ten years old, Daddy
and I were on a walk early on a Sunday morning along the
River Breio. At first I was so happy, it had been months since
we'd spent time together, he didn't have the time any longer, or the desire. He was too busy arguing with Mommy,
yelling at Mommy. Daddy had told me to stop shouting because you can damage your hearing but now he was the one
shouting and screaming.

But this morning I was allowed to accompany him. I
woke up early and he was already on his way out. He was
planning to go alone, he said, but when I pestered him, he
gave in and let me come along. It was just the two of us. I
think I talked a lot, tried to ask about things we saw, ani-

mals and plants, but he gave me single-word answers and I didn't understand until later that it was because he really didn't want me with him.

We followed the road along the fjord until we reached a fork. There hadn't been a fork in the road there before, there had only been a single road, but now it forked into two roads, and one of the roads, the old part, continued along the fjord, while the other followed the River Breio up the mountain.

The road was rough and rocky, with deep ruts from heavy vehicles. It was a temporary road for construction; I hadn't seen it before, only heard them talk of it, especially him—the access road. He used to spit the words out, as if they had an unpleasant taste.

And it was an ugly road, I could see that now, an ugly, stony road which ruined the landscape it passed through, lined with hard stones, dirty and muddy, it tore the landscape in two.

But this was the road Daddy wanted us to take. He walked without hesitation, long strides and heavy shoes against the ground, shoes that soon were covered in mud and filth.

When we'd walked a short distance up the mountainside he turned to face me and finally he started to talk. But it was like he wasn't talking to me.

"Aluminum," he said. That was a difficult word; I wondered if it was written *ali* or *alu* or *almi*, like the word *almond*—I wondered about this while I listened to Daddy, but he said the word so quickly that I couldn't distinguish between the sounds.

"Hydraulic power is actually about *aluminum*, about war, because it's the *aluminum* plants that demand an increase in power production and without the production of weapons, eight out of ten *aluminum* plants would go bankrupt. People think this is about electricity—for schools, daycare centers, hospitals, for people's homes—but it's really about weapons and war, Norway's entire development is based on *aluminum* and weapons."

I didn't know how I was supposed to answer.

We stood there with our heads bowed, looking at the river, and near a particularly powerful waterfall, we saw a rainbow shimmering.

"Roygbiv," I said.

"What?"

"The colors of the rainbow. Red, orange, yellow, green, blue, indigo, violet."

"It's enormous," Daddy said, and I thought he meant the rainbow, but he was pointing at the river. "It's the snow from the mountain. The snowfall this year has been extreme. This is the last year we will see the river like that. Next year it will be gone."

"And the rainbow?" I said.

"That too, you understand that, certainly."

It was a silly question. I felt suddenly ashamed—I knew that the rainbow was produced by light that was refracted by drops of water, he had explained that to me long ago and I wasn't one to forget, I stored everything away, especially things he told me.

"But it will still be in the sky," I said, and hoped it would comfort him. "When it rains while the sun is shining, then we'll see it, it will appear, like a bridge across the fjord."

The last thing was something I'd heard him say once and I thought it sounded nice.

He didn't answer, so I continued, raising my voice.

"You said that, do you remember, Daddy, that God painted the rainbow in the sky as a promise to Noah that he would never again let a flood destroy the world?"

He used to like it, that I told him about things I had learned, that impressed him, but he didn't answer me now either.

"Do you remember that? And then you asked me what I thought about it. And then I said it was a fairy tale. Because if the story was true, the rainbow would have to be in the sky all the time. Do you remember that I said that? That it was a fairy tale?"

He gave a slight nod.

"Noah didn't exist," I said. "The flood didn't happen."

He was just as silent.

"THE FLOOD DIDN'T HAPPEN!"

"Good, Signe," Daddy said finally, but his voice was distant.

Shouting didn't help. All my life shouting had usually helped, but now it no longer had any effect on him and I didn't understand why.

The river unfolded before us, a broad piece of fabric that somebody had unwound from a roll of shiny material, I thought, invisible. It could be made into a cloak of invisibility,

a freezing cloak of invisibility and maybe that was the one I
was wearing now, without knowing it.

Suddenly Daddy started walking again, quickly. I trotted
behind him, on the horrible access road, just wanting to go
home, but I didn't dare ask, didn't dare stop.

Further up the mountainside the road crossed the river
by way of a recently constructed bridge that smelled of fresh
woodwork, and out on the bridge he finally stopped again
and now he looked at me.

"Feel that, Signe, can you feel the water flowing?" he said.

"Yes," I said.

"Do you feel it?"

"YES!"

The water caused a vibration under my feet, made me
shake all over.

"Look around you," he said. "Everything around you is
going to change. A tunnel will be dug here and the water will
be diverted away. Down there is where the power plant will
be," he pointed. "And from there they will install enormous
power lines. And the river, it will disappear. In the riverbed,
where it's flowing now, there will only be stone."

"What about the freshwater pearl mussels?"

"They will die."

"All of them?"

"Yes."

"Who will clean the water?"

"There won't be any water to clean."

Then he started walking again and I didn't dare ask about anything else. We continued for yet another hour, maybe two, up a steep incline. My back was sweating. I wanted to ask Daddy to slow down, but couldn't bring myself to do it; he strode along in front of me, all I could see was his back, his narrow shoulders under his knapsack and I couldn't think of anything except keeping up with him, upwards, upwards, the whole time upwards.

Finally we reached the tree line. I was breathing so hard that my throat was burning, but here the landscape flattened out. The cabin on Sønstebø's old summer farm tilted towards the ground, enclosed by a dilapidated fence. The sheep had just been let out to graze; the lambs bleated softly, fragile sounds as they trotted behind their parents. On the horizon I saw Blåfonna, a grayish-white tongue that ate its way into the tussocks of heather, moss and grass.

The road came to an end in the middle of nowhere and, where it terminated, Daddy also stopped for a moment.

"This is where the dam will be," he said. "Everything you see now will be dammed up, underwater."

"Everything?" I said.

"Everything."

He took a few more steps, straight into the patch of heather, but then it was as if he couldn't take any more, because all of a sudden he sat down on the slope without taking off his knapsack, so it was shoved up his back by the mound behind him, giving him a humpback.

He didn't ask me if I wanted to sit down too, it was like he was alone, but I sat down anyway and then he seemed to notice me, because he took off his knapsack, opened it and took out a lunchbox.

"Here. You must be hungry."

I took the sandwich on top. My stomach was growling, I was both hungry and thirsty, but nonetheless it was difficult to swallow.

I held the box out to Daddy. "Don't you want some?"

"Later," he said, and looked at his watch.

"You have to eat, you know, your body needs food to grow strong," I said.

But he didn't hear, just looked around, like he was waiting for someone.

I continued chewing, wishing the bread slices weren't so thick, that there had been more butter, and I wished that I knew what I should say and do.

"I have to pee," I finally said.

"You can go over there," he said, and pointed at a clump of bushes, the only vegetation growing up here.

I hurried over, squatted behind the bushes, but didn't think they concealed enough. He was just my daddy, I wasn't shy, wasn't afraid he would see me. It was rather that I didn't want to see *him*. I sat there for a long time. The trickling between my legs was warm, a few drops hit one of my thighs, turning cold when I pulled my pants on again, two spots against the inside of my pants leg that would stiffen like salt water on my skin and that I would feel until I had the chance to wash myself.

I was about to go back to Daddy when I discovered somebody else who was also out walking on this day. He arrived in a truck that he parked where the access road came to an end. I hadn't heard him coming, the silence of the mountains had swallowed up the sound of him, but I recognized both the man and the truck. It was Sønstebø, and Daddy approached him and I realized that Daddy had come here to meet him. It was Sønstebø Daddy had been waiting for.

They talked, the two men, and the mountain ate up their words. Or maybe they actually tried to speak softly, maybe they didn't want anyone to hear, not even me, because they stood close together, the way lovers talk, the way Mommy and Daddy used to talk to each other before.

I rushed over, listening more closely and then I was able to make out a few words.

"The bridge," Sønstebø said. "The bridge would be better."

Then Daddy looked up. "Hi, Signe," he said loudly.

And Sønstebø smiled at me—far too broadly, I thought— and again I thought of the doll.

"Hi, Signe," he said.

"Hi," I said.

"How nice that you and your father are taking a hike," he said.

"Yes," I said.

"We are heading home now," Daddy said.

"Magnus stayed home today," Sønstebø said to me.

"Oh," I said.

Suddenly I wished that Magnus had come with him, that he was also standing here beside me.

"He's studying for an arithmetic test," Sønstebø said.

"Signe has to go home and write an essay," Daddy said.

I had forgotten all about the essay, even though Norwegian was really my favorite subject at school.

"I can give you a lift down," Sønstebø said.

"Yes," I said.

"Are you sure?" Daddy said.

Sønstebø looked at him in wonder. "Sure? Yes?"

"But do you think ... maybe it's not worth the risk?"

"I'm tired," I said. "I want a ride."

I remember that I didn't understand what they meant, but I didn't ask the right question: what wasn't worth the risk, wasn't getting a ride home worth it? Because I was so tired, now I could really feel it, my whole body ached, the walk up had been too much, far too much, and there was no point in our not accepting the ride, why should we have to *walk* down when there was a car?

"No ..." Sønstebø said and looked at Daddy. "Maybe you're right. It's not worth the risk, we might run into somebody ..."

"But I'm so tired," I said.

"I want for us to walk, Signe," Daddy said. "It will be nice."

"No," I said. "It *won't* be nice."

Then Sønstebø laughed. "Quite a girl you have there!"

And Daddy blushed, even though he usually liked it when I spoke my mind.

"I don't want to walk," I said. "Why can't we go in the car? Why isn't it worth the risk?"

"It will probably be fine," Sønstebø said. "I can drive you part of the way."

"No," Daddy said.

And there was something about him that made me realize that he wouldn't listen to me, that I would have to walk the whole, long way down. Daddy nodded at Sønstebø, and Sønstebø got into his car, started the engine and drove away, and I was tired and cold, it had started to sleet, the drops of pee were sticky on my thigh, shouting didn't help anymore. I just wanted to go home.

Maybe it's not worth the risk—the words got stuck in my head, made me heavier, I remember; it's not worth the risk, the two of them might be seen together. The words weighed on me as we walked home, weighed on me when we met Mommy again and Daddy behaved as if nothing had happened.

I was freezing cold and worn out, and he didn't appear to notice. But Mommy brought me up to the bathroom and filled the tub while I peeled off my clothes. They lay there on the floor, all dirty and damp, she put bubble bath in the water, it foamed up right away and the soap formed a soft white blanket on the surface that I could sink under and hide myself in.

The water was too hot, scorching hot, and I gasped. I could feel the blood rushing to my face, how it turned red and sort of blotchy.

Mommy left. I thought she was just going to fetch something—a bathrobe for me, maybe, or a clean towel, or something to drink or eat—but then she was just gone, because he was out there, I'd forgotten that, he was there, the thing the two of them shared, he was out there, the big, ugly thing and I couldn't stop it, the rising voices, the yelling. I wasn't a part of it, there wasn't anything I could say, nothing that helped. I wished it could be stopped, but if it was just going to continue, at the very least I wanted to be a part of it.

The bathwater slowly turned lukewarm and then cold, my body got wrinkled, my toes turned red, soon fins grew between them. I became a water creature in the bathtub while they were screaming at each other outside, a tiny little water creature in a snow globe full of sticky, shiny fluid and plastic snowflakes. They lifted me up sometimes, shook me, looked at me, but then they put me down again and went away, back to one another, to share what they had in common, the big, evil, ugly thing, which was only between them, the two of them.

A few days later we heard about the explosion. It was Daddy who told us about it, Mommy had just come home. She had been away for a while, maybe she'd gone to Bergen—she went there often, to purchase supplies for the hotel. When she opened the door and came inside, Daddy was standing there waiting for her with the news.

"Svein Bredesen came by this morning," he said. "The chief engineer."

"Hi, Mommy," I said.

"I know who Bredesen is," Mommy said.

She stroked my hair quickly, without looking at me.

"He wanted to speak with you," Daddy said.

"I can call him right away," she said.

"But since you weren't home, I took a message."

"Yes?"

"Somebody destroyed the bridge over the access road. Last night. It was blown to bits."

"What?"

"There's nothing left of it. It will take weeks to repair it, maybe months."

Mommy just stood there. At first she didn't say anything and I tried to give her a hug, but she asked me to wait. Then she said that she didn't understand how something like that could happen, how somebody could do something like that.

"The bridge and the road have to be there," she said. "The power station and the pipes are going to be installed. It's going to happen anyway."

He didn't say anything.

She stared at him for a long time. "Do you know something about this?"

Of course he said no. I remember how he stood there in

the hallway with his hands in his pockets and said no, no, of course I don't.

"But you must understand how angry some people are," he said. "How angry people are. You must understand what you've started with people. Of course they're furious. They're so angry that they blow up bridges."

"Are you defending it?" she asked, in a soft voice.

"I saw a nest yesterday," he said. "A water ouzel's nest. When the river disappears, we will lose the water ouzel."

"There are thousands of them, thousands . . ."

"No, Iris. There are only a few."

"There are thousands of rivers in Norway."

"Many small rivers. But very few the size of the River Breio."

"But do they know who did it? What did Svein say?"

"Svein? Are you on a first-name basis with him?"

"I mean Bredesen. What did he say? What do they know?"

"When the river disappears, the water ouzel will continue laying eggs there, in the old, dried-up riverbed," Daddy continued, almost like he was chanting. "But the roaring of the river will no longer drown out the sound of their young when they cry for food. Predators will find them. They will be killed."

"Bjørn, if you know something, you must tell me."

"Daddy doesn't know anything," I said.

Maybe it's not worth the risk.

"What did you say?"

She whirled around to face me, as if she had only just realized that I was there.

"Daddy doesn't know anything."

"Signe, you don't understand this."

"But he doesn't know anything."

"Of course I don't," Daddy said. "What would I know?"

Mommy was silent, looking at Daddy, then she turned towards me and tried to smile. "Are you hungry? Have you had dinner? Have the two of you eaten yet?"

"I just want dessert," I said.

"I see," she said.

"I said that I don't want dinner. Just dessert."

"Yes," she said.

DAVID

It was not until we approached the camp that Lou calmed down. Drawn-out sniffles, but no tears.

Summoning my resolve, I attempted once again to distract her from the splinter in her hand.

"Dolphins are really smart, you know," I said.

She didn't reply, but I could tell from her eyes that she was interested. "A lot of people claim they are just as smart as people," I said.

"Smarter than the sailor, at least," Lou said and sniffled one last time.

"The sailor?"

"You, Daddy!"

"Yes, smarter than the sailor."

She walked in silence for a while. I could see that a question was brewing inside her.

"Where do dolphins come from?" she said then. "Do they lay eggs like birds? Huge, blue eggs?"

"No. They give birth to living babies," I said.

"Just like people?"

"Yes."

"Oh."

She slowed her steps, looking disappointed. "But huge, blue eggs would have been nice," I hastened to say.

She nodded. "Yes. That would have been nicer."

The sun disappeared behind the trees. It would be dark soon.

I walked faster.

"How big are dolphins' children?" she asked.

"Um ..."

"How do they swim?"

"They kind of slide forward."

"But how? How do they move? Do they flap, like birds do?"

"No, they just slide."

"But how?"

"They wiggle their tails, like other fish."

"Like wiggling your bum?"

"Yes."

I kept trying to answer the best I could. I didn't do especially well.

She should have had a teacher. Should have gone to school. But no class instruction was offered at the camp. I was all she had. And I didn't know anything.

Nonetheless, we agreed to try to find out something about the swimming business. How they actually moved through the water.

Dolphins. I had been interested in them, too, when I was

little, I remembered. There's something about dolphins, it's hard not to like them. Maybe because they smile.

"One day I'm going to swim with dolphins for real," Lou said.

"Mm," I said.

Then I came up with something about dolphins, something I had read once. That it wasn't good to swim with them. That people who jump in with the dolphins to swim with them actually disturb them, agitate them, keep them from searching for food for themselves and their young. But I didn't say that to Lou.

It was almost dark when we reached the camp. I was able to borrow a pair of tweezers and pulled Lou's splinter out without any difficulty. She didn't cry. Then we went to eat. Francis was sitting outside the mess hall holding his food bowl in his good hand. The bowl was completely empty.

"You have to hurry," he said. "If you are going to get food for the youngster. They are running short today."

My stomach growled loudly when we walked in and I smelled food. I was so hungry that I felt dizzy. I snatched up a bowl of brown stew and a few pieces of bread. And a glass of milk. We received one with every meal. But there wasn't enough, there was never enough. We would have to go to bed right away—the only thing that helped was to try to sleep off the hunger.

I poured half of the milk into an empty glass and held the glasses side by side.

"Are they the same?" I asked Lou.

She leaned over to look.

"Maybe a little more in that one."

She pointed at the one on the left.

I poured a couple of drops out of the glass on the right.

"Like that?"

She nodded.

"Then you can choose," I said.

"But they're the same."

"Whoever divides can't choose. That's the rule."

"OK."

She took the glass on the left. I took hold of the other.

"Do you know why you are given milk?" somebody suddenly said from behind us.

We turned around.

"Hi!" Lou said.

"Hi," Marguerite said and nodded to her.

She had also just received her meal and held a bowl only a quarter full in her hands.

"Do you want to sit with us?" Lou said.

I scooted over a bit on the bench to make room for her.

But Marguerite didn't move.

"You know that the milk is for the children?" she said.

I looked at the glass I had in my hand.

"No. I didn't know that. Obviously."

"That's why you only received one glass. The rest of us don't get any."

"I see."

I put my glass down on the table and quickly slid it over to Lou.

"Are they both for me?" she asked.

I nodded. Felt how the blood rushed to my face.

"The milk is for the children," I repeated softly.

"But I don't mind sharing," Lou said.

"Thank you," I said. "But it is apparently for you."

I stared over at Marguerite as I said it.

She held her head tilted to one side, studying me, as if I were a stupid little man-child.

"*Happy now?*" I wanted to say, but stopped myself. It was better to keep my mouth shut.

"I don't need two," Lou said, and pushed the glass towards me again.

And I wanted milk, I did. No doubt it was cold, would cool my throat, my stomach. The only thing we received that was cold. So I took it. Quickly.

"You're nice, Lou," I said.

Marguerite emitted a tiny sound. I didn't care. My daughter knew how to share, had learned to share. That meant something, anyway.

I took a sip of the milk. Waited for the coldness, but it had already had time to become lukewarm.

We've used up all the cold, I thought.

It was Marguerite's fault. She poked her nose in without knowing anything about us.

•

August was only a year old. Lou had never really experienced having a sibling. A baby in the house didn't count. A baby didn't argue about sweets, a baby didn't want to have the biggest piece of cake. All the same, or perhaps for that very reason, she was good at sharing.

"Have a seat," Lou said to Marguerite.

"She probably wants to eat in peace," I said to Lou.

"Why's that?" Lou said to Marguerite.

Who sat down.

Or more precisely ... took her seat. On the bench beside Lou, an appropriate distance away from her, like she wasn't really with us.

Silence. I didn't want to be the first one to speak ...

But it was very quiet.

Perhaps I should say something.

She didn't.

But none of the questions I was accustomed to asking—*how's it going, how about this weather, have you had a nice day*—was appropriate, somehow.

What do you talk about in a refugee camp? How do you make small talk when your life has gone to hell?

And small talk ... that wouldn't hold any appeal for somebody like Marguerite.

She would just laugh at me.

No, she would smile, a crooked smile.

Best to avoid it.

I put my faith in Lou. She would succeed in lightening the

mood. But she was too busy satisfying her hunger. She gulped down her food, even licked the bowl clean.

In the end it was actually Marguerite who broke the silence.

"They haven't received supplies. That's why there's so little."

"How do you know?" I said.

"I've been at a place like this before. In the mountains. That was the first thing that happened, the supplies stopped arriving."

"The first thing that happened before what?"

"Before we all left."

"It will be fine," I said hollowly.

I didn't want to have this conversation with her while Lou was listening.

"I haven't seen a single vehicle come to the camp. Neither yesterday nor today," Marguerite said.

"You've been sitting by the side of the road all day keeping an eye on things," I said and tried to laugh. "Wasn't it really hot? Did you sit by the edge of the ditch or something?"

She took a bite of her food and didn't reply, didn't even grace me with a glance.

"You're quite the optimist," I said.

I regretted the words immediately and hastened to add: "We are fine here. You can tell, can't you, that this is a decent place?"

As if any of us knew whether this was a *decent place*. It wasn't like she had all the answers, like she was the one who knew how things were at every single refugee camp in southern Europe.

For a while we were silent and finally Lou piped up.

"We found a boat."

"A boat?" Marguerite said.

"Not really," I said. "There was no boat, it was just a game."

"But there was a boat," Lou said. "There is a boat. It's big and blue or black. Is it blue or black, Daddy?"

"Dark blue," I said. "But it's just a game."

"Tell me about it, then," Marguerite said and looked at Lou. "Even if it's only a game."

And Lou told her. About the boat, about the pirates, the dolphins and the shrewd captain.

Marguerite scooted over on the bench, closer to Lou, listened, asked more questions and Lou explained. They chattered away as if they were old friends.

And Marguerite laughed, she actually laughed, when Lou told her about the stupid sailor.

There they sat, the two of them, on the bench across from me, laughing at me. I wasn't sure how I felt about that.

But afterwards, when we went our separate ways, Marguerite reached her hand out to Lou, towards her head, like she was going to ruffle her hair. She held it there stiffly, suspended aloft for a second, before pulling it back, and instead just gave the child a slight pat on the shoulder.

That was something, I thought. That, and that she had laughed.

SIGNE

I wake up suddenly, the cold yanks me awake, my teeth are chattering and the sun has disappeared. The sky is clouding over and the wind has changed, become stronger, the boat is heeling more. I sit up; this must have blown up quickly. Or perhaps I've slept longer than I should have—me, the one who never needs an alarm clock at sea. I have always relied on my built-in timepiece.

All around me there is only the ocean, the only thing in sight is an oil platform, all lit up against a darkening sky. Every day they bring up two million barrels of oil, two million barrels. One barrel is 159 liters; I don't have the energy to work out the total number of liters that comes to, every single day. There they are, all those who are constructing Norway, the nation, while simultaneously they are destroying the world. What if they said no, all of them, refused to work, went on strike? One single week would have helped, just one day would have helped, two million barrels fewer pulled up out of the ground and released into the environment.

The lights on the platform grow sharper all the time . . . no, it's the surrounding world that's growing darker, it must be late. The night is surprisingly dark for the bright month of April. I sail into the night, a strong wind from the east drives me away from land.

I take out the wind meter, hold it up, and measure the wind speed, fourteen meters per second.

Fourteen. Such strong winds already.

The wind is blowing harder and harder. I must reef the sail, rolling back an edge of the canvas to reduce the width. I should have done so a long time ago, but first I have to pee, so I do it quickly on the floor of the cockpit—it will be washed away immediately anyway. Then I adjust the wind vane and slowly release the headsail sheet. The sail flaps as if possessed; I grasp the line of the roller-furling system—it's thin, chafes at my hands, I tug and haul at it but it's too heavy, far too heavy, I'm not as strong as I used to be.

I place the line around the winch, my fingers are frozen, every movement hurts, but slowly the wind force in the headsail is diminished and I can heave to. Then I yank the mainsheet out of the quick-release cleat; now it's the mainsail that's billowing wildly, I have to move forward to the mast to reef.

The wind is a wall as I crawl towards the bow. I should have put on the harness, but I climb up on top of the cabin nonetheless and free up the halyard on the mast winch. At the same time, a wave hits the ship, it's like being hit by a train, I hold on to the mast with both hands, the end of the halyard slips and blows out horizontally from the mast, I reach for it, but know I have no chance of snagging it, the wind blows it back and forth, in the end wrapping it around one of the shrouds just beneath the crosstree, dammit, dammit.

I loosen a boat hook I have attached to the deck, hold it out towards the crosstree, but it's no use, of course it's no use. Should I climb up? No, not now, it will just have to hang there, the mainsail is almost down on the boom. I open the shackle on the line; my fingers are numb with cold as I fasten it to the mast and furl the sail. Then I crawl back to the cockpit. It's only then that I'm able to breathe.

A quick trip inside to pull on my sweater, rain overalls and raincoat on top of the windbreaker and trousers I am wearing. I am already soaking wet, it's pouring off me, but there's nothing I can do about it, there's no time to change.

I should secure the containers of ice, they are stacked in the saloon, their weight is still holding them in place, but a big wave now is all it will take to send them sliding off the benches, careening onto the floor and creating chaos.

I find some rope and a few old elastic straps, look around for something to lash them to, and finally stretch the straps and ropes several times back and forth between the pole the table is attached to and some hooks on the wall.

At that moment, the coffee pot crashes onto the floor. I'd left it on the cooker. Water runs out of the spout, I snatch it up, pour the water out, toss it into a cupboard, close the lid on the sink, and shut the valve on the gas cylinder.

How bad is it, really? Do I have to batten down the hatches

and lock myself inside, stay down here with the ice until the wind drops?

No, I'm not going to do that, I can do this—I can put on the safety harness, fasten it securely. I've done this before, survived hard weather conditions, winds up to twenty-three meters a second, a squall, *Blue* needs me, I can't let her drift on her own.

I straighten up, and at that moment a huge wave crashes into the boat, water pours down into the saloon, spraying over the blue containers. I rush to tread the boards into place over the entrance, throw the maps on the table, turn on the map-reading lamp above the instruments, the brightness of the light making me jump—now I am ruining my night vision, but there's no way around it. I must find a safe harbor, seek shelter behind some islands. I can't continue like this.

What is the latitude of my current position? I check the GPS, already at a latitude level with Stavanger, but the wind is blowing directly from the east, towards me, and I can't sail against the wind.

But I can tack; I'll have to tack even if the storm keeps up all night.

Up again, wearing the harness. I let out a few rotations of the roller-furling system, immediately grateful that I invested in it—imagine if I had to move fore to the bow to change the sail now, take the storm jib out of the space under the bed in the forepeak and raise the sail. I would have had to make it all the way to the bow to rig it. Now instead I can just pull on a line and soon I have the sail that I need.

I set my course north. It's heavy going—according to the speedometer between two and three knots. The oncoming sea slows me down, the waves break hard against the bow, again and again, sometimes stopping me altogether, but I have to maintain my course for a few nautical miles and then go about to the south, and continue in that direction before tacking to the north again.

I am glad I slept earlier in the day, there's no time to rest now. I cling to the helm, my eyes firmly focused on the compass and my hearing attuned to the wind, the waves, the sound of them—they break, surging, tearing at the hull, shaking the boat, shaking me, the fiberglass, which suddenly feels so fragile.

The minutes pass, maybe hours. I don't look at the clock, feel only the wind, how it intensifies, beating against the headsail, driving me forward. I have tacked three times, but still can't stay on course—the long, shallow keel is producing leeway. I am moving too far south, drifting southwards along the coast, but not any closer to land.

The mainsail halyard is whipping against the mast, has wrapped itself around it several times, the sound of steel cables against aluminum is like nothing else on earth, damn that it slipped, dammit.

I could have been indoors, in front of a fireplace—warm, yellow light, not a sound except for the crackling of firewood burning, a room filled with the silence of evening, a book, a lap rug, something hot to drink, could have been submerged in a steaming bubble bath, the scent of soap, the mirror misted over. But I'm here, the wind pounding against my face, the water pouring off me, nature clawing at me, battering me.

I grab the wind meter, want to know how bad it is, probably not as bad as I think. I hold out my arm, the needle rises, sixteen meters per second, seventeen, eighteen, nineteen.

High winds, heavy gales and increasing in intensity.

Bloody hell.

I have to reef, the headsail has to be furled all the way, the wind is going to get even stronger, I can't continue.

I tug at the reefing line, but it gets stuck on the roller. I tug and tug, but am unable to budge it, the jib flaps violently. I have to make my way forward to the bow. On deck the wind feels even stronger, just one gust and I'll be blown overboard. I take pains to tether the stays on the safety harness at all times, not moving an inch without securing it. I don't want to think about lying out there, don't think about it, lying there, in the waves, how long would I stay alive, how long would I manage to keep my head above water, for how long would I survive?

The entire world is rolling, there is nothing that isn't moving, nothing stationary, I have to roll with it, can't fight against it. I crawl, my knees on deck, but they're too old for this, they're like a separate part of me, older than the rest of my body, creaking knees; the knees are the first things to go on human beings, it's almost impossible to make them last an entire lifetime and nothing helps, they've already withstood too much, too many steps, all the strain settles into them, they grumble. I try crawling differently but nothing helps, can't think about it, just keep moving forward, meter by meter.

The jib is flapping savagely, like an enormous, out-of-control white bird. I tug at the line—loosen now, come on, help me, work with me, damn line—then it gives way and I can reef.

A powerful wave washes over me on the way back. There is water everywhere, rain in the air, salt water pours off me, the taste of it on my tongue.

All the sails are down, the boat is hurled forward, backwards, I curl up on the floor of the cockpit, the urine has long since been washed away. I can see the helm above me, also being thrown back and forth, back and forth. I curl into a ball, but can't just lie here like this, give up—I can't give up.

A drogue, a drogue attached to the stern, trailing behind the boat, that would slow the boat down, stabilize it. I sit up, open the cockpit's starboard stowage space, digging, rummaging through coils of rope, fenders, pails of old ship-bottom paint, it's such a mess, good God, why haven't I organized things better, I say to myself—although the boat is shipshape, here nothing is as it should be, when you get right down to it. But there it is, finally. I pull it out and find at the same time a long, thick rope, stiff with salt. I fasten it to the drogue, then I crawl astern, tie the rope to the railing and throw the drogue overboard into the ocean. It makes no sound when it hits the surface—it's made of fabric, a huge bag of fabric, and it will take time for it to fill up with water—but then I notice the rope tightening and the boat is finally stabilized. My *Blue*, my home, Mommy's present for my eighteenth birthday. She gave it to me to stabilize something, I think, she put this boat on my internal scales. She perhaps intended it to be beautiful, this attempt to meet me halfway, but actually it was just ugly, an attempt to buy redemption for all the times she'd disappointed me in my childhood.

"An Arietta 31. Brand new," I remember she said, a little proud when she gave me the keys. "Built in Sweden. Olle Enderlein designed it. He's the best there is these days."

Only the best was good enough for me.

My boat, the sailboat *Blue*, Mommy's present, Mommy's olive branch, the gift I couldn't bring myself to refuse, the only gift she ever gave me that I actually wanted. Unlike her, it has never let me down.

I go inside, to stay this time, secure the hatchway, sit down by the map table, and immediately I can feel how I'm trembling. Have I been like this the whole time or is it a delayed reaction? I don't know, but I shake, tremble, as if the wind were taking hold of me, but it's not cold and frost that's tearing me apart—my back is sweating from the exertion—it's anxiety. I'm afraid. This is the first time, I think, the first time I have been overpowered like this. I wasn't prepared, didn't check the weather forecast, idiot, I didn't—you never sail out without checking the weather—I could have known it was coming, could have been somewhere else now, a port of refuge, docked, solid ground beneath my feet, heat, yellow light, a bathtub.

But I managed it, the sails are reefed, the boat and drogue are working together, I'm sitting here; I managed it, I don't need a port of refuge, because I am my own and I have *Blue*. She gave it to me when I turned eighteen, it was her olive branch, and I accepted it, couldn't bring myself to turn it down and she expected something in return, I knew that, she expected a lot in return, an entire life, but I never gave her that.

People like her, like Magnus, they think everything is simple, that if you just buy a big enough Band-Aid, the wound will heal, but if it hasn't been cleaned it's no use, as long as dirt, pebbles and dust are still stuck in the flesh.

The storm lashes at the boat, a horrific racket, the rigging shudders. I am so tired, lay my arms on the map table, lean my head on them, just for a moment, rest for a moment, but I can't, because I can hear how the water is leaking in, surrounding the boat, not just under it, but washing over the deck, pouring down from the sky and it's leaking inside, the sound of dripping water is everywhere.

I stand up again, listen, it's coming from the forepeak; I move up there, the fore hatch is not closed properly, water's trickling in. I try screwing the hatch even more tightly shut but it doesn't help, the water keeps dripping, teeny-tiny drops forcing their way through, stealing their way in, finding their way through invisible cracks.

It's also leaking from the windows in the forepeak. I've sealed them with silicone, but it's not enough, I should have unscrewed them and reinforced them with a silicone rubber gasket, because now it's dripping down onto the berth, cold water on the mattress and duvet.

But there's nothing I can do about it, I won't be sleeping anyway, soon I'll have to go up again, I must check every fifteen minutes, look for other boats, drilling rigs, be on the lookout for other lone lanterns out there in the storm.

I sit down at the map table again. Time stands still, time rages by—no, it's the storm that's raging, the ocean, the wind, a racket like no other, the cable pounding against the mast, it's no longer a rhythm, the sound is now so powerful and rapid that it has become a vibration. Should I call for help, *mayday, mayday*—if I have enough power on the battery to use the VHF radio I can still reach the drilling rig, maybe they can help?

No, I'm not asking for help, I'll ride it out, the storm, I don't need them, I don't need help from any damn oil rig, from un-woke oil workers, at home half the time, million-dollar salaries, I don't need their help, don't need anyone's help.

I have to check again. I pull back the hatch, peek out, a wave crashes over me, hell, my hood isn't up, ice-cold seawater pours down my back, I can't see a thing, all that's out there is the ocean.

I slam the hatch shut.

Sit down.

Shake, tremble.

Keep going.

DAVID

"I want to go see the boat again," Lou said when she woke up.

She was lying in bed, smiling at me.

"Hush," I whispered. "Don't wake the others."

It was the crack of dawn, by my guess. The hall was still quiet. I heard only the sound of people sleeping, breathing heavily. Somebody was snoring loudly, others turned over in their beds. The morning light filtered through the windows.

"But I want to go to the boat," Lou said, a little more softly.

"I thought you said it was a shitty boat," I whispered.

"You're not allowed to say shitty," she said.

"No."

"I'm going to the boat anyway."

She placed her bare feet on the concrete floor and pulled on the pair of shorts that had been hanging over the headboard.

"Maybe later," I said.

"It's our boat now." She came over to me. "C'mon, get up."

"It's not ours."

"But we're the ones who found it."

She leaned over me, pressing her face against mine. Her eyes were two bright slits in her face. God, she looked so much like Anna. She also looked this way in the morning. The same eyes. The sun was always shining in there, regardless of the weather.

Anna.

"Maybe we can go after breakfast," I said, and tried to hide the huskiness in my voice.

She hopped up and down. "Can we?"

"We have to put the tarps back on."

"Of course," she said.

"But first we have to drop in at the Red Cross."

"Oh. The Red Cross."

She stopped hopping.

"Maybe they've found them," I said.

"Yes."

I stood up and pulled on my clothes, taking my time with my T-shirt, hiding my face inside it until I felt that I had my crying under control.

I held out the bottle of antibacterial handwash and she accepted it automatically. We both cleaned our hands. Then we walked through the quiet hall of sleeping bodies, out into an equally quiet morning.

"Daddy?"

"Yes?"

She took my hand as we approached the Red Cross barracks.

"Do I have to go inside with you?"

"Why don't you want to go inside?"

"I want to wait outside."

"It would be nice if you came inside with me."

"I want to wait outside."

"But why?"

"I want to play."

"Play? Play what?"

"Just play."

She threw herself down on the patch of grass by the entrance and sat calmly on the withered blades that had once upon a time been grass, while the sun beat down on her.

She didn't make a sound.

Jeanette nodded at me when I walked in, and before I even had time to sit down she said: "I have nothing new for you today, David."

"Wow," I said and tried to smile. "That was quick."

"Sorry. But you don't need to check in every single day. These things take time."

"I realize that," I said. "But I wanted to stop by anyway. Imagine if something had actually *happened*?"

"You aren't the only one who has to hear this. I say it to everyone, there's no point in coming every day."

"But imagine if something had happened last night, that they'd appeared somewhere, even here. Imagine if they were sick?" My voice rose. "If they were sick and alone. But that they were here—and I didn't find out about it."

I caught myself, made an effort to lower my voice.

"Or imagine if you had found out that they were some-where else," I said. "At a camp nearby, that we could go be with them right away."

"You're in such a hurry," Jeanette said. "Try not to be."

"But it's been almost a month!"

I took a deep breath, was about to say something else. But her mouth curled into a grimace and that stopped me. Not that she was mocking me, she just pulled her lips apart, like a smile but without any joy. A grin.

She could have sighed, probably had every reason to sigh. Sitting here all day long with people like me—who thought we were the only ones who mattered.

"Sorry," I said.

"It's fine," she said.

But I wasn't convinced that she really meant it. Because nothing was really *fine*. For any of us. Not for her. Not for Lou and me. And I should just get out of here, stop pressuring her, pestering, hassling her.

"But I can't help it," I said quickly.

"What?"

"I can't help pestering you. I'm sorry."

"Come back tomorrow," Jeanette said.

"Everyone wants to get inside," Lou said.

We were on our way to the boat and the only ones walking in that direction, walking out of the camp. At least twenty people were standing in front of the entrance to the camp and waiting to be registered. People who wanted to get *inside*. I hadn't seen so many people there before. So many, so dirty, so tired. And some with soot marks on their faces.

Where were they going to live, all of them?

I wanted to hurry away from the camp, taking Lou with me. But I couldn't help noticing three young men who were standing at the front of the line. There was something rough about them, something guarded. They had been on the road a long time, were used to sleeping with one eye open, used to having to watch over their things, take care of themselves, listen for footsteps, look over their shoulder. They spoke quickly. Laughed a little too loudly, the way you laugh when you want everyone to hear how much fun you are having. Like waiting in line to enter a nightclub, the way Edouard and I had done, once upon a time.

Suddenly one of them spun around to face the man behind them in the line and he spoke loudly to him in Spanish. The man was in his forties. Thick-necked, heavy-set, his skin sun-beaten. He took a threatening step towards the young men. And said something, also in Spanish, in an even louder voice.

The two friends approached him. One of them pointed at his buddy's bag, gesturing—it seemed like they were saying that Thick-Neck had tried to help himself from it.

The words began to fly rapidly back and forth between them. Their voices rose. Almost to screams. They stood close to one another. The three young boys on the one side, the adult and another man, who clearly was taking his side, on the other.

I could make out a few words that I understood, *idiot, bastard.*

Thick-Neck slapped his forehead with his hand.

At the same time he moved one step closer. Everyone in the line noticed them and had stopped talking. The woman sitting at the registration table was completely silent. Lou pressed up against me.

"What are they doing?" she whispered.

The young boy looked at Thick-Neck and then at the camp entrance. One of his buddies put his hand on his arm, restraining him, *take it easy.*

Finally the young boy took a deep breath, nodded quickly. "OK, OK."

He turned to the woman at the registration table, attempting a smile as he spoke in broken English: "Can we go in now?"

She didn't answer. She could maybe have said something, about how troublemakers were not welcome in the camp. But it probably didn't make any difference. Those who want to make trouble will do so, no matter what, whether they are allowed to enter or not. Sometimes it's best just to be nice to them.

Hurriedly, I led Lou away, down the road. I had seen things like this before, brawls in food lines, in bars in the evening.

I knew what it was about and that it wouldn't pass any-time soon. They would keep it up for a long time, these men, because it was always men. They would keep it up until their fists hardened. Till they had hit everything they could find that was soft, throwing punches that landed with hollow thuds. Muscles, bones, flesh and organs. Strange moans a split second after the blow, when the body absorbed what had happened, as the nervous system did its job.

Their frustration was intensified by the heat, the heat that never relented, not even during the night. There is nothing that makes people more aggressive than not being able to sleep because of the heat.

The heat did something to the air. Like a gas, we inhaled it without noticing it. Like fungal spores. We absorbed them through our respiratory passages. They were growing inside of us. The fungi grew large and gray. Shiny on top, layers of supple frills under the cap. Poisonous. They spread through us. Altered our nerve impulses, took control of the brain.

But this wasn't my fight, not my conflict. Spain was not my country.

I had Lou. The only thing I could do was leave.

Nonetheless, my feet were dragging. Because hadn't Thick-Neck stuck his hand into the young boy's bag? Hadn't I seen that, really? Shouldn't I have supported them? Sided with them?

I should have. And I wanted to. Show my solidarity with them. Choosing sides means being inside.

"You are walking so slowly." Lou was pulling me.

And I quickened my pace, walking faster, even though I felt I had shrunk. I was convinced that they were staring at us, everyone in the line, that they saw how small we were, what outsiders we were.

He who doesn't choose sides is damn lonely.

Lou followed the right route, the third lane to the left. The gardens were deserted today, the shutters were closed. All the houses looked empty.

As we walked along Lou's steps became lighter. She was looking forward to this. Soon she started chattering. She talked more than she had in a long time, about the boat, about the dolphins. I listened only in part. But then she started asking questions.

"Daddy. Where is there the most water?"

I didn't answer right away. Couldn't bring myself to talk now.

"Daddy? Where is the most water? In the world or in the oceans?"

"The oceans are also a part of the world," I said.

"And is it water when it's salty?"

"Yes, it's still water."

"Are there oceans that aren't salty?"

"Do you remember when we went up into the mountains?" I asked.

"The mountains?"

"Do you remember you swam in a lake up there?"

"In my yellow bathing suit?"

"Yes."

"I went swimming in the yellow bathing suit even though it was too small for me."

"That was the time, yes."

"But it wasn't too small. I was the one who had grown too big."

"Yes ... The water you went swimming in then, it wasn't salty."

"Did we drink it?"

"No, but we could have drunk it."

"Why didn't we drink it?"

"I don't know. I imagine because we'd brought bottled water."

"Why?"

"Well ..."

"Daddy, can we go there? To the lake?"

"It's no longer possible."

"Why not?"

"You know why."

"The drought?"

"Yes."

"And there's no lake like that here without salt? Fresh water?"

"No. Maybe there were lakes here. But now they've dried up."

"Too bad."

"Yes."

"How many freshwater lakes are there?"

"A lot."

"More than ten?"

"More than ten."

"More than a hundred?"

"More than a million. There are even lakes under the ground."

"Under the ground? That we walk on?"

"Yes."

"That's not true. You can't walk on water."

"Yes, you can. It's called groundwater."

"And we walk on it?"

"In some places there's a lot. In South America, for example, on the other side of the Atlantic Ocean, the Guarani reservoir is located underground."

"We walk on it. Like Jesus."

"We walk on the ground, but the water is beneath us, between layers of soil and stone, so it's not exactly like Jesus."

"But almost."

"There's groundwater everywhere. It's under us now, too."

"Now?"

"Yes."

"Here?"

"Yes."

"But why can't we just dig for it?"

"It's too deep. And the water is mixed with soil and stones."

"Can't we try?"

"People did try a long time ago."

"But what about that place in America, then?"

"South America. There you can dig for it. And it's enormous. It extends all the way under Brazil, Argentina, Paraguay and Uruguay."

"Paraguay, Uruguay?"

"It's much bigger than all of France . . . there's enough water for the whole world to survive on."

"Wow."

"For two hundred years."

"Wow!"

"Yes. Wow."

"Who owns it?"

"I don't know . . . I guess it's the people who own the land on top of it."

"But somebody owns it?"

"I believe so."

"How can somebody own water?"

We had arrived. She let go of my hand and trotted away, ducking in beneath the shadow of the trees. *Yippee* her shoulders said. And her braids bounced against her T-shirt.

We walked through the garden, passing the rainwater tank. I would have liked to try to open it, maybe there was a key in the house. But Lou had disappeared in the direction of the boat and I followed behind her.

"We're just going to put the tarps back on," I said. "And tie the ropes tightly. Remember that. The boat isn't ours."

But she didn't answer. And when we were sitting in the

cockpit again, it quickly became clear that we hadn't come to cover up the boat again right away.

Because it was cool in the shade between the trees. There was even a bit of a breeze up there. And almost immediately, Lou was back in the game. She shouted, she screamed and yelled, shot and fenced, laughed and cried. She raised the sail, fought against pirates and found a baby dolphin that was her own. It swam after the boat and was named Nelly. I had no idea where she got *that* name from.

I was an extra. The stupid sailor. I did as she said, took part in her game of make-believe. *And then you, like, said this, and then I answered that, and then you, like, suddenly jumped to one side, and then it was night and you got, like, scared. And then we sailed to the end of the ocean.*

There was never any fire in her games. Even if we were in danger, it was never really scary. And there was water every-where, all the time.

I followed orders. I breathed easily.

But finally it was Lou who didn't want to play anymore.

"I'm thirsty."

We'd brought along a half-liter bottle of water that we'd filled up that morning when the rations were doled out, but it was long since empty. I could feel the dust from the dry soil on my tongue.

"We have to go back," I said.

"No," Lou said.

She was filthy. A thin layer of dust covered her skin. There were grimy streaks of sweat on her face. One of her braids had slipped out of the rubber band and her hair was tangled. We needed water for more than drinking.

"We'll have to fill out the forms again and stand in line, from the looks of you," I said.

"Do we have to stand in line? Won't they let us in again?"

"I'm kidding, Lou."

"Won't they let us into the camp?"

"Yes, they will, don't worry."

But suddenly she was tense, her little body on alert. I regretted making the joke.

"Fine," I said. "We can stay here a little longer if we find water."

"Where?"

I nodded towards the rainwater tank in the garden.

"There."

I tried all the keys from the house. One by one.

"None of them fit," I said.

"Why not?" Lou asked.

"So we have to go home," I said.

"But can't we open it some other way?"

I nodded slowly, realizing how thirsty I was. I thought about the water down there. Clear, dark, cold water.

I struck the padlock again and again. First with a stone, then with a rusty spade I found in the outbuilding.

But the lock was far too solid. They only made things this solid back in the old days.

While I was banging away at the padlock, I tried smiling at Lou—see, it will be fine, the smile was supposed to say, see, I'll fix everything. But I didn't fix anything. I just got more and more sweaty.

Finally I put the spade on the ground and sank down on the lid of the tank.

Lou looked at me with dissatisfaction. Then she reached into her hair with one hand, took something out and handed it to me. A bobby pin.

"That's what thieves do."

Jesus. "Where did you learn that?"

She shrugged. "I don't know."

"Did you see it in a movie?"

"Maybe. I can't remember."

I puttered with the hairpin for a while, jiggling and coaxing the lock. Finally it opened. I raised the lid. We stuck our heads over the edge and peered down into the darkness.

"Yoo-hoo," Lou called.

Her voice echoed.

An old iron bucket was hanging on the inside of the tank. I threw it down. Hollow sounds reverberated against the walls.

Then we heard the sound of a splash far below.

"Water!" Lou said.

The sound of water, it was really water.

I felt the bucket take hold. Tip over. And grow heavier as it filled up.

I pulled it up again and Lou leaned forward in excitement.

Then I lifted it over the edge. We looked inside, both of us.

It was only a quarter full and the contents could not exactly be called water. The sour-smelling liquid was a light-brown color and there were flakes of rust swirling through it.

Lou wrinkled her nose.

"Can we drink it?"

I shook my head, realizing how disappointed I was.

"But I'm so thirsty," Lou said.

"I know that."

"Very thirsty."

"We can't drink it."

She bowed her head, mumbling from between her shoulders. "Mommy always had water."

"What did you say?"

Then she looked at me.

"Mommy always had water."

"She certainly did not."

"She certainly did."

"But it was from the faucet."

I was about to say more, but stopped myself in time. Because Anna *had* always had water. She always remembered to bring along an extra bottle. For the children. For us. But now we were sitting here, without Anna, without water, only Lou and I.

The world was empty—no people, no animals, no insects,

no plants. Soon even the largest trees would die, in spite of their deep roots. Nothing could survive this.

We sat there, alone, and all we had was a quarter of a bucket of undrinkable sludge.

"Daddy?"

I turned away, didn't want her to see how shiny my eyes were. I got to my feet, took a couple of deep breaths. Pull yourself together, David.

"We can't drink it," I said. "But we can at least clean you up a little bit."

I found an old rag in the outbuilding. I dipped it in the rusty water and wrung it out. The water was cool against my skin. It *felt* like water. That was at least something.

"Close your eyes," I said to Lou.

Then I wiped her cheeks and forehead. She stood facing me, completely still and just relishing the feeling of the cold, damp rag against her skin.

"And hold out your arms," I said.

She stretched them out towards me. The inside, the outside. The rag turned brown as I washed her. She kept her eyes shut. Smiling.

"It tickles."

She stuck her tongue out towards the rag.

"No, Lou."

"Just a little."

"No."

"OK, then."

But when I had finished closing up the rainwater tank, I discovered that she had grabbed the rag and was holding it against her mouth, sucking the water out of it.

"Lou!"

She dropped it immediately.

"Did you swallow any?"

"No."

"Are you sure?"

"Yes."

"Positive?"

"Yes."

SIGNE

Up and down on the waves, in and out of sleep, I'm sitting at the map table, my head in my arms, sleeping, waking, drifting, while the storm pummels at *Blue*, I'm here, I'm there.

It was the night Daddy blew up the bridge. He and Sønstebø met up there in the dark, Sønstebø with his truck, Daddy in our car, or maybe he arrived on foot, walked up the mountainside. Maybe it was so dark that he had to use a flashlight, and maybe the cones of light from the truck's headlamps were the first things he saw, two tunnels in the air, sharp disruptions in the darkness … Did Daddy think of me, did he think of Mommy? Did Sønstebø think of Magnus?

Time is elastic. Time and the memories that bind it are two sides of the same coin. Magnus and I, Mommy and Daddy, the glacier and the river, the Sister Falls, and there's so much I don't remember.

I'm just here, in this night. And I'm in another night, the last night Mommy and Daddy slept together, *were* together. I don't remember exactly how much time had passed since the hike, but it can't have been more than a few weeks. I woke up and my throat was scratchy. I coughed gently into my pillow, but it didn't help.

I twisted and turned; I was hot, even though I was only wearing an undershirt, I turned my pillow over, turned the duvet over, lay on my tummy with one ear against the floral fabric, which smelled clean, and the other out towards the darkness, and then I heard something.

A faint, howling sound, something unfamiliar—an animal, was it an animal, someone outside, in the garden?

At first I just lay there, listening to the sound with one ear. The other ear couldn't hear a thing because it was pressed down against the soft fabric of the pillowcase. But the howling continued; I sat up and then I could hear the sound more clearly.

It was not coming from the garden, it came from the house. It was inside, in my house, a wild animal, a night creature, maybe injured, it howled like it was injured and nobody heard it except for me.

I got out of bed, my undershirt went down to my thighs; suddenly I was cold, I got goose bumps, and wanted to be with Mommy and Daddy, even though I had stopped sleeping with them.

I opened the door, and as I did so the sound grew louder; I walked out into the hallway, it was even louder there, it grew louder because I came closer, but also because it, or the person making the sound, was howling louder and louder all the time.

I was afraid, but at the same time I thought, should I be careful? Should I bring something, a weapon, the fire shovel from my room, should I go get it? But I didn't, because in one way or another I knew that I shouldn't or needn't be afraid, that the sound wasn't dangerous, not in that way.

It was coming from Mommy and Daddy's bedroom, I could hear it now, and it was not just the sound of one, but of several creatures, because a lower and deeper moaning had commenced, and it wasn't an animal, it was a person, as if somebody were in a great deal of pain.

Don't think, just look. I hurried towards the door, I *wanted* to see. Then I put my hand on the handle and pushed it down without making a sound.

They didn't notice me, didn't see that the door had opened a crack, didn't notice that I was standing there, in just my undershirt and underpants, that I was watching everything.

It filled the whole bed, the whole room.

Mommy sat leaning back on her elbows, with her knees bent and pointing towards the ceiling and her legs spread apart as far as was possible; her breasts were splayed outward, resting on either side of her torso, as if overflowing, and the space on her chest between her breasts was slick with sweat, the part that in the male body is called the sternum, though in the female body it has no name, I thought, but the thought vanished immediately, because I just had to look at him, look at Daddy, who was on the floor, on his knees, with his head between Mommy's legs.

I didn't understand what I was seeing and at the same time I knew, because once I had heard two of the big girls at school talking and I knew that something happened between men and women in bed at night, something that had to do with children, but I had never imagined that it could be like this, because it was supposed to be about the man, the big girls had whispered, he was supposed to lie on top of the woman, he was supposed to empty something inside of her. But this was all about Mommy, all of it, the entire room, the house, it was all about Mommy, the sounds she made growing louder, rising and falling.

I didn't move a muscle, didn't even blink, while my mouth filled with water, so much water that I was unable to swallow.

Because Mommy was lying there, with him, and it was all about her, about them, and I hated the bed she was lying in, I hated the room, I hated the house. I hate you, I thought, while the black waves filled my mouth.

Maybe they heard the bathroom door or maybe they heard my retching, because when I had wiped away the last strings of slime and flushed for the final time, the house was silent, a pregnant silence.

But nobody came to the door, nobody asked me how I was feeling. Maybe they were ashamed. They should be ashamed, I thought, that they could do something like that, be like that, have something like that between them.

I sat on the bathroom floor shaking, in a cold sweat, with the door locked, as small as one feels only after having vomited. I was all alone, Mommy and Daddy wouldn't be coming with a bucket and a cold washcloth for my forehead. I could dry off my vomit by myself, I thought. I managed it, because they had all of this together, this big ugliness that tore them apart and then this other thing I had seen tonight. I couldn't understand how they could behave like that, how he could gobble her up when he at the same time so clearly cursed everything she stood for.

The next morning, at breakfast, they didn't argue; they ate, as usual, drank their coffee, Daddy slurped a little, the way he usually did, as if nothing had happened.

"The water ouzel's babies are going to die," I said suddenly.

I looked at Mommy, addressing her.

"What?" she said.

"The freshwater pearl mussels, too. Some of them are more than a hundred years old."

"Signe?"

"And Sønstebø, do you know how he feels? His summer farm will be underwater, where will the sheep graze now? His place is 150 years old. For 150 years he has had animals up there. Where are they supposed to go now?"

Nobody answered, so I shouted: "WHERE ARE THEY SUPPOSED TO GO NOW?"

They sat there, gaping, both Mommy and Daddy.

Finally Mommy started talking. She made the same excuses. Better schools, a new old folks' home, a swimming pool.

"A swimming pool," I said. "I would rather swim in Lake Eide."

She tried again. She talked about the hotel, Hauger Hotel, which could barely make ends meet, how good it would be for us, for the hotel and for the family. But I interrupted her then and now I didn't stop, I spewed it out, as if I still hadn't finished vomiting. The river, I said. People have come here to see the river, see the rainbow, which is always there, to go fishing for salmon, and watch the snow melting in the spring. And the fish in the river, where are they supposed to go, and what about the water that's released out into the fjord, it will be cold as ice, are you aware of that, and the water ouzel, what will happen to the water ouzel when there is no longer any waterfall, its nest, where will it build it, and all the stone you will dig up, it will take over, huge boulders. It used to be green, now it's a scree, all the animals here and all the plants, they live around the river, around the River Breio, and you think you can just take over and do what you want to it, it's a river, it's nature, it's birds, insects, plants, now there will just be scree and pipes and tunnels there, stone and steel, stone and steel.

"Everything will disappear," I said. "Everything we love will disappear. And it's your fault." I almost couldn't talk now. I leaned forward. "You destroy everything."

Daddy said nothing, just looked at me across the breakfast

table, over the hard-boiled eggs and smoked salmon, and now he would have to say something, I thought, now he would be forced to finish what he'd started.

But he was silent and I was a teeny-tiny water person in a snow globe. I pounded my hands against the glass and screamed and tried to get out and that's why I also said the very last thing, what I knew that she didn't know, which could be significant, which could break the glass.

"Daddy talked to Sønstebø."

"Sønstebø?"

"He talked to Sønstebø up on the mountain, on the road, the new road, we were out hiking, they met up and nobody was supposed to know about it."

Mommy just stared at me.

"They didn't want anyone to see them," I continued. "It wasn't worth the risk, they said, that someone might see them together."

"Bjørn?" Mommy said.

"It wasn't worth the risk," I said. "They didn't want to be seen together."

It was the night Daddy blew up the bridge, he and Sønstebø met up there in the darkness, that's how it must have been. And maybe the lights from the truck were the first thing he saw before Sønstebø emerged, his black silhouette splitting the light in two. Sønstebø who had been a shot firer as a young man, he was probably the one behind this, or maybe it was actually Daddy, that could be, that my full-of-rage Daddy made contact with Sønstebø, that he was the one who planned the whole thing.

But I was the one who told on him, told Mommy, and after that morning Daddy was alone. He moved to the house by the harbor. His things, his books, wall charts, articles and lithographs of nature scenes, filled it to the brim; the smell of them filled the small rooms and made them into something familiar, even though the walls were alien.

The windows were thin. The sound of the boats penetrated them, the sound of cables striking masts in the wind, the thudding of motors, the banging of fish crates against the decks, skippers calling. The sound of his typewriter couldn't drown out all of this.

I'm going to Mommy's, I said when I left Daddy; I'm going to Daddy's, I said to Mommy. My place was on the gravel road that went through the village, from the cramped house in the harbor to the hotel with its almost one hundred rooms and back again. I remember myself as being infinitely small, lonely, plagued by guilt, and impressionable. I was just waiting for Magnus, without knowing it myself.

DAVID

"Now it's time for bed," I said as we walked towards Hall 4.
Lou replied with a loud yawn.

It was late today, too. Much later than I'd planned, still no system for bedtime.

The young boys from the line were sitting by the entrance to the hall, in a circle around a pot, like it was a campfire. Each of them held their own cup.

"Tea?" one of them asked me in English as we walked past.

The other two snickered.

Maybe it wasn't tea in the pot, maybe they were drinking something else altogether. It was too dark for me to be able to see their eyes, whether they were under the influence.

"Do you all live in here?" I asked.

"We were assigned places here, yes," the first one said.

"He has to sleep on the floor," the other one said and pointed at the third.

The hall had become crowded over the past couple of days.

"We can take turns. Every third night," he said.

"Yeah, right," the first one said.

They had a good laugh about that. A little listless. A laughter that lingered.

They were my age, but nonetheless younger. They only had themselves.

And were they drinking something? Warmth in the stomach, the gradual heaviness, lightness, the thoughts obliterated. The taste of alcohol on the tongue, in the body. It had been a long time.

But Lou was standing beside me. Lou, whose eyes were rolling with drowsiness, who said nothing, but whose presence was strong nonetheless.

I wanted to push her along with me into the hall, but the first guy grabbed hold of my shin.

"C'mon, have a seat," he said.

"Have some tea," the other one said.

"Mint tea," the third one said. "Found it in a garden along the way. It's been hanging from my knapsack, drying out."

Mint tea? Was it only mint tea?

"I just have to put the little one to bed first," I said.

Their names were Christian, Caleb and Martin. They spoke to me quickly, in broken English, just as bad as my own. Christian and Caleb had met in a camp up in the mountains further south, a camp from which everyone had fled. They had picked up Martin along the way.

They came from southern Spain all three of them, from the desert. Nobody could be bothered to say much about the time before. But they had many stories from the road and from the last camp. All the stories ended in laughter, as if the things they'd experienced were from one long road trip with the boys. It was only when they talked about the guy in the line that they changed, that the hardness came over them again. They called him a bastard from the north, a water bastard.

"They have the Ebro, so they think they have everything," Caleb said.

"A tiny corner of Spain that wants to isolate itself from the rest," Martin said.

"They criticize the water countries, but do the same thing themselves, in their own country," Christian said.

"When those of us in the south can't manage to combine our resources," Caleb said, "share what we actually have, how will ... how ..." He didn't finish.

"I don't give a shit," Martin said. "I don't give a shit about Spain. It's not my country any longer. I don't want to live there. Or here. It just keeps getting worse. Soon there will be desert everywhere. I'm going to save myself. Make it to the rain."

They all nodded, they all felt the same way.

But then Martin laughed, started mouthing off and the others played along, partly in Spanish and partly in English, out of politeness towards me.

And it *was* only mint tea. They snickered when I told them I thought it was something else, said that they wouldn't have minded that. Caleb mumbled that he'd heard there was a way to get hold of some, that there was a guy selling it in Hall 3.

I replied that it wasn't for me, that I needed to keep my wits about me, for Lou's sake.

"I have a child to think about," I said.

At that moment I remembered that I'd forgotten to check whether she had fallen asleep. She was accustomed to my being there with her, to our going to bed at the same time. But she hadn't come out again, so it was probably fine. She was probably fast asleep.

I took another sip, but was unable to relax. I had a feeling that something was wrong.

"Sorry," I said and got to my feet.

The hall was in semidarkness. Many people were already sleeping. But Lou was awake. Her little face was pale, and her eyes were open wide.

"Hello there," I said, and sat down beside her.

She just stared straight in front of her.

"Is something wrong?"

"It hurts," she said.

And now I noticed how stiff her body was, lying there with her knees against her tummy. Her entire body was tense.

"Where does it hurt?" I asked, even though I knew the answer.

"My tummy."

"Are you sick to your stomach?"

"It hurts."

I was about to say something. About the water. About the

rag. *I told you so*, I was going to say. Why did she have to go and suck on that damn rag? I had been very clear. It was dangerous. Water poisoning, people had been dying from it in droves in recent years.

But she curled up even more tightly, wailed faintly and I could not bring myself to scold her.

"I'm sure it will soon pass," I said, and patted her on the cheek.

She was cold and sticky, her eyes introspective.

"Do you want some water?"

I retrieved the water bottle and held it up to her mouth. She took a small sip and struggled to swallow.

"Lou?"

I stroked her head. She didn't respond.

"Get some sleep now," I said. "That will help."

I sat down on my own bed. Looked at her. But she didn't move.

I lay down. On my side, facing her. I stared at her the whole time. It felt like it was important that I not take my eyes off her.

She was breathing calmly.

Was she asleep?

It was quiet in the hall. I heard only the low voices of the Spaniards outside. One of them laughed again. Right now I wished they would be quiet. Their laughter drowned out the sound of Lou breathing.

I lay facing her until my own eyes also slid shut.

*

"Daddy!"

"Yes?"

I came to. It was dark. Completely silent.

"I feel nauseous."

And then, before I could do anything about it, the sound came that is worse than any other sound, the sound of a child retching. Half-strangled croaks, underlined by tears. The most painful sound in the world.

She vomited in her bed. It landed on everything. The bedclothes. Her hair. Our clothing.

"Get up," I said. "Quickly."

She got to her feet, sobbing weakly, and stood between our beds, trembling. But she was unable to speak. She retched again. But only halfway. More like a gulp. Nothing came out. But it would come.

A bucket, dammit, we needed a bucket. I looked around me. The water bottle. My knapsack in the cupboard. An empty water glass. There was nothing here that I could use.

"Quick. Out," I said and took hold of her.

But it was too late. She raised her hands, held them in front of her face and caught what came out. The second round of vomit covered her fingers. Her arms.

"Lean over," I said. "Spit up on the floor. We can clean up afterwards."

Obediently she bowed her head and upper body down towards the concrete floor. Another round of vomiting was on its way. I could see the struggle in her body, building up through small spasms.

And then yet another torrent of vomit flew out of her mouth, vomit that had once been food. I recognized the yellow color from some dry crackers she'd eaten this afternoon.

An intense acidic smell.

She retched again and again.

Finally nothing more came out. Just some long strings of slime hung from her mouth.

I found a roll of toilet paper and wiped it away, helped her blow her nose. There was vomit there too.

She was crying. Painful, desperate crying, while her entire little body shook.

"It's because of the rag," she sobbed. "I sucked on it."

"No, it's not," I said. "No, I'm sure it's not because of that."

But she cried, sobbing loudly.

"Shhh, it's fine, Lou. It will be fine."

I stroked her hair, her cheeks. Tried to avoid getting too much vomit on my hands. Everything smelled sour.

Then I pulled off her smelly T-shirt. Turned it inside out and used it to dry off her hair. I managed to clean off the worst of it.

I laid her down in my bed, where the bedding was clean. Peeled the bedding off hers and put it, along with her T-shirt, under my arm.

"Where are you going?" Lou asked fearfully.

"To get a bucket," I said. "I'll be back soon."

"You're nice, Daddy."

She lay her head down on the sweater she used as a pillow and closed her eyes.

I thought she would fall asleep, that it was over now. Nonetheless, I went to find a bucket just to be on the safe side. The hall had a broom closet that was seldom opened. It's hard to clean when you don't have any water.

But when I came back, she was awake. Again she was lying there all curled up. Again her body was all stiff.

"My tummy hurts again."

"It will pass."

"It hurts so much!"

"Try to lie on your back," I said.

She didn't react.

I gently took hold of her.

"Look here, try to stretch out."

I unfolded her body. Placed my hands on her tummy. Massaged it carefully.

But she just cried.

SIGNE

Maybe it started with a snowman. Yes, I think it started with a snowman and nothing more was really necessary, because even though I saw you from time to time, watched you when you came down to the fjord with your father to buy fish at the wharf or shop at the consumer co-op, you still didn't take up much space inside of me.

Not before the party, Mommy's party. I don't remember if it was one party or many, maybe there were many, but that's the one that I remember.

The hotel was all hers now, the way it always actually had been, because old Hauger had left it to his daughter. Daddy, his son-in-law, didn't inherit anything. The almost one hundred rooms, the commercial kitchen, the huge garden that went all the way down to the edge of the water and the spacious, private wing were all hers.

This evening Mommy filled the wing with people and I remember looking forward to it. Mommy associated with so many people, all the time, and now they came, all of them, filled the hallway with the scent of perfume and their indoor shoes in bags and their loud voices: the school principal with his wife and children, the director of the fish-landing station with his wife and baby, the editor with his wife who was expecting, the journalist who was a woman and not married, and all the engineers and building contractors who had moved here in recent years to work at the plant and left behind *their* wives and children in other parts of Norway and therefore were especially appreciative of the invitation to visit someone's *home* and enjoy a home-cooked meal. They spoke about this loudly as they took off their coats, changed their shoes and lit cigarettes and pipes.

Then they occupied the living rooms of the house, with warmth, laughter and cigarette smoke, their sounds filled me, words that rose and fell in the air, jazz on the record player, high heels on the floor in the dining room, where the furniture had been cleared away, while their children ran through the rooms playing, until the youngest fell asleep like abandoned ragdolls in armchairs and chaises lounges.

I was older than the other children, maybe twelve or fourteen, a head taller than them, but nonetheless I wasn't as tall as the women and lacked everything that they had. I had become slender, skinny almost, like a washboard where they had breasts, my arms were long and I couldn't control my legs, but nonetheless I stayed close to the adults. I thought I belonged there, more than with the children. I tried to talk, take part in their conversation, but nobody heard my loud voice and maybe where I was seated was too far away, in an armchair by a wall, outside the circle the adults formed around the coffee table, or maybe my voice wasn't as loud as it used to be.

There was a man talking, I couldn't remember ever having met him, hadn't noticed him before now, had only heard his name. It was Svein Bredesen, the chief engineer, he spoke loudly and for a long time about the work on the power plant; he talked with such pleasure about the barrage that was almost completed and it wasn't supposed to form a lake, as I'd believed at first, as had several of the guests. No, the barrage would dam up the water from the snowmelt, so it was collected there and could be diverted into pipes through the mountain, all the way down to the power plant and to the turbine, which was called Pelton and which he spoke about as if it were a close friend.

I liked him. I remember that, that I liked him.

So, without fully understanding how it happened, as if there were some kind of adult signal or other that I didn't catch, like in a card game where there are secret signals, touching the nose or earlobe to communicate to one's partner the trump one has in one's hand, several people stood up at the same time, Mommy went over to the record player, she changed the music and they started to dance.

Svein held out his hand to Mommy. I'd heard him talk about being married, and he wore a gold ring on his finger, but all the same he clearly wanted to dance with Mommy. She took his hand; there was something about her, the way she held her head, or her eyes maybe, that made me think

she might start laughing, not at him, but towards him, a
sort of bubbly giggle. I waited for the laughter to come,
dreading it, didn't want to hear her laughing like that, but
she remained silent then, luckily, and just danced with him.

Everyone was on the dance floor now. I was the only one
sitting down and I didn't know what to do with my long
arms and legs. I crossed them, my entire body twisted into a
cross, then I untwisted myself again, but nobody saw it, and
anyway it didn't matter because I was invisible. I was the
opposite of Mommy.

Suddenly I thought of her sounds, the howling. Svein Bredesen put his hands on her hips, he spun her around and
her howling echoed in my ears.

The adults danced, their eyes shining and heels hitting hard against the floor. Full skirts sent tiny vibrations
through the air against my face. I could smell the odor of
adult bodies growing warm, of everything they hid under
their clothing, in their armpits, down their backs, between
their legs.

I could have helped myself to a taste of something from
one of the glasses, they wouldn't have noticed, I could have
tasted the alcohol, but I didn't need it, because I was already
dizzy and I smiled like Mommy, without knowing why, and
soon I would also giggle a bubbly giggle without meaning to.

It could have continued like this for a long time, I could
have sat watching the party for hours, maybe I would have
finally also tried to drink. I planned which glass I would

take, one nobody had drunk from for a long time. It could have continued this way, the evening could have turned out differently for me, but all of a sudden I saw shadows on the porch, two silhouettes out there. They staggered around, trampled back and forth, stared through the windows, and I was the only one who saw them. My heart pounded, I was going to point, tell everyone about them, but at that moment the porch door opened and they came in, accompanied by the cold evening air from outside.

People turned around, Mommy last, the record went around and around on the turntable, Svein spun her one more time, but then he stopped.

It was Daddy and Sønstebø. Sønstebø was swaying slightly, while Daddy was steady on his feet. He looked at Svein, at Mommy.

I stood up. Look at me, I thought, don't look at them, look at me. I wanted to talk, use the powerful voice Daddy was so fond of, fill the room with it, say something really loudly, maybe something they could laugh about, something Daddy could laugh about or, even better, something that impressed him, but no sounds came out.

Daddy walked slowly across the floor, towards Svein, towards Mommy—she was still holding his hand in hers, but now she dropped it abruptly.

Maybe they said something to one another, I don't remember, maybe Mommy's voice was low and exasperated, Daddy's clear and cold, or maybe they just stood there like that, facing one another, until he reached out his hand, the way Svein had just done, and took hold of Mommy's hand which was hanging at her side and didn't want to be held, at least not by his. He took hold of it, tugged at her, pulled her close to him, and started to dance.

Sønstebø danced as well, but alone, with his hips mostly while he made faces and noises. I realized what he was doing, what he was mimicking: Mommy's howling.

It happened so quickly—now Svein was there, he said something to Daddy, tried to help Mommy get out of his grasp, but Mommy didn't want to be helped, she said something under her breath to Svein, everyone else was silent, the only sound was the music.

Svein stood there while Mommy danced with Daddy, he was holding her so tight, it looked painful, I wanted to cry, but I couldn't manage that either. Daddy pushed and pulled Mommy around, but then Svein was there again, he grabbed Daddy's arm, screamed something at him. Mommy didn't make a sound, Daddy refused to let go and then Sønstebø moved in from one side. Turning to face Svein, he raised a clenched fist and punched him.

Svein stumbled backwards, but didn't fall, still managed to keep his balance—he was big and strong, I could see that now. Somebody screamed. It wasn't me, it wasn't Mommy— Daddy was still holding on to her, but they weren't dancing any longer, he had stopped and was holding her close and she wasn't resisting. Sønstebø walked towards Svein again. Svein just stood there; go away, I thought, run, but he stood there, sort of bewildered, as if he hadn't been expecting a brawl, and at the very least didn't anticipate another punch coming, but one did, and yet another, and Daddy held Mommy, he held her against him, as if they were slow-dancing.

Again, yet again Sønstebø was going to hit Svein, but then somebody came into the room, another uninvited guest. At first I didn't recognize him, because he'd started junior high school and I hadn't seen him for a while, but now he was standing there and had grown just as tall as his father. But the squirrel eyes were the same.

He said his father's name, not "Dad" or "Father" but his father's full name, and then finally Sønstebø stopped punching and Daddy released Mommy like he had burned himself.

"We're going home now," Magnus said to his father. "Now we have to go home."

He was only thirteen years old, but had the stature of an adult; the minute he walked into the room everyone had to look at him, all the adults had turned to face him and were waiting, as if they didn't have any choice.

Magnus turned towards the doorway, didn't even check to see whether Sønstebø was following him, didn't check to see what Daddy did, if he was coming with him. But they did, both of them, both Sønstebø and Daddy, as if Magnus was the grown-up and they were children.

But before Magnus reached the door leading out into the hallway, he turned around after all, not towards them, but towards me.

"Hi, Signe."

That was the first time that evening anyone had said my name.

DAVID

We didn't sleep, neither Lou nor I. It was just the two of us in the tiny cloth cubicle.

I had hung a sheet over the doorway. It created some form of privacy. Even though everyone could hear us.

I mopped up the vomit on the floor with a dry rag I'd found in the broom closet. I hoped I could find some water to wash with in the morning. My fingers smelled. But I grew accustomed to it, became immune.

But more smells emerged; now it started coming out the other end.

"I have to go to the bathroom," Lou cried suddenly. "Now!"

She wanted to run out but I stopped her.

"Use the bucket," I said.

"No, I don't want to use the bucket."

"We won't make it to the toilet."

She stopped moving. Hesitated. Made a face, and then crouched down. Apparently she couldn't hold it in any longer. She pulled off her underpants and bent her knees, completely naked. Helplessly, she tried to aim into the red plastic bucket.

I held her, helped her hit her mark.

It happened immediately, exploding loudly towards the bottom of the plastic bucket.

I could hear people moving around in the cubicle around us. They knew what was happening. They found the sound of it disgusting.

I was embarrassed, but then I caught myself. It wasn't my damn fault. And above all, none of this was Lou's fault.

She sat down on the bucket. Her bottom was so tiny that she almost fell inside. She defecated some more.

When she finally finished there were red marks on the backs of her thighs from the bucket.

I dried her without a second thought, even though I had stopped doing so two years ago. She had liked learning to do it herself. But now she was shaking terribly.

The roll of toilet paper was almost finished. I had to find more. But the last time I went to the bathroom, I couldn't find any.

I pulled on her underpants. They hung loosely around her hips. I lifted her up. Her body almost disappeared in my arms.

I laid her down in the bed. Pulled the sheet over her. She occupied only a small part of the mattress.

The bucket was left on the floor, stinking.

"Daddy?"

"Yes?"

"What if there's more?"

"I'm going to empty the bucket now."

"But what if I don't make it? If it gets on the bed?"

"It will be fine."

"But what if?"

I pulled out the only sweater I had and tied it around her waist and beneath her crotch, like a diaper.

At one point in the middle of the night I ventured out to the first-aid barracks. I knew they were open round the clock.

But it was locked and the windows were dark. Two bags of trash lay outside. One of them was open and turned upside down; hypodermic needles and soiled bandages lay in the grass.

She wailed.

She retched again and again. Only yellow strings of slime came out of her mouth.

"Drink," I said, and held the cup out for her.

But she couldn't even keep water down.

"I don't want to," she sobbed between heaves.

"It's better," I said. "It's better to throw up water than not to throw up anything."

What didn't come out at one end, came out the other.

The odors mingled. Soon I no longer noticed them.

She slept, woke up, fell asleep again.

Every time she fell asleep, I thought that now, finally, it had passed.

But then it returned. As if somebody had grabbed hold of her stomach. Pulled at it. Twisted it. An instrument of torture being screwed deeper and deeper inside her.

She'd had tummy bugs before. But never anything like this.

I tried to remember what Anna used to do. Things she'd had in the first-aid cupboard. Charcoal tablets. Loperamide. Now I had nothing. And Lou refused to drink fluids.

I had nothing. She only had me.

Anna. Where are you? How the hell can you leave me all alone?

The hours dragged by. I was so tired. So groggy. So afraid. So awake. I lost all track of time, didn't notice how much time had passed until I realized it was dawn.

I heard a sound just outside. Soft footsteps that stopped outside our cubicle.

Anna, I thought. She's come now. She's here. She heard Lou. Her child is ill. She can't be away when her child is ill. It's Anna.

"Excuse me?" a voice said. "Do you need any help?"

It was a man's voice.

At first I was disappointed. Then I felt relieved, just because somebody had come. Anybody.

I pulled the sheet to one side.

It was Francis.

He stared at Lou. His eyes became shiny.

"I could hear her all night long," he said.

"I guess everyone did," I said.

"Don't worry about that," he said.

"She won't drink anything."

"Have you been to the first-aid barracks?"

"Closed."

"Did you get any sleep?"

"No."

"Take my bed. I'll sit with her."

"No."

"Yes."

"I can't leave her."

"You can hear everything anyway."

His bed was neatly made, as if he hadn't slept in it.

I lay down gingerly on top of the sheet, not wanting to wrinkle it. I lay completely still until I drifted off to sleep.

Her whimpers became a soundtrack for strange dreams.

I was in the water again. I was sinking. Above me it grew darker and darker. But I made no effort to get to the surface.

I heard her whimpers from far below and thought I needed to get to her. That sinking was a good thing.

That I wanted to sink.

Francis's voice pulled me up slowly. He was singing to her.

It was broad daylight. The hall had come to life around us, but I couldn't hear Lou.

I hurried in to them, stopped in the doorway. She was sleeping peacefully.

"Go ahead and get some more rest," Francis said.

"That's OK," I said and sat down beside him.

He looked at me. "You need to sleep."

"No, I don't."

I turned towards Lou. She was lying on her back, with her arms over her head and her hair spread across the pillow. She was breathing calmly.

"Nice kid," Francis said.

"Yes. She is," I said.

"You're lucky."

"Yes."

I remembered the bandage he had taken out of the trash can in the first-aid barracks. Was it a kind of keepsake? The only thing he had left?

"Do you have a daughter?" I asked. "A grown daughter?"

He looked away. "I have a daughter ... No, I had a daughter."

"Oh," I said. "Oh, I mean ... my condolences."

The words felt heavy in my mouth. I couldn't remember ever having spoken the phrase previously. Old fashioned, it belonged in a museum. But it was what people said.

"Contaminated water," he said. "Poisoning. It all happened so quickly."

Poisoning. So quickly. So quickly. A dead daughter. Two dead daughters.

"I think this is the same thing," I forced myself to say.

He turned to face me again. "What did you say?"

I drew a breath, and tried to speak normally. "Lou ingested some water yesterday, from a rainwater tank in a garden."

At first he didn't reply. Then he said slowly: "It's usually fine. It was bad luck, what happened to my daughter."

"Bad luck?"

"She didn't have much strength left."

"But Lou . . . She's so thin."

I laid my hand on her forehead.

"Do you think she's very warm?" I asked.

"I haven't touched her," he said. "Just been sitting here."

"Feel her forehead. Please."

He stroked her face with his good hand.

"She's warm"

"Right?"

"But I've seen worse."

"Really?"

"Don't think her temperature is even 39 °C."

"No?"

"It's 38.5. Tops."

"But she won't drink anything."

"Nothing?"

"Almost nothing."

"It's going to be all right."

He looked at me and smiled as if I were a little boy. It made me feel like a child. I was a boy. He was the same age as my father. He could have been my father. I almost wished that he was my father.

"You said you're from Perpignan?" I asked.

"Yes . . ."

"Where are you headed, then?" I asked.

"I was headed here."

"Same here," I said. "We were headed here."

"And then?" he asked.

"I don't know. We're waiting for someone. For my wife. And my son. He's just a baby. His name is August and he's one year old."

"You're fortunate," he said. "You have someone to wait for."

The entire day passed. He stayed nearby. We took turns sitting with Lou. She didn't get better. A few times I got some water into her. It always came straight up again.

She spoke very little. With every passing hour she became more and more unresponsive.

Several times I went to the first-aid clinic. But it was still closed.

I asked a security guard. He didn't know anything, hadn't seen the doctors for several days.

And there was still no toilet paper.

In the afternoon Francis was gone for a long time. I started wondering whether he had given up on us and I had worked up some anger by the time he came back. But the anger melted away when I saw what he'd found.

A soda. A can of sugary soda. I couldn't remember the last time Lou had had something like that.

"Where did that come from?" I asked.

"She needs sugar and fluids," he said. "And salt."

He held out a small bag of kitchen salt. "Before you give her the soda, pour this in it."

He gave me the salt and the can of soda. I sat there holding the can in my hand, taking in the sensation of the smooth metal against my fingers.

The list of ingredients included additives. Artificial sweeteners, with neither fruit nor berries.

But the sugar was the most important thing, after all. And the salt.

She slept for another few hours. But more calmly and she woke up less and less frequently.

Then, around midnight, something finally happened.

I had fallen asleep, and was lying in bed directly across from her, but I woke up immediately when I heard her talking.

"Thirsty," she said. "Daddy?"

I sat up quickly.

"Yes."

I rushed to open the can. The sound was the most beautiful thing I had heard in a long time. The sigh of the bubbling carbonation when I lifted the aluminum tab.

"Soda?" Lou said. "Soda!"

"Wait," I said.

I poured some of the salt into the soda. It fizzed upon contact with the carbonated liquid.

I put one hand under her head and held the can up to her lips with the other.

She swallowed.

She drank. Large gulps.

Finally she was drinking. My child was drinking.

SIGNE

The sound of the storm is in my body. I awaken with a start and it is still roaring in my ears, but then it's gone, because it's the silence that's creating a din inside me now. I am lying on the floor, can't remember coming in here, I must have collapsed from exhaustion, all curled up halfway beneath the table, the ice containers looming over me. My body is stiff and sore. I push myself up into a sitting position and can feel how every part of me aches.

Magnus, you stood there at the party and looked right at me, steady and calm through and through, and after that it was the two of us.

Not dramatically and intensely, but slowly. Years passed before we did anything more than look at one another, before we had a proper conversation, before we held hands and walked down the gravel road in the village, before we sat down at the far edge of the pier, out of sight, and kissed tentatively the first time, before I let go of your hands to touch other parts of your body, under wool sweaters and singlets that smelled of boy, the smooth skin on your back, before we clung to one another with all the desire we still didn't know what to do with, before we walked down the road and talked, talked, talked, about everything, and especially about how there was nobody else we could talk to exactly like this.

We walked, away from the fjord, away from the water and the valley and up towards the mountain, because there we could be alone. The mountain and the glacier were our landscape during these years.

And then we moved away from the village. I remember how we stood on the deck of the steamer, looking at Ringfjorden at the end of the trail that was the backwash, the village growing smaller and smaller and everything inside me growing lighter.

We chose Bergen. He was the one who wanted to move there.

"It's a short trip home," he said.

"You call it *home*," I said.

"It will always be home."

"Not for me."

"I'll talk to you about that in a few years."

"If you're so certain it will remain *home*, we can just as well move further away."

"Bergen is good."

"Bergen is wet."

"Wet is good."

"Home is where the heart is."

"What?"

"They say *home is where the heart is*. But it's a cliché and, besides that, weak, linguistically speaking. Hearts can't be somewhere without the people who have them."

"Fine. I'll stop calling Eidesdalen and Ringfjorden home."

"You can call it what you want as far as I'm concerned."

"You are home to me."

"How sweet."

"Isn't it?"

"And *that's* pretty feeble as well, linguistically speaking."

"I figured you'd say that."

But we stayed in Bergen, I accepted it. I accepted a lot from him during that period. We attended the same university college; he studied engineering, I studied journalism, but our free time was our own and we followed only the minimum number of lectures, because there were so many other things going on. It was as if the city, the country of Norway, had just woken up. We looked towards the world, became a part of a huge movement, fought alongside people from all over the world against the Vietnam War, nuclear power, atomic test bombings in the Pacific Ocean, but also fought our own battles, against the European Community, for legalized abortion and the right to choose, for the conservation of Norwegian natural resources and wildlife.

I remember the back of his neck in front of me in the First of May parade—he always walked a bit more quickly than I did, but unintentionally. He would stop from time to time, catch himself doing it, smile apologetically and take my hand. Then we would walk a few yards together, before something or other distracted him and pulled him ahead of me again and I would walk and look at the back of his neck, thinking that he wasn't wholly mine, but nonetheless knowing that he was. I remember thinking that he walked quickly because of his enthusiasm, his engagement. It wasn't until later that I understood that he maybe just wanted to get it over with.

We each had our own bedsit, but always slept together, usually in his bed—it was wider than mine and his bedsit larger; he had a separate bed recess, almost a separate bedroom. There was something homey about having the living space divided up like that, I thought, something adult, and he had also put more effort into fixing up his apartment, had worked hard to create a home. Mine was just a room where I stayed when I needed a place to sleep and he wasn't around.

The bed was a place we slept, but also a place we lived; after having made love, naked, our bodies entangled, we chatted, sleepily stroking one another's chests, hair, arms, backs, and also before we slept together, full of anticipation, sometimes lazy, uncertain of whether we could be bothered, sometimes we just talked, that was sometimes enough, but usually we still wanted one another. We ate in bed, drank red wine, neglected to brush our teeth, woke up with blue teeth and laughed at one another, but even tolerated each other's morning breath, inhaled that as well, deep into our lungs, because we wanted to be completely filled with one another.

And we talked. His bed became the site for all our conversations and all his plans. Because he made plans, more and more plans, more and more often. He asked me about the future, about my expectations, about my wishes, and he searched through all my answers, sort of casually, for the points where they coincided with his wishes and expectations.

"How do you see it? How will we live?" he asked.

"I don't know ... a garden, maybe?"

"I've thought about that too. A big old wooden house and a garden. And apple trees, I want to have a lot of apple trees, don't you?"

"Sure, if you pick the apples."

"And on the hillside, maybe all the way up in the mountains, we will have a bench and we will sit there when we get old and look at the view."

"A bench?"

"Yes, I'll build it myself."

He imagined us sitting on a bench together when we get old—what a cliché, I thought, and I liked it.

"We will live by the fjord," he said, "then you can keep *Blue* there. You can go sailing while I putter in the garden. And pick apples."

"Nice that you remembered the apples."

He laughed and then he went on talking about us, that he wanted us to have a progressive distribution of labor, where he wore the apron in the kitchen and I came home with the fish, where he made applesauce. He wouldn't be angry if I ended up making more money than he did, he said, and was clearly proud of his own generosity: I will allow you to bring home the bigger paycheck.

He talked and talked, had so much to get off his chest. There's so much I don't understand, he said, it's only after we became a couple that I've been able to bear thinking about all the things from my childhood that I don't understand. What do you mean, I asked; there's so much, he answered, the most obvious, how often I felt the sting of my father's belt. Even though this was also common in other families we knew, that was no excuse. My mom cried too, she stood in the next room and sobbed, I could hear it through the wall, that's how loud it was, as if she wanted me to hear that she couldn't do anything. Even though it was her decision, she encouraged him, he just did what she convinced him he had to do, what fathers were supposed to do. That's how it was all the time, she was the one who made the big decisions, you know, for him, for me, for all of us, she controlled us, with her hands, the hands she wiped on her apron, with those disapproving sighs and encouraging smiles ... or maybe it wasn't her, after all, maybe it was the expectations they felt the world had of them, but which they actually produced by themselves. It still controls them; they say that they want me to become an engineer, do something more with my life than they have done, because they believe it's right, the only way. My mother and father, they are so traditional that it burns me up inside, tears me apart, but nonetheless, that's what keeps *them* on their feet, I think. They know the rules, they know this game, they know what's allowed and what is forbidden, and God forbid they should decide to step over the line.

"I feel bad for them," he once said. "And at the same time, I'm furious with them."

"Don't be."

"Will it make it better if I laugh at them?"

"I don't know."

"It would be better if I could laugh. Maybe the objective should be to laugh, do you think? If I can learn to laugh at them, then I will avoid turning out like them? I will be different?"

"You're already different."

"Are you sure?"

"You've been different ever since the first time I saw you."

"Or was it you who made me different?"

"... I think we should practice laughing."

It's perhaps his laughter that still inhabits me. I can't get rid of it, the way it rocks inside me, along with the waves.

The boat is still moving, but it's completely different now, rocking on gentle swells from the storm that has blown over, slowly, back and forth on the weary waves, sliding away.

My boat, *Blue*, I fell asleep on it. I can't even manage to sleep with one eye open any longer, my body keeps letting me down, maybe because he is still aching inside me, aching because he let me down.

Because when push came to shove, he wasn't as good

at discerning my needs, at seeing the needs of others, as I'd thought. When push came to shove, he was still just a child of his generation and the belt had made its mark. He wanted to move back to Ringfjorden; he grew tired of Bergen, he said, tired of being required to have an opinion on every street corner, tired of having to take a stand on every issue and that it had better be the "correct" stand. He wanted to move back home, wanted to have a garden, a kitchen, but actually I was the one who would be there, in the kitchen, because the whole time he was searching for the thing in me that had brought us together. He was searching for the girl he could rescue.

Everything else about him was just talk.

He was *less* daring than our fathers, he took no chances, because actually he was just like all the other young men at that time, with shaggy beards and gentle smiles who pussyfooted their way through life and talked about how everything was going to be different, without meaning it.

The work we took part in, the demonstrations we walked in, the fliers we wrote together—it was just a game for him. I look forward to seeing his eyes when I am standing in front of him with the ice, when I dump it in his yard, the expression on that padded, middle-aged man-about-town face of his, with traces of red wine from the evening before on his lips and his sweet little wife with a forehead just a bit too smooth, and a smile just a bit too tight, and the grandchildren who no doubt will be visiting. Maybe they are the ones who will stomp the ice into the dust, sully it, because it's their future he is stealing. It is their future his entire generation is stealing... my entire generation has stolen.

Those of us who have only experienced prosperity, never any obstacles.

Yes, perhaps the children should be allowed to do it, because they are the ones he is hurting. But they probably don't want to, because they don't care either, the children of today. They are pushed forward by the generations behind them, feel only the absence of any impediment, they don't care as long as they can have the latest iPhone when they turn seven, and their own large-screen television and an apartment on their twenty-first birthday. They won't care, they won't even look at the ice melting on the ground, much less stomp on it, because something else will get their attention, a screen beeping, a phone buzzing. And besides, their feet could get cold.

My head spins.

I need food, I need water.

Finally I get to my feet. I go to fetch a coffee cup, find one in the closet; it's a mess in there, all the unbreakable dishes have been tossed around and deep inside it is damp—water must have leaked inside here, too. The closet is situated where the deck meets the hull—it can't be fully watertight there either.

I step on the foot pump for fresh water and muddy water drips into the cup; the water has a faint odor of diesel, like almost everything on board, but I am used to it and drink quickly.

I open the door to the stowage space for dry goods and find a mess in there as well. The lid has fallen off the can of flour and everything is white and damp: bags of powdered soup, canned goods and packages of pasta are covered with sticky flour. I dig out a package of spaghetti and tear off the plastic, can't bear to wait for the water to boil, can't bear to look for a pot, but chew some of the hard strands right out of the package, along with a piece of crispbread that has become soft from the moisture.

I eat half the package, find a chocolate bar, too—palm oil, I know it contains palm oil, but bought it anyway, can't manage without it out here and nobody can see me, I think quickly, but catch myself doing it. Signe, c'mon now, there are limits.

I open the hatch, not knowing what to expect—chaos, the rigging destroyed, the dinghy blown overboard? But everything is as it should be—the rigging, cordage, everything is hanging in its place, as secure as before, the boat has weathered this, held its own, without my doing a thing, and I know it, that long-keel sailboats like this one can withstand a lot, can be knocked down and get back up again. They aren't like modern boats with deep fin keels, which can lose the keel, be tossed about and capsized. *Blue* was designed for this, for recovering in a storm.

I stand there in the cockpit, a soft wind caressing my cheeks; the ocean is growing calm, the sun breaks through the clouds, the water on deck evaporates, and the floor is slippery. When the ocean is peaceful, mirroring the sky like this, I could be anywhere on earth—nothing about the ocean here, about the sky, tells me that I'm located on the North Sea. The surface is identical, here and in the Pacific Ocean, an ocean is an ocean is an ocean, until you go *beneath* the surface. It is then that you will see the species, the seabed, hollows and seamounts that make every ocean unique, the way mountain formations and animal life on land create the variations and characteristics of different regions. The surface of the ocean is the sky for the underwater world, above high mountains and deep valleys, for thousands of creatures we have never seen.

I tear myself away, walk on deck, over to the mast, put my feet on the mast rungs and climb upwards, two thirds of the way up. It's easy to loosen the halyard from the crosstree; I look down, the deck is small below me, just water everywhere, the horizon, the sky and the only thing I have is this boat.

Blue, my *Blue*, I think immediately, you saved me when I couldn't save myself, you took over when I couldn't take any more. But then I shake it off, snort to myself. How sentimental, it's just a boat, just aluminum, plastic and fiberglass, wood and ropes. I am the skipper, this is a skilled profession. I would never have managed had it not been for an entire lifetime of experience.

I climb down again and go inside; everything is in disarray, cupboards and drawers I thought I'd secured have opened, knives and forks have been thrown across the floor. I have to clean up, but first I must check my position. I have no power, the fuse box may have short-circuited, I should troubleshoot, but can't bring myself to do it. I hate the small shocks I sometimes get and perhaps it will dry out on its own. I must bank on that, have experienced it before, I just have to wait, until the sun and the air do their job, once again prevail over the water.

Map, pen, paper and sextant, I bring all of it up into the cockpit, look at the clock, exactly 13:06 hours, check the tables, gauge the position of the sun, find the degree of longitude. I know how to do this too—I am clever, I think, I am clever, there's nothing wrong with telling myself that I'm clever.

But it takes time, good God, what painstaking work, it's been a long time since I have used these ancient methods, but finally I establish the degree of latitude and a position.

I sit there looking at the "X" I drew on the nautical map—there's the boat, there I am.

And now I understand where the wind has taken me, that in the course of the storm it changed directions, came from the north, and it has helped me, carried me south. I'm already at the same latitude as Flekkefjord. Thank you, wind, thank you, ocean, thank you, weather. Again I can raise the sail, I can move on, set my course for the English Channel.

DAVID

Lou chewed and swallowed. It was the most beautiful thing I'd ever seen.

She chewed quickly and swallowed even more quickly. Couldn't get enough. We were sitting in the mess hall. For the first time she was strong enough to accompany me here. She woke up bright and early because she was hungry and we had made it here before the rush. The tables and benches around us were still empty and the temperature was tolerable.

"Is there any more?" she asked when the dish was empty.

She'd had most of my bread, too.

"I'll go ask," I said.

Even though I knew this was all we would get.

At that moment Francis came over. He must have heard our conversation, because now he handed her another piece of bread and sat down with us.

"Thank you," I said, because Lou was too busy eating.

"Come on, let's go," I said when she was finally finished.

"Where?"

"To the Red Cross."

She stretched out her feet in front of her, looked at them and not at me. "I don't need to."

"Yes. You need to. We haven't been there in four days."

"There's just a long line, nothing else."

"She can stay with me," Francis said.

"Yes, I can," Lou said. "I can stay with Francis."

"No," I said. "You have to come with me. Imagine if they've arrived."

"They haven't," Lou said. "You heard what the lady said. They'll let us know if Mommy comes."

"We're going now," I said.

"No," she said and lifted her head.

She stared at me, eyes shining.

She was really well again. I had nothing to offer in response to that no.

So I went. Alone. Angry and pleased at the same time.

I couldn't remember the last time I was alone, just walking like this, without holding Lou's hand. I opened and closed my fingers.

I was able to breathe again. She was fine. I had managed it. Taken care of her, brought her through the crisis. Without Anna.

Without Anna. My heart started pounding even harder.

Today, today they've learned something, today they've made contact. Found them. Today Jeanette will have good news.

But when I entered the barracks, it wasn't Jeanette who was sitting behind the desk. It was a man I'd never seen before.

He didn't even look up.

"There's nothing new here," he said to the screen.

"But you don't know who I'm looking for."

"There's been no contact with anyone since yesterday and no new arrivals have registered. You'll have to wait for a few days."

"But many days have passed since the last time I was here. Where is the woman who's usually here, Jeanette? She knows my case."

"She left," he said. "Replaced."

"Why is that?"

He didn't reply, taking a cookie from a can under the desk instead.

"Sorry," he said as he crunched away. "Need something to keep me going. Half rations for us as well."

I walked outside again. By the entrance there was an overflowing garbage can. It stunk in the heat. I turned around. A wire supporting the tent in front of me had come loose, the canvas was hanging askew. And a little further down along the row someone had painted slogans on a barracks wall. Portuguese? Spanish? I didn't understand the language, but the letters spoke to me anyway, the way they were painted, jagged, brash, hot-tempered.

The lack of toilet paper. The first-aid clinic that was closed. Jeanette's disappearance. I had seen it, but hadn't really given it much thought before now. I continued walking aimlessly between the barracks. I had to get back to Lou, but couldn't manage it, saw only how many things were not as they should be. People were dirtier, thinner, there was garbage everywhere.

As I wandered around, my heart pounded harder and harder.

Lou was well, I had managed that. But we were still half a family. I was still bloody well alone. And now the camp was falling apart.

It makes no difference what I do, I thought suddenly.

Nothing makes any difference.

I can fight for my life. I can fight for her. But it makes no difference when there's no longer anywhere to live.

All of a sudden I heard loud, angry voices.

I changed direction, drawn towards them.

Around the corner of Hall 2.

There, in the blistering heat, stood the man from the line, Thick-Neck, crowding another man, almost on top of him. It was Martin. Both were shouting, screaming, red in the face like cartoon characters. But there was nothing to laugh about here.

At that moment Caleb and Christian came walking by. They stopped for a moment when they spotted Thick-Neck, before they flew at him.

Then everything happened very quickly. A wave passed through the camp; everyone who'd been sitting so quietly, moving so slowly, for so long afflicted by heat-induced lethargy, now all at once became a fury of movement, flying at each other's throats.

I stayed out of it, watched Caleb and Christian pounding their fists into Thick-Neck. Men poured in from all sides to join the brawl, taking opposing sides. As if on cue.

As if they'd been waiting for this.

And I, too, had been waiting for it. I had been so sluggish for so long, so sluggish and cautious. Always with Lou there holding my hand.

But now there was nobody to take care of. And nothing made any difference.

I took a step forward.

I could feel my heart pound. Hard. Hard.

Took another step.

Now you must choose. Are you in or alone?

But I was spared having to choose, because somebody came running up from behind. They pulled me along with them. Pulled me in and I didn't resist.

I ran towards Caleb, Martin and Christian. Became a part of what they were.

Adrenaline filled me. I exploded again and again. Something in me that had been suppressed rose to the surface. Something that had been there all along.

Arms, legs, everything happened so fast. Loud voices. My own, theirs, so loud.

Running footsteps, more and more people kept joining in, everyone with a clear aim, all their energy focused on this.

It was so easy to raise an arm. To punch.

Move your feet.

Punch again.

There were more of us. But they were quicker, larger, crazier. Something about them reminded me of the worst boys at school, a wildness. With guys like them you never knew what you would get.

And I was clumsy. Slower with every punch I threw.

I missed.

I was hit.

The pain erased all the thoughts in my head. It was quick. A pain like that I could take, I had time to think. This is tolerable, because it's so quick, it passes right away.

But then it didn't stop. It spread outward, heat prickling everywhere, throughout my entire body. It didn't disappear, but increased in intensity, obliterating all other pains.

Hard to breathe. It was difficult to breathe. My chest contracted.

And around me people were fighting on all sides. The brawl was just a sound, a single sound. A sound that swallowed up everything else.

I sat on the ground. Shaking. I had drawn my knees up against my chest and was holding my hands open in front of me. They were covered with red stains from the blood dripping from my head.

Christian was lying doubled up on the ground. Caleb was sitting with Martin, talking softly, in a daze.

It was so hot, the pain and the heat all at once. Sweat on

my back, on my forehead. Salt on my face. Pain. It hurt like hell. My body ached all over.

Then someone crouched down beside me. I'd almost forgotten about her. But she was still here, with her protruding collarbones and slender fingers.

"Come," she said.

She was staying in a hall that was smaller than ours. A sign outside stated that it was only for women. She pulled me inside a cubicle like mine and Lou's.

"Sit down."

Marguerite pointed at a bed.

I did as she said. She left me there, without saying a word.

I sat there, feeling her bed beneath my thighs. She slept here. Her body lay here every single night. In what position? On her back, securely, in the middle of the bed? Curled up like a newborn baby? Or on her stomach, turned away from everything?

I bet that she slept on her stomach.

She wasn't gone long, and in her hand she had a first-aid kit. She put it down next to me on the bed and opened it.

"Here you go."

"What?"

"Here you'll find what you need."

"Can't you—?"

"You got yourself into this mess. Now you can straighten it out as well."

I blinked, and a rivulet of blood trickled down from my forehead.

"But it's hard to see."

"That's your problem."

"Can't you—?"

"Do you want Lou to see you like this?"

"No."

"Then get to it."

Lou. She was with Francis. He had kept her away from the fight. He must have.

But now she must be worrying about where I was. Maybe she regretted refusing to go with me to the Red Cross, and was sitting with Francis in despair. Blaming herself, for the entire fight maybe, thinking it was her fault, even though nothing in the world was her fault.

Hurriedly, I opened an antiseptic towelette.

I had to be quick.

I dried my cheekbone where I could feel that it was bleeding.

She was surely safe with Francis, they got along so well, surely she hadn't heard anything, hadn't heard the screaming, hadn't noticed how much time had passed. And she was too young to blame herself.

I took another towelette and quickly rinsed the knuckles on my right hand. They were already starting to turn purple.

"Do you have a mirror?"

"No," Marguerite said.

She remained seated directly across from me. She watched to make sure I removed all the blood, nodding now and then in confirmation, but made no sign of moving.

"Would you mind?" I handed her the ragged towelette.

"You've gotten rid of most of it now," she said, without accepting it.

"Thanks."

I took a strip of Band-Aids and a pair of scissors out of a box and clipped off a piece. Five centimeters, approximately. That would have to do.

Peeled off the backing, stuck it to my cheek.

Marguerite gave me a curt nod. I had apparently put it in the right place.

I pulled up my T-shirt, ran my hand down my ribs on my left side. Pressed my fingers against my rib cage. First gently. Then a little harder.

I tried to keep from moaning.

I stood up, and my right leg almost buckled under me. I had taken a blow there, a blow so hard that it felt like the muscles had snapped.

I took a couple of cautious steps.

It hurt like the devil.

I stretched my arms out in front of me, over my head.

I bent over.

Bloody hell, I was sore!

But everything still worked. Nothing was broken. I'd been luckier than I deserved.

I turned towards the first-aid kit, picked up after myself and closed it.

"Where do you want me to put the kit?"

"I'll take it."

I put it down on the floor beside her bed.

"Thank you," I said again.

I was about to leave. But then she stood up, too.

"David?"

"Yes?"

We stood there facing one another.

"I was looking for you," she said.

"Oh?"

"I wondered how you were doing, you and Lou."

"Lou has been ill. We've barely been out of the hall."

"Ill?"

I could see that she was frightened. That she cared.

"She's fine now," I hastened to say.

"I'm happy to hear that."

"Me too, that is, I mean, of course I am ..."

David, shut up. Now you're just making a mess of things.

She didn't reply, but held my gaze. And suddenly a little smile appeared.

"You look terrible."

And then I noticed that I was trembling, how shaken up I was. Sore. Beaten to a pulp. Everything in my body felt loose and soft, as if I weren't put together properly and had lost all coordination.

To think I'd ended up in a fight. Just like that.

And with a child to take care of and everything.

Idiot. Weakling. Feeble. As much willpower as a goldfish.

I swallowed. Swallowed again. Was not going to cry. Not now and not later.

I was a loser, now and forever. It was a miracle that I even stood on two feet, as weak as I was.

Marguerite could see how I was shaking.

Her smile disappeared and she took one step forward, lay one hand on my arm, her right hand on my left upper arm.

Her hand was cool, but it burned against my skin.

I moaned again.

Everything hurt, all my movements, even the faint summer breeze, even the air itself.

And her hand, when it was on my arm like that, it was almost unbearable.

"Don't take it away," I said.

And she left it where it was.

SIGNE

All the sails are set and the wind drives me forward, at five knots for the third day in a row, soon it will be six knots, the boat maintains maximum speed. The northern wind has again shifted slightly to the east, but still permits me to set sail for the south and the power is back on, everything on board is functioning as it should.

I am in constant movement, a feeling of a restlessness inhabiting my body. I yawn abruptly and involuntarily, my jaw creaks, I fill my lungs, am so tired, really very tired, have lost count of the number of days without consecutive hours of sleep and, with no relief in sight now, I am approaching the English Channel. The vessel traffic is increasing, so lying down and trusting that it will suffice to check the fairway every half-hour won't do here. I must live in the cockpit now.

I have showered. There is still a lot of water in the tank, my hair in the salty sea air smells of shampoo, my body, my skin, dry and smooth, no longer sticky with sweat, the air temperature is 23 °C, an early morning heat. I am wearing only shorts and a T-shirt, but my hair, my just-washed hair, is not held in place by grease and salt water, but instead sticks to and irritates my face when the wind loosens it from the ponytail. I should get a haircut, most women my age have short hair. I could take a pair of scissors and be done with it, right now . . . no, because then perhaps he wouldn't recognize me. Then perhaps Magnus wouldn't recognize me.

Recognize me? Signe, why are you thinking in this way? As if it makes any difference. The most important thing is that he recognizes the ice, the ice that I am going to dump at his feet, throwing his betrayal and his weakness right in his face.

I should have realized how different we were from the very beginning.

My life was in Bergen, but Magnus was constantly pulling me towards Ringfjorden and Eidesdalen. He spoke about our villages, about friends who settled down there and had children. He spoke warmly and at length about unity, simplicity and nature, about its fantastic beauty. He used words like that, like some tourist.

He let me know that he saw my mother from time to time. Whether it was by chance or design, I didn't know, didn't want to ask; later I thought I should have known more about the kind of contact they had, about what it meant to him, but the whole time I told myself that she wasn't an important part of my life, that I wasn't interested in what she was up to, and for that reason neither could she be an important part of his.

It was my father I spoke with. I called him at least once a

week. I was always the one who made contact with him, from the telephone in the hallway of the block of bedsits.

But one day the landlord knocked on the door and told me that I had received a phone call. This time it was my father who was calling me.

"Signe? Hello?"

"Hello, Daddy."

He got straight to the point: "The company Ringfallene wants to develop the Sister Falls."

"What?"

I sat down on the hard chair beside the telephone. The summer sunshine poured through the window and illuminated the dust in the air.

"Ringfallene purchased the water rights on the falls at a bargain price, when development of the River Breio commenced. And now they want to make use of them."

I was unable to respond immediately, could feel how I wasn't relaxed on the chair, but rather prepared to leap into action.

"Signe?"

"I'm here."

"You understand what this means?"

My mouth was dry.

"The Sister Falls will disappear," I said.

"Yes. The Sister Falls will disappear. Seven hundred and eleven meters of free-falling water obliterated, as if it had never been there. Norway has no other waterfalls like those two and now they are going to be diverted through a pipeline."

I drew a breath.

"And the water?" I asked.

"They are building another dam on the mountain, a few kilometers from the last one. And they want to channel the water down into a tunnel from this one, too."

"But ... where? Channel it where?"

"To the power plant, of course," he said, and laughed a short, brittle laugh. "Towards Ringfjorden."

"Away from Lake Eide?"

"Lake Eide will be drained, Signe. And the majority of the revenues will go to Ringfjorden."

I couldn't make sense of it and asked confused questions that caused him to talk even louder, even faster.

"It's your mother," he said. "And Svein. They are the ones who will profit from this, Signe, with all their shares in Ringfallene. The Sister Falls will make them extremely wealthy."

Mommy. Svein.

"Signe?"

"I'm here."

"Do you understand what I'm telling you?"

"What about Sønstebø?" I said. "Magnus's parents?"

"Sønstebø lost the summer farm last time. This time he's losing his entire livelihood."

*

We went home the following weekend. I drove. Magnus wanted me to, didn't want us to be one of those traditional couples where *he* always did the driving. I drove even though my body was too agitated. I was too angry, too restless. He, on the other hand, was apparently unperturbed, speaking about the view, about the weather, about nothing. I didn't understand how he could be so calm.

The sun broke through the clouds as we approached Ringfjorden, the road clung tightly to the mountainsides, narrow and curving, almost at sea level, wet from the rain, a shiny snake in the terrain. I tried to concentrate on getting there, but when we reached the crossing where the road to Eidesdalen turned off, a sudden impulse caused me to turn and take the road leading to the mountain.

"Aren't we going to Ringfjorden?" Magnus said. "Isn't your father waiting for us?"

"I want to see the Sister Falls," I said. "I have to see them."

We drove through Eidesdalen where the lake lay before us, huge, silent and blue on that summer day, where the fields were green and the trees in the orchards full of ripening fruit, past Magnus's family farm, Sønstebø's farm, without letting them know we were here, and all the way to the waterfalls—the two, parallel, silver strings on the precipitous mountain.

I stepped out of the car and could feel immediately how saturated the air was; it felt like dewdrops on my face, the sound pounded against me, thousands of liters of water

every single second, a push, a scream. The falls frightened
me. Every time I stood here, images flew through my mind of
people under the torrents of water, of children who tripped
and fell on the slippery stones, landing where the water hit
the ground. Water has power, a force. I had considered it
to be invincible. But not any longer, not when encounter-
ing human hands, power shovels, steel pipes, tunnels, not
in the face of license revenues, industrialization and the
welfare state.

Magnus had come up behind me, lifted his arms and
slipped them around my waist.

"They're powerful," he said.

"Is that the only adjective you have in your repertoire?"

"What do you mean?"

"Of course they're powerful. They're also beautiful. Gor-
geous. Magnificent. Dramatic."

"What are you getting at now?"

"Have you seen the latest tourist brochure? *Bridal Veil*, it
says there. You could say that ... you could say that they are
as beautiful as twin brides at the photographer's. Doesn't that
sound wonderful?"

"Signe—"

"And then you have to say *useful*. Did you forget that one?"

"It wasn't the adjective that came to mind, but of course
the falls are useful."

"Not so much the falls in themselves, but the water that
comes from them."

"The water that comes from them is useful."

"The falls are exceptional."

"That too."

I got back into the car and he did the same.

"We're driving to the dam," I said, without asking whether he minded. "I want to go diving."

He didn't say anything until we reached the mountain. We had to park the car and walk the final stretch, because the road leading to the dam was no good.

We followed the riverbed which was a dry gash in the mountain, and stopped at the top. I could sense that old feeling of something lifting; that it became easier to breathe when I no longer had to crane my neck to see the sky.

He stood there looking at the power lines that cut through the mountain landscape.

"Can I say something about this?" he asked and pointed at the huge constructions.

I smiled. "Fine."

"The adjective I want to use is ..."

"I can hardly wait."

"Hideous."

"That was a good choice of words."

"I know, right? But ..." He fell silent, glanced at me quickly. "Am I allowed to say that it's also beautiful?"

"Beautiful? Where did that come from?"

"In some way or another it's beautiful. The human grandeur. How we take on the world. It is perhaps the engineer in me that's talking now, but it's all of this that has lifted us out of poverty. That has made progress possible."

At first I didn't reply. Where was he going with this?

"Human grandeur," I said finally. "A contradiction."

"What?"

"A contradiction in terms. The words *human* and *grandeur* do not belong in the same sentence."

"It must be possible to have two opposing thoughts in your head at the same time."

"Have you ever said something like that to your father? That you think the power lines are ... formidable?"

"Mom and Dad ... they have actually managed just fine without that summer farm. It didn't turn out to be the catastrophe they feared—they received compensation, it was done by the book, even *he* had to admit that."

Magnus's gaze followed the high-tension cables that were running through the mountain wilds and pointed. "This is a result of man's ability to plan ... that we are able to imagine a future, provide for ourselves, our children, our old age. And for those who will come after us. And it's even clean. The energy is clean."

"And for that reason we are superior to other species, because we know how to plan?"

"Like all other species, we take care of ourselves. It's instinct," he said.

"So what drives us? Instinct or intellect?"

He hesitated. "Both."

"But the development of hydroelectric power is the result of intellect?"

"... Yes."

"I would say that it's rather a result of instinct."

I started walking again, didn't want to look at him any longer.

"You don't plan enormous hydroelectric power plants instinctively," he said and hurried to catch up with me.

"But if we agree that humans instinctively provide for themselves and their own children ..." I said.

"Yes?"

"Then these developments are a result of instinct ... an instinct that is faulty."

I stared at the road in front of me. It was still just as ugly.

"Faulty?" he said.

"You say it's in our nature to provide for our descendants," I said. "But we are really only providing for ourselves. Ourselves and our children. At the very most, our grandchildren. We forget about those who will come after them. While we are also capable of making changes that will have an impact on hundreds of future generations, that will destroy things for everyone who comes after us. Ergo our protective instinct has malfunctioned."

"You're a pessimist, do you know that?"

I was walking faster now. I wanted to get away, but couldn't stop myself from answering him. "No. I'm a determinist. There is nothing to guarantee that everything will be fine. For the human race. For the world."

"Nothing?" he said. "Think about the Second World War..."

"We have to go back to the war, yes." I tried to laugh, but it sounded hollow.

"Think about the post-war years, of everything we have accomplished," he said. "Everything Europe has achieved in an incredibly short period of time. When people combined their resources."

"That was brilliant, wasn't it?"

"And how can you be a determinist when you want to take part in protest marches every single weekend and spend all your free time handing out fliers?"

"I said I was a determinist. I didn't say I was logical."

"And I say that you're allowed to have two opposing thoughts in your head at the same time."

He stopped, took hold of me and pulled me close to him, but I didn't return the hug, because suddenly I could feel how angry I was.

"Signe?"

He held me.

"They are going to drain off all the water in Lake Eide," I said. "I can't believe we're walking here discussing whether power lines are beautiful."

"Yes ... I know ... I know. Sorry."

"Determinism or not, we don't own nature," I said, and disentangled myself from his embrace. "Just like it doesn't own us. We don't own the water, nobody owns the water. But all the same, we persist. And even though I don't think it will help, in the long run, I will continue taking part in protest marches and handing out fliers, as long as I have feet to carry me and hands to distribute them with."

We stood facing one another on the road. Suddenly I wished that I was taller, because he looked at me, at my fierceness, as if all of a sudden he thought there was something strange about it. As if I were a strange and not particularly attractive animal.

"But we can," he said calmly, "we can do what we want, Signe. That's what makes us human beings, what distinguishes us from animals. It must be possible to think both ways at the same time, that it's brutal, but also fantastic, that these installations make life better for thousands of us, now and for many decades into the future, that we are creating civilization."

I was unable to say anything; there was a pressure in my chest. "You've been away from here for too long," I said finally and tried to smile. "I think we have to move back, before you turn into a city boy through and through."

"Maybe you are the one talking like a city boy . . . Or maybe you've become a city girl?" he said. "I've always thought that city people have a more romantic relationship to nature, that those of us who are from here actually see its utility value also."

"Are you serious?"

I turned and walked away, while he stayed where he was.

"Signe?" He didn't follow me, just stood there calling me, in a low and controlled voice, as if he were talking to a child.

"Come on, Signe. You have to accept that we don't agree about everything."

I could accept our not being in agreement about everything, of course I could, but I couldn't accept that we didn't agree about this. So I kept walking and luckily he followed me, finally. My back must have made an impression on him, because now he tried making some rude comments—silly, harmless, trying to show me that the conversation didn't bother him—and I pulled myself together, answered him, wanted to demonstrate the same thing, but the whole time his words kept spinning inside me, I wanted to scream, hit him on the head with my arguments, because this was a betrayal on his part, talking like this, talking like everyone else and at the same time taking the bite out of his words by making me the difficult one, the immature one, making me the one who couldn't allow any disagreement, the uncompromising one who failed to see that there was more than one side to any issue.

We reached the dam, the man-made concrete dam, the strange, artificial lake created in the middle of the mountains. The sweat was dripping off my body and I tugged off my clothes without looking at him.

"Are you really going swimming?" he said.

I didn't reply, took one step out, balanced on a rock, the water came up to the middle of my shins, ice-cold meltwater, at its highest level now in June.

The lake was huge and silent, deep and shiny, the water

exceedingly clear. I thought I could discern the old summer farm far below.

I leaned forward, summoned my strength and jumped.

The shock as I broke through the water surface, the biting chill against my skin ... I swam away from shore, kicking hard, without another look at him, swam until I was directly above where I believed the summer farm was located.

Then I dove under and floated face down with my eyes open just below the surface and, even though the water made everything unclear and foggy, I was sure that I could see it.

I stuck my head out of the water again and now I forgot about being angry.

"It's here!"

"What?" he shouted.

"The summer farm. The water's clear. It's easy to see."

Then he too tore off his clothes and threw himself into the water, gasping at the cold, but he still swam quickly in my direction.

"Here," I said, treading water above the site.

He dove under, floated below the surface for a few seconds and came up again.

"I can see it too," he said.

And he smiled, he had already forgotten everything. "Are you going to dive?"

I didn't reply. I simply dove into the water.

With steady strokes I swam towards the bottom.

I could make out more details all the time. The cabin was

overgrown with plants, as if grass were still growing on the roof. The gate in the traditional fence around it was closed and I headed towards it.

There was energy in my strokes, I would make it, but at the same time I could feel the suction from the intake tunnel. It was covered by a screen, protecting the facility from leaves and trash, and now I could feel the water current, pulling me towards it. How much water, I thought, how much water disappears down into the tunnel every second, every minute, disappears down through the pipes, downwards, downwards, while the pressure increases more and more, meter by meter, until it finally reaches the power plant in Ringfjorden? And the water around me now, it's headed there, will become a part of the pressure, of the power, disappear into the turbine, contribute to producing its rotations, become a part of the moment when the fall energy of every single, tiny drop is transformed into kinetic energy, passing through the generator, disappearing, transformed into electric signals, and that is where it's pulling me, too.

But I didn't allow myself to be pulled there; I resisted, continued on towards the summer farm, released a little air, the bubbles rose to the surface. I could feel the beginnings of a pressure in my chest, the lack of oxygen, but the gate was right in front of me now and the air I had would be enough.

I reached out my hand, took hold of it, the woodwork slick beneath my fingers, not like wood, like a snake. I took hold and tugged, bubbles came out of my mouth, they flooded out uncontrollably, the gate was slippery and heavy to pull, but I could do it.

And then it was open, the sheep, no ... the fish could enter.

I let go of the gate, kicked away from it, tried not to release any more air—the more air I held in my lungs, the more quickly I would rise to the surface—but the pressure in my chest was growing, no time to equalize, my ears popped.

I saw Magnus far above me, keeping an eye on me.

Upwards, upwards, I would make it.

And finally.

I gasped, inhaled, the water stinging my lungs, my nose, a buzzing in my ears and the cold penetrating every single cell.

"Did you see that?" I finally managed to say.

"God," he laughed, fearfully. "I was trying to recall everything I know about lifesaving up here."

We swam to land, climbed up onto shore, both of us shaking, our feet frozen.

Finally I caught my breath and turned towards the dam, towards the hydraulic construction.

"Admit that it's ugly," I said.

"Ugly? Right now I'm thinking that it's dangerous," Magnus said.

I lifted my hand, placed it on his back, feeling the warmth under my fingers.

He didn't move, didn't react, not until I pulled close to him. "Admit it. It's ugly."

Then he finally put his arms around me. "Fine, fine, it's a damnable dam."

"The entire construction?"

"The entire construction."

"Finally you're on my side."

"Are there sides?"

"You know there are sides."

"Then I'm on your side."

I believed him, in spite of everything he'd said, even though he so clearly demonstrated that he was moving away from me. I was perhaps naïve. But I wanted to believe in him, maybe, or else he made it impossible not to, because he squeezed me tightly. I grew warmer, from the sun, from his skin. We were alone up there. There was only us, the sky, the mountain and thousands of liters of water and maybe our argument had made the day different from what I'd envisioned, but I still loved him and thought that his words didn't mean anything. I even tried to forget them, because we had to be able to handle an argument. There was no reason to hold back, I remember thinking, no reason to be careful.

And afterwards, when we were lying close together, out of breath and naked, on top of our clothing that was like a patchwork quilt over the prickly heather, I can remember that I thought I was happy.

I was happy when we made our child.

DAVID

"Have you turned in already?"

When I saw Lou, I was taken aback. During the past few days she'd had more energy and refused to go to bed early. But now she was lying in bed, curled up on her side, her body forming a C under the sheet and with her face towards the entrance.

The hall was almost empty. The majority of the residents were still sitting outside in the hot evening air. They needed to be outside after hiding from the sun all day long. Only the sound of an elderly couple having a hushed conversation could be heard and the breathing of someone who was already asleep.

I sat down on the edge of Lou's bed, but then she gave a sudden start and contracted her body into a ball under the sheet she had over her like a blanket.

"Is something wrong?"

I tried to whisper, not wanting to disturb the elderly couple.

"No," she said.

She answered far too quickly.

What had happened today? I reviewed it quickly in my

mind. I had been to the Red Cross. She hadn't wanted to come along, saying she preferred to stay with Francis.

At the Red Cross everything was as usual. They had no news for me. The same answer as before. Every time I went there it became more difficult. But I kept going anyway. What else could I do?

When I picked Lou up afterwards, she'd been happy. She and Francis were laughing about something. I didn't ask what, didn't even think about asking.

Then we went to the boat. We went there every day now. It was the only place where I could escape from my thoughts. The only place where I found some relief. And it was good to get out of the camp. During the past few days the halls had filled up. There were beds everywhere. Many people were being pressured to share cubicles with strangers. Fortunately, for the time being, Lou and I were left in peace.

The food rations had been reduced. I had almost become accustomed to going hungry. To the growling of my stomach. A craving throughout my entire body. The thought of chocolate, bacon grease, hot cocoa with whipped cream, French fries, deep-frying fat, breast of duck, lasagna, pâté, fresh bread, just fresh bread with butter.

There were rumors of how no supplies had been delivered for a week. That the camp was depleting its food supply.

And the morale. The piles of garbage, stinking in the heat. More slogans were written on walls all the time.

More and more frequently I saw small groups of people

huddled together, speaking in low voices, closing ranks among themselves.

The very sound of the camp had changed. There was a constant, oppressive hum, which threatened to grow louder all the time.

But the worst part was the water. They had cut back the rations even more. We couldn't shower, couldn't wash our clothes. We received only exactly as much as we needed to drink.

I woke up and thought about water, drank a few lukewarm drops, saving it for Lou. I slept and thought about water, my tongue parched. I tried breathing through my nose so as to preserve as much saliva as possible.

I hadn't seen much of Marguerite. I stayed away from her. Or she stayed away from me.

After the brawl, after Marguerite's hand on my arm, I caught myself walking around looking for her in the camp. All the time I thought I spotted her back in front of me in the line, or heard her voice from around a corner.

I wanted to see her again. And I didn't want to.

I fantasized about what could happen. What would have happened if she'd continued? If she had moved her hand a little further up my arm. Stroked my neck, my throat. Pulled me close to her ...

But I hadn't spoken with her today either. We had stayed at the boat until dinnertime.

In the evening Lou disappeared with Francis again.

They had a game, she said, an appointment to play a game. She was so happy and enthusiastic, it was good to see her like that.

While she was away, I sat with Caleb and Martin outside the hall. I was unable to think of anything but how hungry I was, talked about nothing, about everything, joked.

I didn't notice that Lou had come back, but suddenly she appeared beside me. She'd smiled. Slyly? Yes, she had smiled slyly. And she'd gone straight inside. Then she'd said she wanted to go to bed. And now she was lying here hiding something.

I tried to move closer, but she didn't want to make room for me.

"Lou?"

She didn't reply.

"Lou, what are you up to?"

"Nothing."

She didn't dare look me in the eyes.

"Sit up."

"No."

The elderly couple spoke more softly, realizing that something was happening.

"Lou."

"No!"

She shook her head fiercely.

"Get out of bed now."

She curled up again like a hedgehog in her bed.

I threatened her, but it didn't help. Now the elderly couple was silent.

"Lou!"

"No!"

Finally I had to lift her entire body out of bed.

She squirmed in my arms. Fought back. But without a word, without making a sound. Just soft, belabored breathing.

"What is going on with you?" I whispered.

I sat her down hard on my own bed. I turned towards hers, pulled off the sheet.

But there was nothing there.

Lou had clearly given up fighting back. She just sat there, a limp heap, with an expression on her face that was so guilty I almost had to laugh.

And now I saw what she was hiding. A lump in the mattress. She'd hidden something under it.

I lifted the mattress.

It was a tin can. A picture of yellow corn shone back at me from the label. It felt heavy in my hand.

At that moment the elderly couple walked past in the hallway.

I quickly hid the can from them behind my back.

"Nothing here," I said loudly. "That's good."

Then I dropped the mattress back in place, took hold of Lou and led her outside with me.

I pulled her with me away from the hall, between the rows of tents and barracks, past clusters of people. Behind the sanitary barracks I finally found a calm spot. We sat down there. I put the can between us.

"Where did you get this from?"

Lou stared down at the ground.

She pressed her lower lip beneath her upper lip, so it almost disappeared, but said nothing.

"Did someone give it to you?"

Still no answer.

"Lou? Did you get it from Francis?"

She shook her head.

"Somebody else? Someone who wanted to do something nice for you?"

I could hear my voice trembling. There were so many single men here, especially among the most recent arrivals. Damaged men. Thick-Neck, I thought suddenly. Men like him. And little Lou. Her lack of shyness, the underpants she just pulled off without thinking about who could see.

"Who did you get that from?"

"I don't remember."

"Have you had it long? How long have you had it?"

"I don't remember, Daddy."

"I told you not to accept things from people you don't know. You can never know what they want, I told you that. You mustn't believe what people say."

I had a lot more on my mind. I wanted to reprimand her. Because she was so naïve, she trusted anyone. I wanted to shake her until she told me who had given her the food. Who wanted something with her, who wanted something from her? Because nobody gave anything away without wanting something in return. Especially not here. Not now. But she interrupted me.

"But nobody *gave* it to me."

And then suddenly I understood.

"... You ... you took it?"

"No, I didn't. No."

"You took it from somebody."

I was unable to say *stole*.

"Daddy ..."

And I didn't need to hear her say it, because her entire little body communicated it.

Her face was bright red. The tears pressed forward between her eyelashes, trickled rapidly down her cheeks. A child's huge, guilty tears, hard to resist.

I tried to strengthen my resolve.

"Who did you take it from? Who is it that won't have any dinner today because of you?"

"But there's tons of them," she stammered. "In a gigantic room. There are a lot of cans there. You should have seen it, Daddy. Many, many cans. And I just took one."

A storeroom. The camp's storeroom, all there was left, now that the supplies were no longer being delivered. And she had stolen from there. We could be thrown out for something like that.

Suddenly, I felt cold.

"Weren't there any security guards?"

She answered quickly, no longer trying to hide anything: "I got in from the back. Under the canvas. It was just big enough."

That slender body. She could wriggle her way in anywhere.

"Did anybody see you?"

She shook her head. "Nobody. I'm sure."

My child stole. How had she learned that? Why?

Everything I should have said. Ought to have said. I ought to have said something that would have ensured that this didn't happen and wouldn't happen again. But I was too hungry.

"Don't do that again," was all I managed to get out.

Then I took a can opener out of my bag.

It scraped against the metal.

We used our fingers like tweezers, the index and middle finger, picking one piece of corn at a time out of the can. Taking turns.

The sweet, crisp, yellow taste, the crunching sensation of every single kernel of corn, I guided each one into place between my front teeth with my tongue, tried dividing them in two, before I pushed them further back into my mouth and chewed properly.

We emptied the can slowly, in silence.

I fell asleep more quickly than usual. The corn stuck to my ribs. The sounds of everyone we shared this hall with disappeared, the hushed talking, the breathing, the beds creaking, the rummaging through bags and suitcases, the snoring. Sleep took me away from all of it. I sank down into the water. It felt as if I would stay there a long time.

But something yanked me awake, almost immediately. Sounds pulled me to the surface. I fought back, wanting to remain down there. But the sounds grew louder, turning into screams.

I sat up in bed. Lou was still breathing calmly. Children can sleep through everything.

I pulled the sheet over her, stood up and went outside.

Caleb was standing there, as vigilant as a bird. His arms were crossed over his chest.

"It's him again," he said. "That bastard from the north. Christian and Martin couldn't stay away."

A loud bang and somebody yelling, followed by ominous howls. And then Caleb also set off at a run.

"Wait," I said.

But he ran to join the mob.

I stayed behind by the entrance to the hall. I wanted to run after him.

But Lou was lying in there, alone. I couldn't abandon her again. Couldn't explain more bruises, blood and Band-Aids to her.

And what if she woke up, what if she came out?

The intensity of the racket increased, the screams grew louder. More people came running. I tried not to listen.

Tried not to hear the swearing. The threats. Tents being

knocked over. Clothing being torn, loud crashes from things being broken.

But it was my people who were being threatened.

Caleb, Martin, Christian.

My muscles tensed. My heart pounded.

I had to protect them. Be one of them. I owed them that.

We'd already been in a fight together, it was my duty to do my part.

I was about to start running.

But then Marguerite was there. She arrived rapidly, short of breath. Appeared by my side.

She laid her hand on my arm, again she laid her hand on my arm.

At first I thought she was going to restrain me. But then I realized that she was afraid.

"They're in my hall," she said. "I can't ... I couldn't stay there."

I took her hand in mine and pulled her along with me.

It had been so long since I had held hands with anyone except Lou. Marguerite's hand was so big. Even though she was thin, it filled my hand completely.

We stopped just inside the door to the hallway. She was breathing more easily, but didn't let go of me.

Without another thought I pulled her inside with me. Into our cubicle. Where Lou was fast asleep.

We sat down on my bed.

She lay down.

I lay down with her.

She had this thinness about her, also when I was lying close to her.

I was lying close to her.

There's something wrong, I thought.

There's something wrong with me, if I can do this.

If I can lie here and feel her, feel the differences between her and Anna.

All the ways they are different, all the ways they are similar. There is something wrong with me.

I have to stop now.

I kept going.

It was like the fight.

I stopped thinking.

Thought about everything.

Skin under my hands. Another body against my own.

I didn't want it to stop.

Didn't want anything else except that it would stop.

That somebody would stop it for me.

We didn't make a sound. Lou was sleeping. They were still at it out there, but it was far away, the din rose and fell.

They made sounds for us. Their sounds became ours.

Her body was taut and thin, only her abdomen was different, scarred. There were marks from her navel to her pubic bone, where the skin had been stretched.

Somebody had been inside her, somebody she no longer had with her.

I ran my fingers over the stretch marks, wanting to ask but unable to do so.

Hoped she could say something.

I stroked the stretch marks. And that was the only time she took my hand away.

SIGNE

Do you remember, Magnus, when you found out that I was pregnant?

We were in Bergen again, living our lives as usual, the weeks slid by. It was summertime, we were getting up early, working nine-to-five and talking about how we were looking forward to the autumn and student life. At the same time, plans were being made back home in Ringfjorden. I spoke with Daddy almost every day, it's getting there, he said; it was growing, two national organizations had become involved, and this time we would mobilize. People were on their way from Bergen, from Oslo. All over the country nature conservationists were talking about Ringfjorden.

I had just come home from my summer job in a cafeteria the first time I noticed it. I was on my way up the stairs and suddenly felt a heaviness in my breasts. With every single step I took I could feel them, the tenderness, like I was about to get my period, but more extreme, and how long had it been since my last period, four weeks—no, five. I should have had my period the week before.

I let myself into the bedsit, which was silent and dark. I didn't turn on the light but went straight into the bathroom without taking off my shoes.

It was only then that I turned on a light.

I stood in front of the mirror, pulled up my sweater, my undershirt.

This heaviness, discomfort, I had never felt this way before, as if my breasts needed support. I would have to start wearing a bra—no, I couldn't, nobody wore a bra unless they had to, only old ladies and housewives.

I looked the same as always, everything was the same as always, but nonetheless, something was different, and while I stood there in the cold glare of the bathroom light, with my sweater pulled up under my arms, I felt the other symptoms, too, those I knew would come, which I had already been afflicted with for a few days without really paying attention to them: fatigue, my mouth watering, the stirrings of nausea.

I stood in front of the mirror with the sweater, an apple-green wool sweater, pulled up under my arms. I held it up, my arms were two pointy angles in the mirror, like wings, and suddenly I knew that I was pregnant and there was such a lightness in me—my arms were wings, I could fly, but I didn't know if I dared.

We met at my place that evening, I asked him to come. I wanted to be here, in my nondescript bedsit, not in his apartment.

He noticed that I was quiet, and I told him almost immediately.

"I think I'm pregnant."

He was so thrilled that at first he couldn't speak. Then he asked if I was sure.

"Sure?" I said. "How do you define sure?"

He laughed. He had to stand up, jumped up and down on the floor in front of me, then he hauled me up from the bed I was sitting on, hugged me so tightly that my feet were lifted off the floor, he carried me, but then he stopped himself.

"Sorry, I didn't think about the one inside there."

"If there is someone in there."

"If? But don't you know?"

"Yes, I think so. My period has always arrived like clockwork."

"There's someone in there."

Then he placed his hand on my abdomen.

"Just a lump of cells," I said.

"No. A child. Our child. Do you think it's a boy or a girl?"

"I'm not thinking much of anything yet."

"Signe!"

He laughed again—a loud, strange and very happy laughter. Then he leaned forward, kissed me and pulled me towards the bed.

Afterwards we lay side by side in silence. He stroked my forehead and cheeks.

"Signe. I think you should give her a call."

I turned towards him. "Who?"

"You know who."

"Now?"

"Daughters need their mothers. Especially when they become mothers themselves."

"I'm not thinking about how I'm about to become a mother yet."

"But you are."

"It's too early to think that."

"Call her."

"All I need is to be free of my childhood."

I pressed my nose against his arm.

"Acting as if it doesn't exist," he said, "isn't the same as being free of it."

He gently twisted his arm free and tried to make eye contact with me.

"I'm not going to call," I said.

"You grew up in the midst of a conflict but that doesn't mean that it's yours," he said.

"When did you become a psychologist?"

"... I'm your boyfriend."

"But you think I need to be in therapy."

"I don't know ... maybe. What do you think?"

"I don't have time for psychoanalysis."

"Signe, I didn't say that you should start therapy, just that you should call home—"

"Two times three hours a week, a monologue on a couch . . . I don't have those hours. Or the money. Besides, I have more faith in a behaviorist approach. I am a rat. I have learned that contact with my mother produces frustration. Ergo: I stay away from her."

"You aren't a rat."

"She's a lever. When I press it, I get a shock. And I want you to stop being Skinner."

"I'm not Skinner."

"You want to put me in the laboratory again."

I twisted away from him and rolled over onto my back to stare up at the ceiling. It was stained yellow from cigarette smoke and time.

"I should paint," I said.

"What?"

"The ceiling."

"Why?"

"Why does one paint a ceiling?"

"You're changing the subject."

"I'm done talking about it. I have been done with it for many years."

". . . Are you going to spend money on this shabby bedsit?"

"I'm sure the landlord will cover the cost."

"But we aren't going to live here, are we?"

"Why not? It's cheap."

He laughed. "And after a while it will be pretty crowded."

"It's still just a lump of cells."

I twisted towards him again, caught myself in time ... Stop it, Signe, you know what he wants and he loves you, why are you pushing like this, why do you keep insisting?

I laughed softly, to emphasize that it was a joke, and hugged him.

But he didn't return the hug.

"I want you to call it something else," was all he said.

"Fine."

"Fine."

"Sorry."

"And call Iris."

Iris, not *your mother*.

"I would rather lie on a couch six hours a week."

"It's cheaper to call home."

"I don't want anyone to know yet. Not her, not Daddy, not your parents."

"But I want to tell people."

"Not yet. Please. We don't know yet how things will go."

"Fine. We'll wait. But you can still call her."

"Maybe."

"Think about it. I just want everything to be fine when the baby comes."

"I'll think about it."

But I didn't have a chance to call because a short time later we were summoned to Ringfjorden by Daddy. It was happening now.

*

The rooms in the little house by the wharf had formerly seemed so small; now it was as if they'd been expanded. There were people everywhere, loud conversations, a woman was cooking a vegetable stew in two enormous pots and the floors had been cleared to make room for the painting of signs and banners:

NATURE CONSERVATION

STOP THE CONSTRUCTION WORK

WITHOUT SISTER FALLS EIDESDALEN WILL DIE

Daddy had let his beard grow out; it made him look younger, more like the many male arrivals surrounding him. He introduced me to all of them, spent the longest time on Lars, who was Daddy's age, but had a longer beard and apparently a leading role in the protest. They talked and talked, all of them, especially Lars, especially Daddy, as quickly as only people from the capital can. Daddy was beaming with enthusiasm, for the struggle had only just begun and we had the most powerful tool of all. He talked about Gandhi, about non-violent methods, about the power of the Indian model, passive resistance, civil disobedience based on the religious concept *ahimsa*.

"To prevent injuries. Non-violence . . . that's the only way one can be heard," Daddy said. "And now, soon, the eyes of Europe will be turned towards Norway. Towards the Sister Falls, towards Eidesdalen."

He pushed his glasses further up on his nose—they were round, not unlike Gandhi's, not unlike Lars's glasses. I could feel the warmth radiating off him and I wanted to throw myself into the work. I grabbed a paintbrush and got down on my knees. With a steady hand I began filling in the pencil lines forming the word "Eidesdalen," using a bright-red oil paint with an acrid odor that filled the room and made me slightly dizzy, and perhaps it was not good for the baby, but I didn't have time to think about that.

In the evening Sønstebø came; he and Magnus hugged each other stiffly, the way they used to, as if they didn't know each other very well and at any rate not like father and son, before Daddy separated them with his torrent of words. More people were on the way from Oslo, he said, from Bergen, tomorrow the camp would be set up.

"We will win this fight! For the Sister Falls, for Eidesdalen."

"Yes," Sønstebø said. "Good."

"And the people of Eidesdalen," Daddy said. "Are they ready?"

"Yes," Sønstebø said, "yes, they are."

"Great," Daddy said. "How many are coming?"

"A few," Sønstebø said. "I don't know … They have farms, all of them."

And he didn't say much more than that. I didn't notice when he left, I was sitting with a student from Oslo. She was my own age and had, like me, quit her summer job to help out. I was moved when she told me that.

We slept on the floor at my father's place, Magnus and

I, side by side between other bodies; it was uncomfortable and safe.

The next morning we packed up the car. We were given Daddy's old tent; he'd bought a new one. I had brought sleeping bags and a Primus with me from Bergen. Then we set out for the mountain.

DAVID

I was awakened by a bewildering sense of relief. She had left in the course of the night. She had not said anything about why, but it was probably because of Lou. And that was for the best.

Yet it was as if Marguerite were still there, beside me in the bed. The warmth of her, the hollow in the mattress where she'd been lying.

I turned towards Lou, who was waking up. I smiled at her, wanting to suggest something: a walk, a game, a picnic. A game of tag beneath the trees. A treasure hunt—perhaps I should create a treasure hunt for her.

"Today I can go with you," Lou said.

"What?"

"I don't need to stay with Francis. I can go with you and ask about Mommy. I can go with you to the people who find people."

Anna.

August.

His four tiny baby teeth. The big movements he makes with his little arms when he pounds a toy against the floor. And the joyful sound he makes over the rhythm he creates.

Anna, her smile in the morning, her narrow eyes sparkling

at me in bed. And rosy cheeks. She had always had rosy cheeks when she woke up. As if she'd been outside in the fresh air.

What was I doing?

"Fine," I said, and sat up quickly. "Fine. If you want to come with me, that's terrific."

We went outside together. She was Lou, herself. Chattering away, but not about the can of corn. Maybe she had forgotten about it already or forgotten that she was supposed to be feeling guilty. Or perhaps she understood in one way or another that I was feeling even guiltier.

She was the way she'd been yesterday, stepping lightly across the dry grass, across the dirt. She was here.

While I ... I was floating somewhere else, without solid ground beneath my feet. I floated, rising and drowning at the same time.

There was no line today. A woman—I'd seen her before, one of the many who came here often—was standing at the door looking inside when we arrived. Then she pulled the door shut and left without looking at Lou and me.

I took hold of the door handle and pushed it down. The floor—the nice, clean floor—was covered with dust.

There was only an empty space where the desk had been. A clean square on a gray surface, like when a picture is removed from a wall. In the middle lay an extension cord that had been connected to the computer, dead and useless.

"They've left," Lou said. "The Finders have left."

"No, they haven't," I said. "I'm sure the office has just been moved somewhere else in the camp."

Lou didn't say much more as we trawled through barracks, tents and halls. I talked all the more because of it.

"Look here, here they are, I'm sure, around this corner. No, but what about this? And him, we can ask him, I'll bet he knows something. Let's go to the entrance, maybe they know something there. The main office, then, they must know something there at least. No, you know what, nobody knows anything here, but we can manage on our own, we can figure it out, right? We can manage on our own. We will find Mommy and August."

I talked, not solely to keep my own spirits up, not solely to reassure her, but to hide what I saw.

Things had gotten even worse. Garbage cans filled to the brim. Clean laundry torn down from a clothesline, soiled with dirt and dust. Dirty pots thrown into a ditch. Personal possessions, a bag, two cups, a bra, a book, scattered across the ground between two barracks.

Two guards were standing in front of the warehouse, both wearing uniforms, both wearing helmets and Kevlar vests and holding machine guns. I kept talking as if they weren't there. But Lou squeezed my hand, tightly, while looking in the other direction, neither at me nor at them.

But I don't think she saw the very worst. Because when I discovered it, when I discovered the water tanks, I took her away from there in a hurry.

They were located in the very back of the camp and had been refilled on a daily basis. I had never seen them less than three-quarters full.

But now they were only half full of water.

I hauled Lou away.

"Wait," she said.

"Yes," I said. But I kept tugging.

We should leave, move on, get away from here.

But I didn't know where to go, because the war was advancing from the south, and north of us the borders were closed.

To the west, that was the only direction open, but there lay the ocean, only the ocean.

We could leave. Try to get onto a boat.

But the ocean was many miles away. And we didn't have any water. We couldn't just start walking without water.

And then, the most important thing of all, Anna and August ... they had to get here. We had agreed on that. Sooner or later they would have to arrive.

We had no choice but to wait.

Wait. Keep waiting.

I dragged Lou out of the camp with me. To the boat again, the only place where we could get away from everything.

I didn't notice that Marguerite had followed us. I was too busy talking, shooting my mouth off to avoid having to talk about what I had seen.

We had made it a good distance down the highway when she suddenly appeared. She was out of breath, as if she had been jogging to catch up with us.

"Hi."

She smiled. A bit shyly?

My heart beat a couple of extra beats, an idiotic teenager's smile forced its way across my face.

"Hi!"

But I couldn't smile at her like that, what was I doing?

"Hi," Lou said and looked back and forth between the two of us.

"I was calling you," Marguerite said.

"Ah," I said.

"The Finders were gone," Lou said.

"She means the Red Cross," I said.

"The people who find people," Lou said.

"But they've probably just relocated," I said to Lou. "Or are taking a break."

"Probably," Marguerite said, without conviction.

We'd stopped and stood facing one another. Lou stared at Marguerite. I would have liked to know what the child was thinking. Had she picked up on something?

"Are you going for a walk?" Marguerite asked.

Hush, I wanted to say to Lou. Don't say anything. But I didn't have a chance.

"We're going to the boat," she said. "You can come along."

*

Lou climbed up the ladder expertly and swung over the railing.

I let Marguerite climb after her, wondering whether she would hesitate, say it was too high, ask questions about whether the ladder was stable.

But she did none of these things.

She was wearing only a tank top. I could see the muscles tightening in her neck and back as she moved.

While I was climbing I could hear them laughing softly at something up there.

"We were waiting for you," Lou said when I peeked over the railing. "Marguerite and I were waiting for you."

She pulled the board off the entrance hatchway and crept down into the saloon.

"Ladies first," I said to Marguerite and regretted it immediately.

But she smiled. The second smile of the day. "Thank you."

It was very cramped inside. I hadn't noticed it before when it was only Lou and me. But two adult bodies took up too much space.

Everywhere I turned, there was Marguerite. I tried to avoid contact with her, but my bare arm still brushed against hers, I could still smell the scent of her hair as she moved past.

I didn't want physical contact with her. Didn't want it. Though it was all I could think about, that and only that. I even imagined Lou not being here.

Anna. Anna. Jesus. What kind of a man am I, what kind of a partner, what am I doing?

Finally I sat down at the map table. There was no room for anyone else beside me there.

Lou showed Marguerite the toilet.

"Daddy says that it works, for sure," Lou said. "He checked the pump."

"How nice," Marguerite said.

"But we can't use it here," Lou continued. "Because it will fall into the garden."

"Gross," Marguerite said.

"Yes, gross!" Lou laughed.

They continued chatting.

Laughing more. Enjoying themselves.

Having far too nice a time.

I turned towards the map table. Something that was covered with old plastic bags was screwed onto the wall.

I took them off, one by one. They concealed instruments. It reminded me of the control room at work. I quickly read through the names: echo sounder, VHF, GPS.

Then I discovered that the tabletop could be opened. I raised it. Nautical charts. Large transparent plastic folders containing maps.

I picked them up, spread them out before me.

White ocean, light blue along the shoreline, gray where it was the shallowest. The land was light brown, almost golden. That made sense. Dry. The ocean was covered with numbers, there were numbers everywhere. It took me a while before I understood what they represented: shallows and depths.

Along the shore the numbers were close together, in many places just one to two meters, but at sea, on the white patches, the open sea, the numbers were further apart. And it was deeper: two hundred and fifty meters, three hundred, four hundred.

How much water made up an ocean? How many liters? An ocean three hundred meters in depth, an area of one thousand square kilometers. How much water was that?

The calculations made me dizzy. An infinite amount of water. And all of it completely undrinkable.

Dead water, Thomas, my boss, used to call it. Not good for anything. You can't water your plants with it. You can't water yourself. Salt is death.

He had been proud of the job he did. And his pride was infectious. "Salt water is the future, David. Water into wine is all well and good, but what we're doing is even better. We are the magicians of tomorrow."

We just didn't wave our wands quickly enough. There weren't enough of us. The plant was too old, too run-down, too small.

And then ... I remembered the flames when the building caught fire. It burned so well, almost brightly. That something that contained so much water could burn so well ...

"Where has it been?"

Marguerite was standing over me and pointing at the maps.

"I ... um ... what do you mean?"

"The maps show where the boat has been, don't they?"

"Oh. Yes. Maybe they do."

I glanced down at the map I had lying in front of me.

"This is France."

"The Atlantic coastline," she said, and pointed. "Bordeaux is there."

I opened the folder and took out more maps. They covered every part of the same coastline, overlapping in some places, from Bordeaux via La Rochelle to Brest. Large portions of the maps were white. Ocean, the Bay of Biscay.

"Are there more?" Marguerite asked.

I took out the other plastic folders containing charts, opened the first one, took out four more sheets of paper, tried spreading them out, but they were too large for the tiny saloon table.

"Let's take them outside," Marguerite said.

Lou helped to spread them across the dry grass in the garden. Marguerite laid overlapping charts on top of each other, showing Lou how they could be fitted together like a puzzle.

There was a slight breeze, the maps fluttered. Lou and Marguerite found stones to hold them down.

I stood there watching. The two bowed heads. Marguerite explaining calmly, Lou talking loudly and eagerly, while the entire western coast of Europe slowly appeared before our eyes on the ground.

"From the north," Marguerite said finally. "She came from the north. Far north."

"She?"

"That's what you call a boat. She's a woman."

"But it's a boat," Lou said.

Marguerite laughed. I felt a stabbing inside of me. How rusty it sounded, that laughter. As if she wasn't used to laughing.

"From the north?" I asked.

From the water countries.

I gazed at the maps, following them upwards, the English Channel, Le Havre, Calais, Ostend, Vlissingen, Den Helder, Cuxhaven, Sylt, Esbjerg, Hirtshals, Egersund, Stavanger, Haugesund ...

I walked over to the maps of Norway, stopping by the one furthest north.

What a coastline, so different from France. The landscape at home was a straight line facing the ocean compared to this. The Norwegian coast was jagged, fragmented, made up of thousands of islands. And long, dramatic fjords that continued inland for miles.

"We're here," Marguerite said, and pointed at a place in the grass, off the charts.

"Where is the ocean?" Lou asked, and looked around her.

"Far, far away," Marguerite said.

"But how did the boat end up here?" I asked. "In the middle of the countryside?"

"Come."

Marguerite walked away between the trees. She stopped for a moment. Sunshine and shadows flickered across her face. Then she seemed to notice something between the trees behind the house.

"Here."

She nodded at us, encouraging us to come along. And we followed her into the tangled underbrush, where she pointed out an almost overgrown cart road.

It followed a dried-up brook, with smoothly polished stones where the bed of the river had once been.

Soon the riverbed sloped downwards. We walked down a gentle incline.

We reached a dilapidated construction beside the riverbed.

Marguerite stopped at the sight of weathered planks and rotting wooden boards.

"What was it?" she said.

I was puzzled. "Didn't you ever build a dam as a child?"

"No," she said. "I never built anything."

No ... women like her didn't build ... they didn't need to— you don't need to build when you are given everything.

We continued on along the path, and soon the landscape opened up. And there, between the trees, we saw it.

A belt of mud, almost dried out.

"A river?"

"A canal," Marguerite said. "Canal de Garonne. It continues on to the Canal du Midi. At one time they divided France in two."

"In two?" Lou said.

"The canals divided France, but connected the oceans, the Atlantic and the Mediterranean."

"Where is the water now?"

"The canal has dried up. But it will be filled up again if it starts raining."

"When it starts raining," I said.

"What?"

"The canal will fill up again *when* it starts raining."

Marguerite looked at me, was going to say something.

I stared back at her, hard. She would have to understand this, thank you very much. We couldn't talk like that around Lou.

She corrected herself.

"*When* it starts to rain," she said to Lou, "the canal will fill up again ... all we need is a little rain."

We walked home together, Lou in the middle between us. I suddenly expected her to reach out her hands, one hand for each of us. That she would get us to hoist her into the air. Jump. The way she used to, with Anna and me.

But she walked without taking either of our hands. And that was good. Because she shouldn't hold hands like that, not with Marguerite.

We passed a tractor. It was parked on the side of the road. Abandoned.

Somebody had vandalized it. Cut up the leather seat with a knife—the foam rubber was spilling out.

Marguerite looked at me, above Lou's head—was it safe, she was thinking maybe, to walk along these roads alone?

We walked faster, hurrying back to the camp.

"Thank you," Marguerite said when we arrived. "For letting me see the boat."

"Yes ..." I said.

"You're welcome," Lou said.

"Good night," Marguerite said. "See you."

"You can come with us tomorrow, too," Lou said.

"I'm sure she doesn't want to do that," I said.

"Don't you want to?" Lou asked.

"I would like that very much," Marguerite replied.

But she didn't wait until the next morning.

She came back that very same night.

She was there with her body. The rippling tautness beneath my fingers. The bony softness.

You're here, I thought.

You're here, under me, over me.

And I can't stop myself. See no reason to hold back. I am incapable of thinking about why I should hold back.

Anna was a hole in my head. August and Anna a black hole into which everything disappeared.

But Marguerite filled me up again. A little, a little bit.

We didn't talk. I wanted to, wanted to know everything about her. Wanted to hear everything.

But we couldn't talk. Because Lou was sleeping quietly.

We could only lie here. Beneath each other, on top of each other. And I wanted to gasp. Howl. Scream. But I was as quiet as I could be.

While I hoped the hole would shrink.

While I hated that the hole shrank.

SIGNE

No wind. I turn on the engine, sailing at a low rpm. I can hear better then, stand tall, stretch, but I can't see much.

Thirty-three point one kilometers at the narrowest point, in the strait between Dover and Calais, France on the port side, England on starboard. I stay close to the British coastline to avoid the ferry traffic. It feels like the land along the shore is closing in on me. The wind drops and the fog seeps in, from England of course, the homeland of the fog.

England, England, there you are again. I've never been back, have avoided the country, the odor of deep-fried food, cigarette smoke, the aftertaste of brick dust in my mouth, the eyes of the receptionist, am not going there either, not ever, not even if I need a port of refuge. I would rather founder.

There is a tunnel under the Channel; it's inconceivable, every single hour hundreds of people travel by train beneath me, with millions of liters of water over their heads. To think that they dare make that journey, those who every day board a train and willingly and knowingly allow themselves to be transported under the seabed—there is no place more claustrophobic or tomb-like.

The mist grows heavier and heavier, clouds that love the land, Daddy said, he liked the fog, but the fog here ... now ... I get to my feet, my visibility is obscured, the sea evaporates before me, behind me, I can no longer see the sky.

It is dark, a peculiar gray darkness; I turn on the lanterns, but it doesn't help much. I do it mostly just to have done it, use the fog horn; its faint howl is swallowed up by the air thick with moisture, one long and two short blasts, one long, two short.

But I know my position, I have the compass; if I just continue on exactly the same course, sounding the fog horn, I will be safe.

I cling to the helm, my knuckles whiten, my eyes on the compass needle. It is completely silent, like in a vacuum, like in outer space, the moisture in the air prevents the sound waves from traveling. I try the fog horn again, but the sound is so faint, almost nothing.

I keep going, on the same course, maintain a low speed, three knots—at this speed it will take several hours to pass the Strait of Dover, but I don't dare try to go any faster.

And then I hear it, the engine of another boat ... no, not a boat ... the pounding, enormous engine of a ship.

I turn around.

Where is it coming from?

Just the same gray wall on all sides.

The ship draws closer, the sound grows louder, but where is it coming from? I turn my engine off, stand rigidly, my jacket makes a noise when I move, the material of the jacket squeaks, while the ship, the ship still doesn't exist except as a pounding, heavy rumble, gradually, inexorably increasing in volume.

I listen, the sound is coming from the starboard side, I turn my head, no, it's coming from the port side. My damn hearing, the right ear weaker than the left; I stood too close to a megaphone once, or maybe it was the angle grinder during the protest in Alta. Alta, yet another loss, they spent a day removing the chains. We thought we were going to win and in just one day they cut all the chains. But now I don't need my hearing any longer, because now I can see the ship, it's emerging, a huge, gray shadow, like a mountain right in front of me.

Heading straight for me, to my port side.

My fog horn screeches, one long, two short, again and again, but it is smothered by the sound of the big ship's engine; they haven't seen me, just keep going. I shift the helm forcibly, set the engine at full operating speed and . . .

There are just a few meters between me and the ship, I can glimpse the patches of rust on the side of the vessel, the weld seams in the steel construction.

He has presumably not seen me, the skipper up there on the bridge, he doesn't know, will never know, that on this day he almost ran down a sixty-seven-year-old lone sailor from Norway.

But then he disappears again, then the ship disappears behind me and I think I can see it growing lighter, or perhaps it's just white spots floating before my eyes, because now I finally remember to breathe again.

And I laugh, a loud laugh of relief.

The laughter carries actually, even through the fog, it carries and lingers.

I'm unstoppable, I think.

I am, and have always been, quite unstoppable.

Unstoppable.

Especially in the fight for Eidesdalen, infected with anger and with the child growing inside me. I remember how the anger grew along with it, how it burned and warmed me, became stronger with every passing day.

Unstoppable but not happy. There are people who live their entire lives with a glint in their eyes, they move slowly, walk securely through the world, able to take pleasure in a nice meal, an evening spent with good friends, a hike in the woods with people they care about. They collect such experiences, carry them inside to turn to when life turns against them, cling to them, use them to warm themselves on. I think this ability must be innate, genetic, like a talent for numbers or words.

But I was happy up there. I remember that I was happy. We set up camp at the end of the access road up in the mountains, 1,100 meters above sea level, where according to the plans the new dam was going to be built. But there would be no dam, no tunnel, no pipeline down to the power plant, we thought, because every day more demonstrators joined us, soon there were more than 500 of us, mostly young people, even some children joined us, because it was summertime and school was out and the children roamed about as if they were attending an unusual kind of summer camp.

The tents, all of them low mountain tents designed for conditions such as this, were scattered across a large, stony area. The weather was rough up there, so far above sea level, and it rained often, because the area was located where the clouds from the ocean met the mountains. But it made little difference to us. The days were long, there were many hours of daylight and we shared everything: food, coffee, cigarettes, stories and political engagement. We gathered around a huge bonfire in the evenings, filled the silence of the mountain with singing and reading letters and newspaper articles out loud. Everything that came to us, everything that was about us, we read. Every day we received declarations of support in the form of letters, newspapers and food, all of it airlifted to us by light aircraft. All these things were signals letting us know that we were being noticed, that we were taking part in something historic—never before had the Norwegian struggle to protect the environment found expression in a demonstration like this. And best of all, our protests were reverberating beyond the borders of Norway, because soon Swedish, Danish and even German newspapers were writing about the demonstration.

I have never felt as much at home anywhere as I did up there and I hoped it would last forever. But the memories didn't turn into something I could warm myself on, because soon it would all come to an end, along with the rest of my life as I knew it.

The beginning of the end ... that was perhaps the morning when the sheriff from Ringfjorden arrived. He had been hired just a couple of years ago, so neither Magnus nor I knew him, a young guy with a Stavanger dialect. He had with him three men and a megaphone, through which he stammered his prepared statement.

He asked us to leave, was heartfelt, earnest, speaking without anger; he made reference to the penal code, which he claimed we were all violating and that we were at risk of being fined or even being put in jail.

"You are hereby ordered to evacuate the area immediately so the work can continue."

I squeezed Magnus's hand.

"Forget it," I said softly to him and to myself.

Because we stayed, of course we stayed, we were going to remain here until they had to carry us away.

But the sheriff continued: "You have communicated what you wished to communicate, you have achieved what you wanted to achieve."

"What language," I said.

"I thought you liked it when people expressed themselves correctly," Magnus said.

Daddy stepped forward, smiled at the sheriff.

"We understand that you're here because you have no

choice," he said. "But you only represent Ringfjorden ... I don't see the sheriff from Eidesdalen up here ..."

"I don't see many people from Eidesdalen either," the sheriff said.

"They have farms to run," Daddy said. "And we're not just here for them. We're here for the environment, for the water ouzel, for the freshwater pearl mussels."

The sheriff stood there, hesitating, the three policemen vigilant behind him. Nobody seemed to know what to do with their hands. There were five hundred of us, four of them.

"I believe I have said what I had to say," the sheriff said, and took a step back.

"And we have heard you, but we are not going to obey," Daddy said.

"I can only hope that this will have a peaceful resolution," the sheriff said.

"We support non-violent protest," Daddy said.

"If you mean that, you should heed the warning and take down the camp."

There was something helpless about him, now that he no longer had a piece of paper to read from.

"Poor guy," Magnus murmured.

"Nobody's forcing him," I said.

"It's his job," Magnus said.

"All right, then," the sheriff said loudly. "See you soon."

"You know where to find us," Daddy said.

The sheriff nodded to the three officers and they retreated.

We cheered, all of us, when the car started and they drove away.

"One–nil for us," Daddy said.

Magnus didn't say anything, just walked to the tent and I hurried after him.

It had started drizzling.

"Are you hungry?" I asked.

He shrugged.

I went to get the camping stove and took it outside, suddenly noticing how cold I was, my hands shaking when I went to pour denatured alcohol into the burner. The bottle was already half empty, we would have to get more tomorrow.

I took out a can of beef stew and started heating it up directly over the flame. I didn't really like the smell of canned food—everything hermetic had a particular flavor, as if it tasted first and foremost of the can, and now the steam rose from the mushy mass in the can, forcing its way into my nostrils. This diet made my nausea worse and it could not possibly be healthy for the child I was carrying.

Magnus was sitting in the tent opening. Behind him the tent was crooked; the canvas hanging between the poles wasn't properly secured. He just sat there, like a sack of potatoes, even though the dented aluminum plates we were going to eat from were still dirty.

"Aren't you going to do this?" I tossed him the plates.

"You don't need to yell."

"Will you wash them, please?"

"Signe, you know that sooner or later we will have to leave."

I didn't answer, kept stirring the stew; it was starting to stick to the bottom, the thin aluminum the can was made of was flimsy.

"Can't we just leave?" he asked. "Now."

"Dinner is ready. You have to wash the plates," I said.

"Signe?"

"The stew is burning."

"Can't you at least take a trip down and talk to Iris?" Magnus said.

"What?"

Again, her first name, *Iris*.

"She's unbelievably sad, Signe."

"Have you spoken to her?"

"Please ... can't you meet her halfway?"

Meet her halfway?!

"No," I said.

"I was there yesterday," he said.

"When?"

"In the evening."

I hadn't even noticed that he was gone.

"She's so sad that you ... both of you ... are taking this so personally."

"As if it were anything but personal."

"She's still your mother."

"Don't you take it personally? It's your family. Your valley."

"I am trying to separate the issue from the people involved."

I couldn't help but laugh, a short cough of laughter. "I don't understand how you think I am supposed to take this. If it's not personal, what is it, then?"

"The people who came from Oslo, from Bergen," he nodded towards the bonfire. "They've maybe understood it. They've come for the cause."

"No," I said. "You're the one who hasn't understood it. They take it personally, too, it's their waterfall, their water, their valley, even though they're not from here."

He stood there a little while, and a kind of dullness came over him. Then he reached out his arms towards me, smiling wanly. "Sometimes I don't understand how you can be bothered, Signe."

"Be bothered? As if I have a choice?"

When evening came, I crept into my sleeping bag as usual, but falling asleep was impossible. It was so damp, so raw; it didn't make any difference how tightly I laced up the bag. It felt like I couldn't get away from the tent canvas, it was far too close to my face all the time. The taste of burned canned stew and denatured alcohol was still in my mouth, and all of a sudden I was incredibly fed up with the taste of denatured alcohol, the smell of denatured alcohol and with the rain that was still pouring down, the dampness that penetrated everywhere, but I couldn't share this with Magnus, who was sleeping with his face turned away from me. That would be admitting he was right.

DAVID

"We're feeding the wood," Lou said.

We'd found sandpaper, oil and brushes in the toolshed. Now we were spreading oil on the surfaces of the cracked benches. The wood absorbed everything it was given, like dry soil absorbs water. The oil altered the surface. Softened it. Turned it a warmer shade of brown.

It was the three of us and the boat. I never found out what had happened to the Red Cross. I just wanted to stop time.

We cleaned out the cupboards. Found old books, some cans of food, bedding.

Marguerite dragged a stack of cushions into the cockpit. They smelled moldy.

"The sun will take care of it," she said, and put the cushions out to air.

While we were working, I thought about Marguerite. About her lips against mine.

I wanted so much to kiss her, constantly, to put my arms around her waist and bury my face in her hair.

But then Lou was there. With her high-pitched voice and

those quick eyes of hers that didn't miss a thing. Or missed everything, I couldn't tell.

And I didn't want her to leave us alone, because I liked seeing her close to Marguerite. I liked hearing them talk. Hearing them laugh.

Three days passed.

We didn't talk about the day before, Marguerite and I, didn't talk about the day that would come, about the drought, about how long it had been since it had rained.

We just talked about what we ate, the water we drank, about the sun in the sky, the trees along the roadside. About the boat.

Every time we approached another subject, I made sure that we stopped. Or she would, as often as I did. Even Lou helped out, with her chattering and laughter.

She talked a lot about Francis. They had a game, she said, were in the midst of a game. But I didn't ask what the game was.

Three days passed and then the fourth day came.

Suddenly Lou didn't want to come with us to the boat. She was going to play with Francis, she said, all day. They had agreed on that.

I gave in. Far too easily. Because I knew what this meant, that we could be alone, Marguerite and I.

We walked to the boat. Neither of us said anything along the way. I didn't look at her, only at the road in front of me, at the dust that was stirred up by the hot wind. We didn't walk close to one another, didn't touch one another, but nonetheless at all times I could feel her body beside mine.

Then we climbed into the boat.

She undressed. It was the first time I had seen her naked in broad daylight.

This time she didn't remove my hands from her abdomen, from the stretch marks.

I wanted her to tell me, but she said nothing. Said nothing, but didn't stop me either. Let me get close to her.

It had been a long time since we had showered. We were sticky, salty. A layer of dry dust coated our bodies, was between us, became a part of us, a part of *it*.

Afterwards we lay there in silence.

I couldn't resist looking at the marks. I stroked them again.

There had been someone inside her. But she wasn't going to tell me about it.

Just as I didn't say anything about Anna.

Anna. Suddenly, I was unable to look at Marguerite.

My Anna ... after the pregnancies her stomach had been round. But no stretch marks. And her breasts ... She claimed they had changed. But they were the same as before. Small and round, they fit into my hand. The feeling of them against my palm ...

Anna wasn't shy. Could argue with me without any clothes on. We shouted and screamed at one another. Argued often. Probably more often than most couples. She distracted me with her tits. Stood there with them pointing straight out. The young, pert breasts. And then she might suddenly laugh, in the middle of the argument. Because she discovered how my gaze flitted back and forth, from the screaming mouth to the smiling tits that resembled two eyes in the middle of her body.

Marguerite sat up, reached for her dress. She pulled it over her head, covering her freckled, pale skin. Anna tanned easily. Golden brown. She never used sunscreen.

A deep sob struggled out of me. I curled up, turned away. I couldn't let her hear it.

"I'm getting up," Marguerite said.

"Yes," I said.

"You coming?"

"Mmm."

But I was unable to move, closed my eyes, could see only Anna.

Anna when we went running. Anna with August on her arm.

I had lost her. I had lost August. I left Argelès without them. What kind of man does such a thing? What kind of father?

And now I was lying here fucking another woman. A much older woman, to boot. A woman who just happened to be here. Who was available. I had fucked her for one sole reason: because I needed a woman.

That's the kind of guy I am.

I got out of bed quickly, pulled on my clothes and went out into the cockpit. I had to escape from myself. Had to do something.

Marguerite was sitting on the recently aired-out cushions

and looking up into the trees. She'd done up only half the buttons on her dress and I could make out the cleavage between her breasts. She didn't turn around when I came out.

I thought I could hear the stand under the boat creaking when I moved outside. A stranded boat on a stand. It didn't belong here. It was just as out of place as I was.

And suddenly I knew what I should do.

"We have to move it," I said.

"What?"

Now she looked at me.

"We have to move the boat back to the canal."

"We do?"

"It has to be ready for when the rain comes."

She looked at me in wonder.

"It's going to start raining," I said.

And suddenly the words poured out of me. "The rain will come back. Sooner or later it has to start raining again. I don't mean a pathetic kind of rain like we've had the past four winters. I mean a proper autumn rain that lasts, weeks of rain. All the rain we haven't had. Sooner or later it has to come back. Sooner or later. I will do everything I can," I said. "So the boat will be ready when the water comes."

Marguerite still didn't say anything, but she got to her feet. And buttoned up her dress all the way.

"Will you help me?" I asked.

"Of course I will," she said.

*

It took us two days.

I invited Caleb, Martin and Christian to lend a hand. They accepted the task without asking any questions. We're happy to have something to do to fill the hours, they said. To get out of the camp, where everything is just getting worse.

We broke into a couple of barns and found what we needed: materials, tools, an old cart. Caleb attached a log to the wall of the house. He'd gotten hold of some pulleys, drilled deep holes into the wall. Constructed a mainstay.

We used all the old ropes from the tarps, throwing out only those that had decayed the most. Wound them around the boat, again and again. They would have to support the full weight, they *had* to hold.

The second night we broke into the generator cabinet in the camp and pulled a long power line all the way out to the road. We charged the abandoned tractor, stealing no more power than we needed, just exactly enough so it could drive the few meters to the house and from there through the underbrush to the canal.

The key was in the ignition. The tractor started immediately and drove without complaint down to the yard, over to the boat.

Caleb had converted the old cart into a trailer. On it he had built a cradle. Now we attached the trailer to the back of the tractor.

The air stood still when we hoisted up the boat.

The hull rested solidly on floral couch cushions from the abandoned house.

It was so big and heavy. The weight would stall the tractor, I thought.

But when I turned the key and started the engine again, it pulled the trailer easily. Both the tractor and the boat on the trailer rolled forward.

Through the garden, down the path, towards the canal.

Lou ran beside me.

Marguerite took her hand. "It's working. It's working."

"Come on, Daddy!"

I backed up to the canal, had to keep turning around in my seat to keep my eyes on the boat at all times. My hands were sweaty. Imagine if it didn't work, if the cradle collapsed, if the trailer didn't hold?

It was steep, too steep.

I closed my eyes and continued. Could feel the boat pulling. It had gained momentum.

Was on its way down towards the canal.

I no longer needed to use the gas. The trailer was rolling by itself. Gravity did all the work.

"Stop!" Martin shouted.

"Brakes!" Christian howled.

I did as they said, but the weight of the boat produced its own momentum.

Now it's tipping over!

But it didn't tip over.

It just slid out into the canal. Exactly the way we had planned.

The trailer hit the muddy bottom.

"Wait," Caleb called.

As if I had any choice.

The back wheels of the tractor were on the bank of the canal, about to roll down.

Caleb and Christian ran over to me and loosened the trailer. I put my foot on the gas pedal and drove a few meters forward, back towards the yard.

"Hurrah," Lou called, and jumped up and down.

Everyone clapped.

Because there was the boat, in the middle of the canal. Resting solidly in the cradle on the trailer, which was now securely stuck in the mud.

There it would remain. Berthed in the mud.

As stable as a post, until the rain came.

Caleb, Martin and Christian didn't want any payment for the labor. Not that I had anything to give them.

"But the tractor," Christian said, "you don't need that, maybe."

"Just take it," I said.

Christian took his seat behind the wheel.

"Come on," he said to Lou in his broken French. "*On y va.*"

She ran over and climbed up beside him.

"You too!" He turned towards us.

We piled onto the rusty vehicle, all six of us, and drove back to the camp.

The thudding sound of the tractor vibrated inside me.

To move like this, without any exertion … it was so given and yet something I'd never thought about before, back when I was driven and transported around all the time, by cars, busses, trains and airplanes. I hadn't needed to make an effort, no energy was required to move from place to place.

It had been so simple.

I took pleasure in sitting like this, carried along by the noisy engine.

But the tractor didn't hold out for long. Just a few hundred meters. Then it ran out of electricity.

We left it behind, in almost the same place we'd retrieved it from, and had to walk the rest of the way to the camp. But we walked with light steps.

SIGNE

The fog lifts, the wind picks up and I take hold of the line to unfurl the headsail, but something—a disturbance in the water—causes me to stop. The surface remains unbroken, but nonetheless there is something down there, far below me.

A sound, a loud sound, of rushing air; I whirl quickly around towards the port side and there it is: about fifty meters away from the boat, a tall geyser is rising out of the water. The whale sings, has its own language, but the song can't be heard up here, only this strange, almost mechanical sound of water gushing out of its blowhole.

The bluish-black back draws closer, glides towards the boat; it's long, God, so long, maybe twenty meters, twice as long as *Blue*, a finback whale, it must be a finback whale. The second largest species on earth after the blue whale, found in all waters. I've seen whales before, but never one so large, never at such close range.

The body is an arc on the surface until it slides underwater again and is swallowed by darkness.

Where are you, where are you? Disappear now, swim calmly away from here.

But then it returns, just a few meters away from me, swimming alongside the boat. It must be a female, they grow the largest, maybe fifty tons, maybe sixty, compared to the Arietta's meager 3.5 tons. A single flick of its enormous body and *Blue* will be destroyed, a mere flick and there's nothing I can do, it's so huge, so heavy, it can hurt me if it wants, hurt the boat, place its back against the hull, capsize *Blue*, taking me along with it.

How long would I survive in the water, how cold is it? Maybe eight degrees, maybe ten—at ten degrees I would remain conscious for one hour, it would take three hours to freeze to death unless my panic kills me first and I start breathing through my mouth, swallowing water, throwing up, suffocating. Most people who drown are able to swim; it's the panic that does them in, not the cold water. Or maybe the whale just pulls me under, long before I've had time to get cold, tossing me around, playing with me, a heartless game driven by an animal's incomprehensible impulses, and there is nobody here who can save me.

Again the whale exhales through its blowhole—an intense, loud sound; the column of water is so powerful that I can feel the drops where I'm standing. Should I do something, make noise, maybe that would frighten it? Or agitate it?

I don't do anything.

It glides underwater but just for a moment, then it's back once more, only ten meters away now, headed straight for me—it's going to capsize the boat, I will tumble overboard, it will drag me under, drag me under . . .

But at that minute it dives away, again it disappears, is centimeters away from making contact with the broadside, as if intentionally, as if it's playing with the boat and, as if on cue, now it surfaces again starboard. I jump in response to the powerful gush of its breathing.

It swims away from me, but turns, returns to me, glides through the water along the hull of the boat, as if it wants to come up against it, caress the boat, but it never touches it and slowly my fear ebbs away.

Usually they travel in pairs or in groups, in the winter 400 whales were beached in New Zealand, they were beached and couldn't leave because they waited for each other. The smallest whales could have managed it, at high tide they could have swum away, but they stayed, never abandoned their parents, stayed with the pod, dying with the others instead.

This whale can't be alone either, it's bound to have a partner or a child nearby and, anyway, it has the entire ocean beneath it, with all the life it contains, the unimaginable number of species, only I'm alone up here on the surface, only me and the huge surface of the ocean and an infinite emptiness above me. I am a cross on a map, a dot on a surface, insignificant, almost invisible, as we all are, because from a distance, from above, each and every one of us disappears; from outer space it is water one sees, the ocean, the clouds, the drops that give the earth life, the blue globe, different from all the other planets we know about, just as alone in the universe as each and every one of us down here.

You have to stay, dear whale, you have to stay here with me, just stay.

But at that moment it disappears, without warning it's gone, no ripples on the waves, no bubbles in the water, just the sheer, flat surface is left behind, the enormous, unwieldy floor of water with its incomprehensible system of waves and streams, not impenetrable, but closed all the same.

And the whale doesn't return.

I'm unable to move, just stand there, feeling the solid deck beneath my feet, how cold my hands are, the lightness of the wind, the humidity in the air.

It's just me—me and the surface.

There have been periods in my life when I thought I had a pod—Eidesdalen, Alta, Narmada—but actually, there's only been me, alone, now and always.

I think I've been alone ever since the night Daddy blew up the bridge. I think it happened on that night.

They met up there, he and Sønstebø, in the middle of the night, in the dark. I wonder what Daddy was thinking as they attached the sticks of dynamite to the freshly cut timber of the bridge, if he thought about Mommy and about me, or if he just thought about what he had between his hands, the blasting caps, the explosives, about Alfred Nobel who invented dynamite sometime in the nineteenth century—it would be typical of him to think of Nobel ... And when they

had driven the van away, when they got into position to deto-
nate the charges, did he think of us then, of me? Did Sønstebø
think of his child, of Magnus?

Or did the two men think that they were at war, that all's
fair in war, was it a war they were fighting, the two of them,
up there on the mountainside that night?

I snitched on Daddy. When I told Mommy about him and
Sønstebø that was the beginning of the end. I bore the guilt,
I bear the guilt for my own loneliness, I have chosen it myself,
am condemned to be free, can't shirk my responsibility. But it
was him, it was the two men who attached the sticks of dynamite to the bridge. That was actually what happened first.
I was a chubby little girl with a voice just a bit too loud. I was
stuck inside a snow globe and merely did everything I could
to escape.

You didn't know a thing, Magnus, about the bridge, about
that night that brought us together. I was alone, you were
an interruption in all my years of solitude, but maybe everything would have been different if our fathers hadn't
blown up the bridge. Perhaps the interruption would have
lasted longer.

Or maybe we wouldn't even have found our way to one
another. And I would have been without that interruption,
without the years we actually had.

Would I rather be without them?

Would I rather be without Magnus?

*

Stop it.

Stop it, Signe.

I have to raise the sail. I take hold of the line again, bend over, and am about to pull when I make a clumsy movement, hitting my knee against the cockpit bench. The pain radiates from my knees, hot shocks in my feet, up along my thighs, through my entire body. I sob; it hurts more and more, and I can only think about the physical pain. For a while that's all I need to think about.

DAVID

We could smell the smoke long before we saw the entrance to the camp.

It was so harsh. Familiar. The acrid smell of fire. It had been there all along.

The smell of smoke was something massive that had infiltrated and inhabited me. The stinging in the throat, eyes, the pressure in the chest.

Marguerite started to run. I took Lou by the hand and ran, too.

When we arrived, people were running in all directions, carrying away the few personal possessions they had or running towards the fire, hoping to help.

Caleb pointed.

"It's the sanitary barracks," he said. "Someone has set the sanitary barracks on fire. It's those bastards from up north, I'm sure it's one of them."

"Is that the women's shower?" Lou asked. "Daddy, is the women's shower burning?"

We ran closer, Christian, Caleb and Martin in the lead. I followed right behind them, holding Lou by the hand. Marguerite took up the rear. And we stopped only when we could feel the heat of the blaze.

For the time being only the barracks were burning. It looked harmless. It looked like something that could be controlled.

"No, the trees," Christian said.

The trees, the shady trees that had kept the camp cool, were a firetrap. The branches stretched towards the ground. If they should catch fire, that would be the end. Then we would have no other choice but to get out of there. Run away, as we had run away from Argelès.

People were running back and forth with half-empty buckets. Some stood with hoses in their hands. Feeble streams of water were sent into the flames, only to evaporate and disappear.

"The water," Marguerite said softly. "They're using up the water."

She was right. The fire was consuming the last of the camp's water.

The woodwork caught fire, the flames ate their way inwards, upwards and disappeared in a tail of thick black smoke.

Martin, Christian and Caleb had also thrown themselves into the fire-fighting effort. They carried a plastic water tank between them, a few liters sloshing at the bottom.

"More for the hoses," Caleb shouted.

More people ran past us, so close to me that somebody

rammed into me, a hard shoulder against my own. I almost lost my balance.

Lou tugged at my shirtsleeve. "Daddy? We have to help! We have to stop them! We have to stop the fire!"

But then she discovered something. "Francis."

She walked a few steps closer. "He's doing it!"

The light from the fire illuminated him.

He was standing, strong and tall, holding a hose in his hands. Suddenly he was a man, no longer an old-timer.

He walked steadily forward, fighting the flames, in the front lines. He gave orders and everyone did what he said. He, too, was on fire.

He shouted that everything around the barracks had to be removed so there would be no fuel for the fire.

Caleb and Christian started taking down a tent while Martin joined those who were spraying water onto the flames.

I walked further ahead, away from Marguerite and Lou. Marguerite stood with one hand on Lou's shoulder. Taking care of her.

I have to help out, I thought. I must do something, too. But there were no tasks in need of doing. Everything was already being done. There was nothing I could do.

So dizzying. The smell of smoke. The heat from the flames. The ashes descending like snowflakes to the ground. The sound of the fire, a creaking, crackling roar.

All I managed to do was stand completely still.

But suddenly somebody was screaming, drowning out everything else. "The child! No!"

At first I didn't understand what they meant. Then I spotted Lou's purple singlet on its way into the burning barracks. And after it: a hose she was dragging with her, a green garden hose that was being pulled into the roaring building.

She was inside.

I heard nothing but my own breathing, heavy, rasping, as the smoke filled my lungs and my chest contracted.

Lou in the flames. Anna in the flames. August's face in the light of the hot tongues of fire.

It wasn't illness that would take Lou from me. Not a water shortage. It was fire. I would also lose her to the fire.

My entire world would burn up. And there was nothing I could do.

"David."

Marguerite thumped hard on my arm. I still was unable to move.

"David!"

And she ran towards the flames herself. That woke me up.

I ran after her, towards the heat.

But Francis got there before us. He was quicker. He jumped lightly over a burning beam on the ground, followed the hose, and disappeared in the direction of the purple singlet inside.

Time stopped, time flew by.

I just stood there.

And then he finally came out.

I had no idea he was able to move so quickly.

She was on his back. I couldn't see her face. She hid it. His back became a shield for her.

He ran towards the flames that separated them from us, ran straight into them, protecting her with his body. And in that way he saved my daughter.

In the meantime, the flames consumed the barracks behind them. Soon there was nothing left.

But I was no longer staring into the flames, only at Lou, whom I held in my arms.

I brought her to the first-aid barracks. Somebody had opened the door, broken the lock. There were a number of people who needed help, who had burns on their hands from fighting the fire. But no doctors or nurses were to be found.

Instead people helped each other. Took what they needed in the way of Band-Aids, bandages and pain relievers.

Lou was the only child there and everyone let her through. Children still came first. Some things were still as they ought to be.

Every single injury from the fire was dressed and bandaged by Martin, who worked with practiced hands. He had apparently done this before.

Lou didn't ask about Francis. Maybe she had already figured out what had happened. That he was lying in the next room, that Marguerite and Caleb were with him, that they were doing what they could.

No, he wasn't what she asked about.

"The women's shower, Daddy, did it burn down? Did everything burn down?"

She could hardly sit still on the hospital cot where Martin had left her. The whole time she wanted to jump down and run away.

"Wait," Martin said. "The barracks burned down but nothing else. We were able to put out the fire before it spread."

But she wouldn't listen.

"We have to go, Daddy. We have to go back. There's something I have to check."

Martin rubbed some ointment on her and put on a final bandage. Far too big for her minor injury.

"There's no fire damage in the rest of the camp," he said calmly. "You mustn't be afraid. Hall Four is fine. Your bed is still there."

But Lou clung to me. "I have to go and see. We have to go now."

Finally Martin let her go. He smiled at me apologetically.

"I did the best I could."

I didn't have time to answer. I had to run after Lou.

It was starting to get dark. Smoke still hung over the camp like a dry, scorching fog.

Embers lay glowing on the ground where the sanitary barracks had been. Christian and a number of other people my age were sitting in a circle. All of them were covered with black soot, and they were grimy and exhausted. Several were holding half-empty water buckets in their hands.

They were guarding the fire. If they saw any stray embers, they put them out immediately.

Water, water, even more water wasted.

Lou ran all the way to the smoldering ruins before she stopped.

She stood in front of it, scanning the blackened ground.

Then she put her hands over her face. A tiny sob escaped. "Everything's gone!"

Gone? What was gone?

"Lou?" I placed a hand on her shoulder.

"It's all burned up," she said without looking at me.

She grasped a scorched wooden stick with one hand. And then she started walking in, across the red-hot rubble, while poking with the end of the stick.

"Where was the women's shower?" she asked.

"What do you mean?"

"Where was it?"

She kept going. Her shoes gave off the stench of burned rubber. She used the stick to push aside charred woodwork.

"Lou, what are you doing?"

She picked her way through the rubble, placing her feet between glowing embers. Her face was red from the heat.

"Lou? Stop!"

And at exactly that moment she stopped, but not because I had told her to.

With her stick she pushed aside a huge floorboard made of some kind of plastic material.

Smoke poured out and I couldn't bear to think about how toxic it was.

In two steps I was at her side.

"Now you have to stop!"

But then I discovered what she was standing there staring at.

"They're destroyed. All of them burned up!" she said.

At her feet, hidden by the board, by what had previously been the floor of the women's shower, were tin cans that had exploded. The contents oozed out. Yellow corn turned gray from ashes.

It smelled of fried ham, baked beans. Tomato sauce.

She squatted down.

"There must be something left!"

Using the stick, she started digging through the destroyed cans.

"There? No. What about that one?"

But they were all destroyed.

I pushed at the cans with my foot and the food got stuck on my shoes.

Finally, at the very bottom, we found four undamaged cans. The labels were destroyed but the cans were in one piece. I took the stick from Lou and dragged them towards me. Then I peeled off my T-shirt and used it as a pot holder.

We brought them with us, went away from there and sat

alone a little way away from the burned-out ruins. I opened a can that turned out to contain beans.

They were steaming.

We shared the beans. Once again we shared her booty. And I didn't manage to say anything today either. I was too hungry. I gobbled up the food like a dog.

We were dogs, all of us.

Lou was sniffling as she ate, drying her tears with quick movements.

"They were supposed to be for us, Daddy. For us and the boat. We were supposed to take them with us and live there. Francis helped me. We collected the cans and hid them under the floor of the women's shower."

I was unable to answer. I was afraid I would start crying myself. And besides . . . what would I say? She knew that stealing was wrong. All children know it. Anna and I had taught her that. But all the same, she had stolen again, because her hunger was controlling her thoughts. Overpowering everything else.

And me. Regardless, I had nothing to say. Damn dog that I was.

She stood up. Brushed the ashes off her clothing. "I want to go to bed now."

Hall 4 looked the same. Our beds were waiting just like before. The bag in the closet. Our home was intact, I caught myself thinking.

But this wasn't a home. Just an old warehouse full of military cots.

And we were refugees. A refugee has no home. *Home* was what we had lost.

Lou fell asleep right away. When Marguerite came in I was still sitting at Lou's bedside, just as passive as before, just as listless.

I'm a lump of meat, I thought. There are no bones in me. No skeleton. Just flesh, fat, a soft mass.

Marguerite stood beside me. She said nothing. It took me a while to turn around and look at her. She was crying.

"Francis . . . he's . . ."

And then she said it, using many words to express something very simple. I didn't look at her, heard only how she fretted on and on. I knew from the start what she was going to say. Knew it the minute I saw him emerge from the flames, that this wouldn't end well.

"Sorry," she said softly. "I said we should leave, wanted to take her away, but she just ran. Straight in."

"I never asked you to watch her," I said.

There was a coldness in my voice, coming from I didn't know where.

"We should have realized it," she said. "She said it, after all, *we have to help*. We should have realized that she was talking about herself as well."

"*We* shouldn't have realized anything at all."

The cutting words flew out of my mouth, but it was the

only reply I could muster. For there wasn't any we. There was only Lou. Me. Lou and I. Marguerite wasn't a part of it.

But Marguerite didn't leave, she sat down with me. She continued.

"We have to leave, David."

I didn't reply.

"We have to get out of here."

We. Still *we*.

"David?"

I got to my feet. "I'm not going anywhere."

I left the room, left her sitting there, left Lou who was lying in bed. The embers were still smoldering at the scene of the fire. The smell of wet, charred wood filled the camp.

Christian, Caleb and Martin were sitting in the soot on the ground. A jar of pills changed hands.

"We stole it from first aid," Caleb said when I sat down. "Everything is up for grabs now."

"One will do away with the pain, three with the anxiety," Martin said, his voice already listless.

I took four.

Everything was all right, for a while everything was all right.

My mind became sharp, my body simultaneously slow and quick.

The words pouring out of my mouth were sharp, witty, clear.

I was only interested in being. Here. Now.

I danced, on two legs, on all fours.

Rolled around with Caleb and Martin, the dirt sticking to us. I could smell the odor of soot and human beings.

Girls arrived, several of them. I took one of them, rolled around with her, too. Pounded hard inside her. I heard moans, but whether they came from her or from me, I couldn't say.

I never saw her face, it was too dark. Or maybe I was blinded by woodsmoke.

Everything was all right. Everything was forgotten.

SIGNE

The approach to Bordeaux reveals a gently sloping land-scape, apparently innocent, welcoming, but I still have to wait twelve hours before I can put into port, the tide takes everything with it, the waves move back and forth, the ocean rises and ebbs. I've seen surfers rush forward on this brown, brackish water before, but today there aren't any here.

The moon controls us; every six hours and twelve minutes it pulls the ocean up or down. Out here, tables are everything, one lives according to the tide table. I have it on my phone, update it all the time, a dot shows me where I am in relation to low and high tide at any given moment. The moon is rising now, large and yellow as I sail carefully in along the strait, let-ting myself be steered by its pull, drawn towards land while the sun sets into the ocean behind me, as if it is the one I am abandoning.

The landscape around me is living two lives, twice every single day the coastline is drained of water; only a broad strip of sand, mud, shore crabs and oysters remain, where aban-doned dinghies await side by side, stranded on the seabed, moored to buoys that have no purpose, no longer afloat.

And then, twelve hours later, the water is back, the boats bob on the surface, have come to life, and woe to the one that happened to be in the wrong place at the wrong time, that was taken by the tides.

I step onto the quay in Bordeaux, solid ground beneath my feet after such a long time, a feeling which never ceases to surprise me, because my body is used to the rocking, has long since adapted, only knows of a world in constant movement, and now I'm standing here feeling how the movement continues and it's as if the ground beneath me, the wharf's concrete structure, comes towards me. How rudely and unyieldingly it meets my feet, meets my body, jars against my inner turbulence with its stability.

I make the boat fast using an extra spring line, put out all the fenders I have, but don't think it's enough. There are huge heaps of old tires on the quay, abandoned by other boats that have used them in the canal. I carry a few over to *Blue*, ease them down between the hull and the wharf, toss a couple extra on deck, thinking they may come in handy later.

A bistro by the wharf draws me in, no vegetarian dishes on the menu; I can't bear the thought of fish—no mussels, nothing from the ocean right now—order boeuf bourguignon, can't remember the last time I ate red meat, but I'm so thin, my body is all angles and hard edges. I'm hungry, I gulp down chunks of meat, carrots, mushrooms and onions in red wine sauce, a hot meal, a rich meal.

A glass of beer to drink, it goes straight to my head. I almost regret it—the world rocks even more and, strictly speaking, beer is not the right choice. The waiter makes this clear, wrinkling his nose when he puts it on the table—you should have ordered red wine here, of course, that's what Magnus would have said, a full-bodied Bordeaux to go with the solid meat dish. But no wine for me; on the rare occasion when I do drink, it's beer.

A man comes over, around my age, maybe a little younger, his skin tanned, a blue and white striped sweater, Top-Siders. A little pathetic, dressing like a sailor to signal his maritime connection to everyone.

"Can I sit down?" he asks in English, with a French accent.

"No."

"*Please?*" he says.

"Why?" I ask.

"Have you sailed here from far away?"

It's been a very long time, many years, since I last experienced this and it always made me angry, that a woman, the second sex, can't sit alone at a restaurant, have a meal, without being disturbed, without a man storming over with a peculiar and vague agenda of protecting her from her own company, maybe also from other men, and hoping that this heroic deed will lead to further enjoyment in another, more intimate setting, preferably in a bed.

"I'm not looking for company," I say.

"I didn't mean to—"

"Yeah, you did."

"Are you the one who came in with the Arietta?"

Is he really not going to give up?

I stare at him, *evil eye*, I think suddenly, and catch myself grinning, and the combination of a hard stare and a confusing smile is fortunately enough, because now he starts to walk away.

"Let me know, then," he says. "If you change your mind. I'll be over there." He points at a bar stool.

I return to my beer, would like to drink it in peace, but am unable to think about anything but the man now. He's sitting at the bar doing everything he can to avoid looking in my direction. He's attractive, to the extent that men my age are attractive; perhaps he's been at sea for a long time, sailing the kilos off him, slender, almost no paunch whatsoever, strong hands, thickly muscled and full of all the tiny cuts and injuries you get from sailing for weeks in a row, cuts that heal slowly when they are constantly exposed to salt water.

I could have gone with him to his boat. There's nothing stopping me. Maybe it's every bit as tidy and maritime as he is, dark blue with copper trim, weathered only in the right places. Or maybe it's big, a forty-five-foot Hallberg-Rassy, a stylish cliché, white as chalk, except for a single, dark-blue, snobbish stripe, and with a bed twice as wide as my own, good mattresses, clean sheets, another body against my own, another's warmth . . .

But no. Such an ordeal—the undressing, the bashfulness, the discomfort, embarrassment—maybe he has hair growth in the wrong places, I do at any rate, maybe he smells rank, alien, maybe he'll think I'm too haggard, too wrinkled, at the end of the day, with all my scratches, scrapes and dents. And what about him, what about his scratches? No doubt he doesn't give them a second thought, he's a man, the positive and neutral being. The word for man in both French and English also signifies human beings in general, while I'm the negative, *woman represents only the negative, defined by limiting criteria, without reciprocity.*

I empty my glass, stand up, pay at the bar, stop for a moment. Shall I say something to the man at the bar, shall I give him a piece of my mind? No, I can't be bothered, am too old for anger, too many have tried to rescue me.

Magnus also wanted to rescue me—he rescued me with a snowman, he rescued me at a party. It was maybe for that reason alone that we were together, because he continued to live off the good deed he had done when he was thirteen, when he had behaved like an adult. Maybe he had tried to live off that moment, tried to find it again and perhaps also tried to find his way back to the same helplessness in me.

Or was it me, was I the one who based our relationship on this, who was searching for the same thing again? I know that memories are unreliable, just as unstable as fiction. But whatever it was, it wasn't enough to base a life on. He was an interruption only, an interruption in everything else that is really me. I have to trust it, because what can I trust if I start second-guessing my own history?

I unlock the boat and walk into the saloon, where the containers dominate the space completely. I want to sit down, but there's no room, so I walk out into the cockpit again; it's damp there, condensation on the benches, a cool evening, I miss the saloon.

I return below, pick up one of the ice containers. I can put them on deck; the mast has to come down tomorrow, to be disassembled for the trip up the canal. I can put them beside it. There aren't any waves here, no storms to wash them overboard.

The feeling of plastic against my palms—I don't dare open them, imagine if it has all melted, imagine if there's no ice left . . . and have I started coming undone, imagine if I can't do it, don't have the strength, am too old, too slow, have lost the rage required to see this through?

No, no I haven't, and it's just as well if the ice has melted, then I can pour it out across his courtyard; it was supposed to melt anyway, sooner or later, the way all ice eventually melts and I can say that, I can shout that to him.

All ice melts.

DAVID

I was awakened by the first rays of the sun. It had absorbed the moisture in me, even if it was only early morning. In my mouth, the taste of dust, a dryness so intense that my tongue was paralyzed. And the smell of fire. All of me stunk, like a piece of smoked meat.

I lay with my cheek against the ground. The soil shifted beneath me. I could see the stripes in the landscape that was as wrinkled as the skin of an old man.

The dry wisps of grass still held the soil in place, but they would soon surrender, crumble into dust. And what once had been topsoil, arable land, would be blown away.

I got to my feet. At the bottom of a bucket someone had tossed away I found a few dirty drops. Dirty water, shouldn't drink dirty water.

But I couldn't help myself and poured them down my throat.

Spittle formed in my mouth. And a taste, which either came from me or from the water. As foul as poison on the tongue.

I walked to the hall. Gathered our things, the few clothes, a little food I had saved. Quickly packed it up.

I moved as quietly as I could. Marguerite was sleeping heavily and soundlessly on my bed.

Every time I bent over the backpack, my head pounded, the nausea rose. But I did nothing to prevent it. I *wanted* to feel the nausea, the headache. I deserved it.

Then I pulled on my backpack and picked up Lou.

Finally I was the one carrying her.

Today I was carrying my daughter. I should have been the one carrying her yesterday.

And I should have been the one who carried my son, August. I should have carried him too. He was too heavy for Anna. She must have stumbled. He was too heavy.

No.

Just this, just now. Lou. My child in my arms. She was alive. She was here. I could carry her to the ends of the earth.

There was nobody sitting by the exit when we passed. I didn't see the guards when I left what had once been a camp.

I didn't turn around to look back. Didn't look anymore at the scorched ground, the sleeping people who would soon wake up to the drought—the drought and the flames they had fled from, but which had now caught up with them.

I moved slowly, with my backpack on my back and Lou in my arms. All of this was too much to carry, too heavy, but at the same time, too light.

I stopped from time to time but never sat down. Just stood

there, motionless, breathing, waiting, and then continued walking when I felt I was up to it.

I stopped at every single farm we passed, put Lou down in the shade, and searched. Found food in a couple of places, but water in only one place, in an almost empty tank. I filled up some battered plastic bottles and put them in the knapsack.

My load grew even heavier, but I could take it.

Lou awoke from time to time. She didn't say anything; she blinked, but never focused her gaze on me.

The boat was waiting for us, in the middle of the canal, safe and sound in its cradle. The ladder was leaning against the stern, as if it were welcoming us.

We can stay here, I thought. We can boil the muddy water at the bottom of the water tank. It must be drinkable if we boil and filter it.

We can stay here, Lou and I. We can play. We can play so much, play so hard that everything else disappears.

I can play like that. It's perhaps the only thing I know how to do.

I put Lou down on the ground by the boat and shook her gently.

"Lou? Lou . . . You have to wake up, I can't carry you up."

Finally she came around. Got to her feet and waited, swaying. I put my arms around her. I wanted to hug it away, the entire night, the flames and Francis, who had carried her out.

But she didn't respond to my hug, she was completely stiff.

Finally I released her. She continued to stand in the same position, staring at me.

"We must go to the camp," she said.

I didn't answer. She was thinking of August, of Anna. Of how they might come.

"We have to go back now," she said.

"Are you thirsty? I have water. Here."

"I'm not thirsty."

"We will find Mommy and August," I said. "We just have to rest a little. Stay here for a little while."

"No."

"Do you want to sleep some more? You can sleep in the boat."

"We have to see how the others are doing."

"The others?"

"Marguerite. And Francis. And everyone." Her quiet voice was full of stubbornness. "We have to go now, Daddy. We have to go." She turned and took a few steps. Her steps were heavy and her neck determined as she walked across the muddy bed of the canal, up onto the bank.

"Lou?"

"We have to go there, Daddy."

And she started walking more quickly on the cart road between the trees.

"Lou, no."

I hurried after her.

"I'm going back," she said.

"We can't."

"Can to!"

I pulled her close to me, wanting to hold her tight, but she twisted out of my grasp.

Such strength—I had no idea she was so strong, so tough.

I took hold of her again. But she struggled against me, she scratched, screamed and bit. At first without a word. Only a low hissing, fierce whimpers and moans accompanied her exertions.

But then the words began. Everything she was carrying. A lot of it I had heard before, but some words were new. *Idiot! Shit father! Damn Daddy!*

I restrained her by force, the force of a father, hating it, that I had to hold her like this. I'd never held her like this before. If a father holds his child like this, does it constitute abuse? Does it?

I held on to her, tighter and tighter. She screamed, louder and louder. Finally it came:

"I hate you. I wish you were dead. Just like August! Just like Mommy!"

It was only then that I released her.

I released her so abruptly that she fell down. Her body hit the ground with a thump.

And there she remained, breathing hard where she sat. Her hair hung over her eyes. I couldn't see her face, and I wondered if she was crying, but she wasn't sobbing. Only breathing, more and more slowly.

I could have screamed, too. Yelled back at her. Denied it. Objected. Put her in her place. Called it delusions.

Or comforted her. Said that you mustn't think like that. Given her hope.

But I didn't say anything. Because there wasn't anything more to say. She'd said it all.

Finally she got to her feet. Turned away from me. Started walking again.

But she didn't walk far. Because she knew I wasn't following her.

She just walked a few steps into the forest, to a spot in the shade.

There she sat down, folding her legs underneath her.

"Lou?"

"Go away. Go to the shitty boat."

And I turned away. Did as she said. Because she wouldn't leave me, no matter what I did. She was a child, she couldn't leave me. Hiding here between the trees for a little while was the extent of her daring. And that in itself, that I could rest assured that she wouldn't leave me, was almost the worst part. The most unfair thing of all.

I climbed up onto the boat. Crawled into the forepeak.

When I opened the ceiling hatch, a breeze swept over me. A slight draft.

I lay down on the berth, feeling the woolen fabric in the mattress prickling against my skin.

And then I cried.

Then I cried.

I cried for everything I'd had.

The cramped apartment by the wharf. The rooms that were sticky in the heat. The tiny kitchen with clutter in all the cupboards. The sofa bed we argued on, made love on.

Mommy, Daddy, Alice.

Anna, her eyes, her mouth laughing, yelling. I cried for her body, the hollow in her neck, her breasts, everything I wanted to bury myself in.

I cried over August, God, how I cried for him. Our baby, the gurgling sounds he made, which nobody else managed to imitate. The porridge he spit out, how he laughed while spitting. His tummy, the belly button bulging against the world. Even his diapers, I cried for his diapers, which I hated changing.

And I cried about myself. My bungling. My voice that was too loud. That I always came home too late after a night on the town. I cried about the time I'd forgotten to pick up Lou from the babysitter's. About the key hook I never put up in the hallway. About being the kind of person who was unable to pull out in time.

I cried over what had been a life, over how it had been taken away from me.

And while I was crying, it was no longer possible to keep that day at a distance. The day Anna and August disappeared.

Anna had wanted us to leave. She talked about it every day. Almost nobody we knew was still in Argelès. She wanted to go north, showed me photos of the camp near Timbaut. We'll be safe there, she said, we can travel on from there.

The streets were empty. The stores closed. We had hoarded, but the food would soon come to an end.

But I couldn't bring myself to leave. We had an additional responsibility, those of us who worked at the plant. That's what we told each other, that's what I told her.

And we had water, as much as we needed. As long as we had water, we could manage.

All the same, more people left, also those who worked at the plant. Finally, only Thomas, my boss, and I remained.

The electricity came and went, cut off for increasingly long periods of time. And without electricity, no production.

Thomas laughed about it, about how well we had messed things up for ourselves, we humans. It was the electricity production from coal-fired power plants that had contributed to creating global warming and the water shortage in the first place, and now we needed even more electricity to produce water.

He laughed about such things. He laughed about a lot of things. Even when we put too much pressure on the machinery and blew the fuses, he laughed. It's just as worn out as I am, he said and chuckled.

But Anna wasn't laughing any longer. She cried when I came home from work. She was startled by the tiniest noises. She just sat on the tiny balcony in our apartment. Vigilant. It was as if she knew something was going to happen.

Both of us knew that something was going to happen.

I had just eaten lunch that day. A chewy croissant I had taken out of the freezer in the break room. The last one. I turned off the freezer but didn't unplug it.

The croissant had tasted like mold. I had nothing to put on it. The taste of mold was still in my mouth.

I was on my way out with the trash, it was my turn to take it out. We had to take turns. The cleaner, an Algerian refugee who had lived in Argelès since long before the five-year drought, had quit many weeks ago. He didn't understand how we dared to stay. He had already fled from another drought many years ago.

The trash bag was half full. There weren't many leftovers any longer, we ate every last crumb. The garbage cans were located a short walk away from the plant. I had to go all the way out onto the main road. They stunk in the heat. Nobody had emptied them for months.

The bag of trash in my left hand, clutched tightly between my fingers, white plastic against my palm, a knot. And then I noticed the smell.

I turned around. At first I saw only whitish smoke rising into the sky. Like a fog.

But it quickly grew darker.

Then the flames came. Small tongues over the buildings.

It was only then that I moved. Thomas, I thought.

He hadn't had lunch with me. He ate on his feet, not taking breaks.

The last time I had seen him he was standing by the control and monitoring panel. There was something that wasn't working, he said, something that had broken down again, yet another overloaded mechanism, another broken part. But he would figure it out, the way he always did.

I started running towards the building. Smoke rose towards the sky, towards me. More and more smoke billowed out all the time. Toxic smoke. And Thomas was inside.

It was only then that I dropped the bag of trash.

I ran, but the fire was spreading quickly. The flames blocked the main entrance.

I ran around the building to the rear. But the door was locked.

Back to the front. Spun around. Time passed.

The flames took hold. Ashes were already falling to the ground like snow. On me.

Water. Water. I needed water. A hose.

At that moment I heard someone calling from behind me.

"David?"

I turned around. It was Anna. She was holding August on her hip and Lou was running just behind them. They must have run out of the house the minute she noticed the smell of smoke.

Tears were running down her face and she screamed.

"David! Wait!"

"I have to go inside," I called. "I have to find Thomas!"

"No," she said. "No!"

With one bound she was at my side.

"You're not going in there!"

"I have to!" I said. "Thomas is in there."

But then she handed me August. She lifted him towards me and forced me to take him.

Then she lifted Lou onto her hip and Lou hid her face against her shoulder. I could hear her crying.

"Now we have to run," Anna said. "You see that. Now we have to get out of here!"

I stood there holding August. He smiled at me, understanding nothing. A smile with four white teeth. I don't understand a thing either, I thought.

"David!" Anna said.

"It's growing," Lou said.

I turned towards the plant.

The fire was a raging beast that ate everything.

The sparks spread, setting the dry grass on the dunes and the bone-dry trees behind them on fire.

The flames devoured everything in their path, they were a beast growing with everything it swallowed, growing ever larger and more powerful and at an ever-increasing pace.

Then finally I managed to run. August thudded against my hip. He laughed, thinking it was a game.

"Will we make it to the apartment?" I asked.

"Yes," Anna said. "We have to make it. Our passports are there. Everything is there."

We ran towards the city. Our breath tore at our throats, our eyes were stinging. We rushed down the esplanade where the old summer villas were, locked up and covered in dust.

We were faster than the fire.

"We're going to make it," I said. "It will be fine. We will make it. It will be fine."

Again and again I spoke exactly those words, like they were a jingle.

Through deserted streets, past boarded-up stores. Up the stairs towards our apartment. It smelled so good, I thought. Home, I loved that smell.

Then I caught sight of my reflection in the mirror. A white man, covered in ashes.

"Here."

Anna moistened a towel with water from a barrel and tossed it to me. I wiped the worst of it off me. At the same time she stuffed some clothing and a little food into a bag.

"And the passports," I said.

"Yes," she said. "I already packed them."

"Good job," I said.

Actually I wanted to say more. Ask her for forgiveness. I should have apologized.

Apologized for making us stay. For not listening to her. For our still being here. For having to leave our home like this, without anything.

But I didn't have a chance to say anything, because now a sound could be heard outside. A buzzing—no, a faint roar that grew louder all the time.

"It's coming," Anna said.

"But it can't come here, can it?" Lou asked.

We didn't reply. I picked up the bag. Lifted August. Anna took Lou's hand. We ran outside.

"Mommy, don't you have to lock up?" Lou asked.

But she received no reply to that question either.

We continued into the town, away from the beach, away from the plant.

I turned around. I couldn't see the flames, only the smoke. There was a light breeze and a black wall rolled into the town on the wind.

My heart in my throat, breathing hard, August in my arms. He wasn't laughing any longer.

Anna pulled Lou behind her but they weren't moving quickly enough. She picked her up.

She balanced her on her hip. But that slowed her down even more. Lou was too heavy.

"Here," I said and held August out to her. "You take him."

We swapped children. That was when it happened. It was Anna and August. Lou and me.

Then we continued running.

We approached the downtown area. The bike rental. Ran past the smiling plastic figurines in the small amusement park on the corner. Past the pharmacy. All the ice-cream parlors. The hamburger restaurant that had once been the most popular place in Argelès. Engulfed in smoke so thick I could barely breathe.

Lou kept her face hidden against my shoulder. I could hear her crying. But I couldn't console her. I just ran.

And forgot to turn around.

"Mommy?" Lou said suddenly.

It was only then that I noticed that Anna was no longer behind me.

I called for her in the smoke. Screamed. Yelled.

Lou screamed even louder than me, her voice high-pitched against the deepness of my own.

"Mommy?"

"Anna?"

"Mommy!"

But Anna didn't come.

Then I turned around, ran back, towards the fire, towards the roaring.

They had to be here somewhere.

She had stumbled, I would find her.

"August? Anna? August?!"

No sign of her and no sound of him crying.

Soon there was only the sound of crackling flames. They spread with a swiftness that I wouldn't have believed possible.

Spread through the dry landscape, which had scarcely seen rain in five years.

Everything could burn. And everything did. My entire world burned.

SIGNE

Some break-ups happen slowly. You can't put your finger on the moment when it's over, it's a gradual, silent transition, while other break-ups ... I know the exact day I lost Magnus.

No. The day he lost me.

I remember the minute, the second, when I realized it was over.

The tide is about to turn. Right now, for a short while, the river is still and flat beneath me, beneath *Blue*, until once more the pull of the tide returns. It's like driving on freshly paved asphalt, the engine pounding in my ears, allowing me no peace, only the sound of a monotonous droning. If I turned it off I would be at one with nature, able to hear the birds, the light wind I see blowing in the trees onshore, the gurgling of water in motion. But the engine is the only thing I have now.

I have put out tires as fenders along the entire broadside and the mast is lashed securely to the deck. *Blue* is a sad creature, amputated, bandaged and bound on a brown river.

Water itself is colorless. It's the world around it that gives it color, reflections from the sky, from the surroundings; water is never just water.

Water absorbs and whirls around everything it meets.

Water is humus, sand, clay, plankton.

Water is given color by the bed it covers.

Water reflects the world.

And now the water is reflecting the blue sky above me and the tree branches reaching across the river, while its color also comes from a sludgy bed I can't see.

At Castets-en-Dorthe, the first lock rises in front of me, a vertical wall many meters tall, and the river is banked by a muddy shore.

As I sail closer, I can hear the rushing sound from inside, torrents of water in continuous man-made motion.

A lock-keeper comes out onto the edge, looks down at me.

"Are you going in alone?"

He looks at me skeptically, as if he wants to finish the sentence with "old woman"—*are you going in alone, old woman.*

I feel the urge to retaliate, tell him about the storm I just weathered, about the fog, about all the voyages on the open sea, the demonstrations, the nights spent in a holding cell. What's a lock compared to that?

"It's prohibited," he continues. "The current gets too strong when the sluices are filled. You won't have a chance of keeping the boat against the wall on your own, you won't stand a chance."

"You have anyone on standby?" I ask.

"Huh?"

"Someone who can come with me, you know someone?"

"No."

"Me neither."

"But it's prohibited," he says, a little more meekly.

"I'm going in," I say.

"Idiot," he mumbles.

I start to answer but suddenly begin to doubt whether he actually said anything; the water is making too much noise and he has already turned half away, given up. He lets me through.

All the water is drained out of the sluice chamber, everything is electric here, but I know that further up the canal the locks are manual; the lock-keepers must open the gates.

The water gushes out into the river with an enormous force. I heave the boat to while I wait, then the gates open and I can sail in.

A metallic creaking sound can be heard as the gate slides into place. The smell of damp stone walls greets me, confined, stagnant; it's called a chamber and I understand why—right now there's no way out.

There's just me and the water and I can manage this by myself. I throw two lines up to the lock-keeper; I can control both lines using the primary winch in the cockpit, but I've also set them up with natch blocks in the bow and stern, so I can pull in the slack on the lines as the boat rises.

But he doesn't give me a nod of appreciation from above and I have time to wonder whether it will work before the water starts streaming in.

Slowly the water rises and *Blue* along with it. I pull in the mooring lines, pulling and pulling. I must at all times make sure that the boat stays up against the wall of the sluice. But the force of the water gushing in and filling up the sluice pulls at *Blue*, pulls at me. I curse the long keel that makes *Blue* especially difficult to handle as the water takes hold, trying to force the boat all the way back into the chamber, to throw us towards the gate I just passed through. The line slips on the winch. I lunge forward and grab hold of it again.

The lock-keeper shakes his head up there, swears and throws up his arms dramatically in a typically French manner. I turn away, can't be bothered to pay any attention to him, concentrate on the lines, on pulling in the slack.

I don't make any more mistakes. The sweat pours off me, I concentrate wholly on the lines, on keeping the side of the boat against the sluice's one chamber wall and *Blue* is steady now, until the water stops streaming in, until we've risen several meters—it must be at least five meters, maybe ten.

The sluice gate in front of me opens, it creaks even more, as if it were in the process of rusting completely to pieces; now there's yet another chamber and I will have to go through the whole process one more time.

The engine has been idling and, when I can finally sail out

into the canal, I put it into gear. The water is greener here, maybe it's because of the trees growing close together along the shore, the leaves reflected in the surface, or maybe because of the sea grass growing down there. A single blade has come loose and is floating on the surface and I must be on the alert for this sea grass. It can get into the backwash inlet, clog it, like hair in a drain.

I can't see the bottom, but nonetheless it feels as if it were pressing towards me. The Arietta extends 1.35 meters below the waterline. The water level should be at least two meters in the canal now, but that also depends on how much the farmers in the area are draining from it. If the vegetables need water, the water level will be low, so I keep an eye on the water at all times, as I creep further and further inland.

An oncoming boat from time to time, otherwise there's nothing to do, nothing to concentrate on, just this calm movement forward through this placid landscape. I miss the ocean, I miss the waves, the concentration they demand. Here it's impossible to escape from myself.

Magnus, I know exactly when I lost you and you lost me and it took me by such surprise, a shock, even though I should have known beforehand. Yes, I should have seen it coming. Because you didn't participate actively in the protest like the rest of us; more and more frequently you left us up there on the mountain and drove down to your valley, to the farm, to your parents. Didn't you feel safe with us, were you frightened or were you just fed up—with the discussions, the songs, the warmth?

One evening when you came back you brought your father with you.

Daddy welcomed you, the way he welcomed everyone who came. In his large, dark-green parka, with a heavy sweater underneath, he looked larger than before; for the first time his name Bjørn, meaning bear, suited him.

He shook Sønstebø's hand, greeted him, said it had been a long time, but that he didn't blame him, although we all wondered about the absence of the people from Eidesdalen. We knew they had farms, they had animals but still ... it would have strengthened the protest had they been here with us. But Daddy didn't say anything about this and it was a conscious choice.

"So here you are," Daddy said.

"Yes," Sønstebø said.

"Come have a seat, have some coffee," Daddy said.

"Thank you kindly," Sønstebø said.

I went over to Magnus.

"You went to get him?"

"He wanted to come along."

"Good. Finally."

"He has something to say."

It was only then that I noticed that there was something agitated about Magnus; his movements were sharp, his eyes alert.

We sat down with them by the fire and many people joined us. Sønstebø was treated like a guest of honor.

"Yes …" Sønstebø said finally. "It turns out … that … it seems that we, those of us in Eidesdalen, we think you should end this."

"What?" Daddy said. "You don't mean it?"

Sønstebø threw out his arms. "It's an impressive set-up, all of this …" He waved around him to show that he meant the camp. "And we … we are very glad you're doing this for us … but we think maybe it's getting to be enough now. Yes, it's enough. People should maybe start going home again, little by little."

At first, Daddy didn't say anything; several people around them murmured but he was completely silent.

"It's not that we don't appreciate everything," Sønstebø continued, "and we think it's good that the issue has been in the newspapers and that people in Oslo have been informed about what's happening. But the way things have evolved, I think it best if we call it a day. Before there's trouble."

"Trouble? You don't have to worry about that," Daddy said.

"We will have to live with this for many years to come," Sønstebø said.

"That's precisely why it's so important."

"And we will receive revenue. Waterfall rights?" He turned to face Magnus.

"Waterfall rights revenues," Magnus said.

"But you'll lose everything else," Daddy said.

"It's just that ... it's enough now. We don't want any trouble," Sønstebø said.

"Are you frightened?" Daddy said.

"No. No. We're not frightened."

"The man who blew up the bridge is afraid," Daddy hissed suddenly.

Sønstebø started, looked around him and laughed suddenly. "I was a shot firer, once upon a time, yes. You have a good memory. But I never blew up any bridge."

He's lying, I thought, you have to say something, Daddy, he's lying. But Daddy sat in silence, leaned back a little, his eyes narrowed.

"I think you've misunderstood," he said finally. "We're not doing this for you."

"No?"

"We're doing it for all of us."

"Yes. Of course. Yes—"

"For our children. For our grandchildren. The waterfalls are supposed to be eternal. Their destruction will be too."

Sønstebø squirmed. "So you won't leave?"

"No. We're not leaving."

Then Magnus took a step forward. He spoke loudly and a little too quickly. "The people of Ringfjorden are mobilizing, Bjørn."

Daddy turned towards him. "And?"

"The construction workers are losing thousands of kroner every day the machinery isn't running. That's stirred up anger. These are ordinary people, you see, they've invested, they are counting on this development. Waited for it. And with every passing day, they are becoming angrier."

"So much the better," Daddy said.

"You cannot mean that."

"More attention."

"I don't think you realize what you've started."

"What *I've* started?"

"Yes. You."

"I'm not the one who wants to develop the river, I'm not the one who sold the land, I'm not the one who arranged the sale of the waterfall rights. I'm not the one who's married to the head of operations for Ringfallene."

Mommy—again it was about her, again it was about the two of them. There was no end to it. A break-up lasts forever.

"We're going to have to live with this for many years to come," Sønstebø said again. "Enough bridges have been blown up."

He looked at me as he said it.

After that the camp changed, the singing died out, the laughter as well.

We just waited.

Two days later they came, when we'd been up there for twenty-one days.

It was in the evening and the first thing we saw was a gleam of light above the mountain, then we heard the sound of tires against the wet road.

A convoy—we couldn't see the end of it, that's how many there were. They parked in a line along the roadside, the doors opened and men poured out, every single car was full, four or five in each one, some people also came on motorcycles and one even came on a tractor.

They gathered into a group and walked towards the camp. We had gotten to our feet, people came out of their tents, stopped their cooking, hushed the children, left the guitars in their cases, shoved pipes into the pockets of parkas.

They looked like us, we looked like them; I recognized farmers, fishermen, colleagues of Svein at the plant, familiar faces, people I associated with the place where I grew up, associated with security, predictability, men whom I'd perhaps laughed at a little—for their taciturn sturdiness, their lack of knowledge, of education—but also respected, for the job they did, the investment, the ability to take pleasure in the life they had been allotted. First and foremost, however, these were men I had never thought about much, just taken for granted—they were there, they hauled the fish out of the ocean, harvested grain, picked apples, day in and day out, in the sun, in the wind, in the rain.

They had brought signs and banners, all of them hand-painted, like ours, but the message was different.

LEAVE OUR VILLAGE IN PEACE!

GO BACK WHERE YOU CAME FROM!

HIPPIES, GO HOME!

We moved towards the end of the road and they followed

suit, approached us from all directions like magnets towards a pole.

A man stepped forward—it was Svein. He had a megaphone in his hand and a thick wool cap pulled down over his ears, he who usually wore a hat. He lifted the megaphone to his mouth and looked around, his gaze swept over me, I was sure he saw me, but it didn't have any effect on him.

"We, the citizens of Ringfjorden municipality," he said, "hereby present you with the following ultimatum."

He took out a piece of paper and started to read out loud: "We demand that the camp be taken down by midnight tonight, so the work on the access road in connection with the development approved by parliamentary resolution can continue without further delay."

Magnus had come up beside me. He took hold of my hand.

Svein continued: "If you *don't* voluntarily clear the road by the above-stated deadline, anything could happen. I repeat: anything could happen."

Then he lowered the megaphone and put away the piece of paper and cheers broke out on his side of the road. The men shouted, raising their firsts in the air.

Magnus squeezed my hand, whispering quietly, "It's enough now, Signe, you see that, it's enough now."

"We can take more than this," I said.

But then he dropped my hand and walked towards our tent.

I was left standing alone. I saw Daddy leaning his head towards Lars and a couple of the others; they were speaking quietly together. I approached them. Daddy's voice was an intense whisper.

"I'm staying here till they have to carry me away."

"No," Lars said. "You see them. What they are willing to do. This is over now."

Meanwhile a disturbance had arisen among the people from Ringfjorden; several of them were screaming and shouting and now they started to approach us, slowly, a huge, crawling animal, and I jumped at the sight of knives gleaming.

They drew their knives on us.

Svein walked forward, positioned himself between us and them, tried to restrain them, but they kept shouting and clenching their knives in their fists.

"Damn Oslo hippies, go home!"

Svein spoke more loudly, asked them to calm down, turned towards Daddy and Lars.

"Give us an answer, then we'll leave right away and let you pack up in peace."

Lars and Daddy had a hushed, intense discussion. Daddy sullen, furious. "No. They're not going to fucking win this."

But Lars spread his arms out before him.

"There are children here. Anger like this ... Nothing good can come from it."

The others nodded. Daddy was the only one who opposed them and I walked over to him and stood beside him.

"If we leave, we lose."

Daddy started.

"Signe, no. You have to leave."

"But you're staying, aren't you?"

Daddy's voice became more high-pitched: "You and Magnus are going to drive down right now, you understand?"

Then Lars grinned. "So you want to protect your own daughter, while the others' daughters don't matter so much?"

I didn't hear Daddy's reply, but as I walked towards the tent, towards Magnus, I could feel the heat rushing to my cheeks. Daddy didn't take me seriously—I was still a child for him, a little girl, it infuriated me and at the same time I was embarrassed for his sake, because I saw Daddy the way Lars had seen him, someone who had said and done everything right, by the book, but who, when it came right down to it, with a knife against his throat, was just as irrational and selfish as everyone else. Daddy wanted to be like Lars, but would never be able to fill his shoes.

I approached the tent. It was starting to get dark and I stumbled on the uneven ground, but managed to recover my balance at the last moment. At the same time I heard steps behind me and somebody calling my name.

She jogged towards me. At first I didn't recognize her. In her ski pants and parka she almost looked like a young boy and she moved with the same lightness as before, as if she weren't a day older.

It was Mom.

Mom and Svein, Svein and Mom, of course she'd come up with him. Else was surely looking after the little boys, my half-brothers whom I barely knew, and Mom had come here to support Svein, support the village and emphasize which side she was on, the hotel's side, but first and foremost, her new little family's side. Unnecessary, I thought, so horribly unnecessary, you didn't need to do it, we know it already, we know where you stand, what you want, how you make your money and how you've planned to ensure your children's futures. Why did you want to come here, to demonstrate it yet again, in yet another manner, why did you want yet again to dissociate yourself from me and everything that's mine, from what you and Daddy once had?

I stopped. I wanted to scream but couldn't, because tears would also come with the scream, I could feel it now, the fierceness with which they were rising, so I just stood there like that, completely silent, and waited for what she was going to say, how she would yet again declare her loyalties, like rubbing salt in a wound.

But she said none of this.

"My dear child ..." She took a step towards me. "My dear, you're dirty."

I swallowed; it was impossible to hold back the tears, because I *was* dirty and Mom saw it and, even though she said nothing more than this, I suddenly knew what she really wanted to say: come home with me and take a bath, come home with me. I'll draw a bath for you, all the way to the rim of the tub, fill the tub with scalding-hot water and bubble bath, bubbles that smell clean, you can help yourself, take as much as you want, and let me wash your hair, with Timotei shampoo, massage it into your scalp for a long time and scrub your back, with the hard brush that removes dead skin cells and makes you soft as a baby, and let me lift you up and wrap you in the largest, cleanest towel I have and rub you down until you're dry and warm and your skin is burning, and let me lend you my bathrobe, the big, thick one, and stay with you all the time, because this time I'm not going to leave you to go scream at your father, I'm not going to forget about you until the bathwater turns cold. This time I will stay with you until you fall asleep.

I could have gone with her, now, immediately, gotten into her clean, warm car with an engine that ran more quietly than any other car's and driven to the hotel, to the wing, driven home.

I drew a breath.

No.

No.

She wanted to bribe me, a double betrayal, she came here to flag her side, show everyone where her loyalties were, maybe even lead them, and simultaneously, she wanted to bribe me. Were there no limits?

I turned away from her, walked away as quickly as I could, towards Magnus and the tent, hoping my back was enough of a rejection, but she followed me.

"Wait, Signe, stop!"

Now Magnus noticed her, he stopped working; the tent was already halfway down.

"What are you doing?" I asked. "The tent stays up."

But he just looked at Mom behind me. "Iris?"

Mom came all the way over to us, raised her arms towards me, as if she wanted to hug me, but I crossed my own.

"Sweetie," she said. "I wish you could understand my thinking. That it's you and the boys I'm thinking about."

"You're thinking about me?" I so wanted my voice to be calm but could hear how it trembled. "How can you be thinking about me when you're doing something like this?"

Then she turned towards Magnus. "I told you it would be like this."

"What!" I said. "Have you talked about this? Have you talked about me?"

"We care about you, Signe," Mom said.

We?

"What is this?" I asked and noticed how my voice came back. "A sewing club where you discuss Signe's well-being?"

I looked back and forth from one to the other, unable to comprehend the bond between them. "I thought this was about the falls," I said. "About Eidesdalen?"

Magnus and Mom held each other's gazes. They stood there so calmly, so balanced, and almost simultaneously they turned towards me and stared at me with the same amazement I had previously seen on Magnus's face. All at once I felt stupid—with all my strong words, my loud voice—and like an outsider. The two of them were the same, I was completely different and this difference they tried to understand, with the best intentions, even though they would never get it. Because the pragmatic human being doesn't understand passion.

"I don't think you should be up here, especially not now," Mommy said.

I turned to face Magnus and now I no longer managed to hold back the tears. He had told her.

"I'm staying," I say to Magnus. "Do you understand—put down the damn tent peg, I'm staying up here."

Magnus threw down what he was holding in his hands, reached out for me with them; whether he was despondent or wanted to make peace, I didn't know, but I didn't care either. I just wanted to escape the sight of him, his calm demeanor, escape hearing any more of that calm voice. But it wasn't over, I still couldn't get away, because he had even more to say.

"Svein has arranged a job for me, Signe. I wanted to tell you before, but then all of this happened. Your mother and Svein want to hire me at Ringfallene, they need engineers and we can move back. The salary is much better than what I could hope for anywhere else. You won't need to work, we'll be able to take care of the child, you can write, sail, do the things you love, we can live here and it will be a good life, Signe. A good life."

This was what he had always wanted, this was what he had imagined, a house by the water, a bench on the mountainside, where we would sit when we were old and look at the view. A garden with a wharf where *Blue* could be docked. I could go out fishing, he could take care of the garden, even spend time in the kitchen on the odd Sunday to prepare food for a party the guests would praise him for, but first and foremost he had imagined the trip he would make every day to and from this house, to and fro. The suit he would wear—the suit, the symbol of stability, respectability—maybe even a briefcase, the office where he would sit, the secretary he would have eventually, the carbon paper, the file cabinet, the promotion, the reassuring scent of ink, freshly brewed coffee, and the paycheck he would receive every single month—a piece of paper, tangible proof of his proficiency, which he would put into the bank where the money would grow, so that eventually he could buy a larger house by the fjord, a nicer car, matching floor lamps for the living room, winter clothes for the children, a girl and a boy.

A wholly ordinary, relatively good life was what he wanted. A life where there weren't too many sharp edges, not too much noise, too much of everything that was me.

How would life have been if I had given in on that day? If I had embraced his dream? Would it still be Magnus and me? Would we have acquired the house by the fjord? The children? The bench? Would it have been a good life, for me, too?

But I embraced neither him nor his dream.

I ran.

I ran, away from Mommy and Magnus, Daddy, Lars and Svein, I passed the protestors, who shouted even more insults at me, a girl they'd seen grow up in the village, someone who had been one of them.

But none of them attacked me; they let me run.

I ran down the access road, past all the parked cars—there had to be more than a hundred, with five men in each, five hundred men had come up the mountain to take us down.

They'd gotten rid of me.

I ran, I walked, I ran some more.

It wasn't until I reached the wharf that I stopped, inhaled the damp air from the fjord, the smell of salt water. But it didn't help.

DAVID

I cried until there was nothing left of me.

Afterwards I sat calmly on the berth, with my legs curled up underneath me, the way Lou usually sat.

There was a new kind of silence in me. Now that I remembered. Now that I couldn't forget. A silence like inside a shell, I thought. A shell, an empty mussel shell.

The tears had left dried salt behind on the stubble on my cheeks. The salt made my skin stiff and dry.

I passed my tongue over my lips. They tasted of salt too.

I was salty from tears, salty from sweat.

Salt.

It dried me out until I started to crack. Until it woke me up.

Salt was perhaps the only thing I knew anything about.

I placed my feet on the deck and went into the saloon.

The only thing I knew anything about.

I opened the map table and found a bundle of maps. I turned them over. The backs of the maps were blank.

On the table I also found a chewed-down pencil with an eraser on the tip.

And then I started to draw.

A pump. I needed a pump. Maybe I could use the water pump on board, in some way or another hook the machine up to it.

A container. I would have to search the surrounding farms. Somewhere or other there had to be something I could use.

And a cylinder. A pipe. The cigar, Thomas called it.

I tried to remember everything he had taught me about reverse osmosis.

And then I sketched it as quickly as I could.

The water was supposed to go into the cigar, where it would be channeled through a spiral-wound module. The water with the finest molecules would be pressed into the core. This water would be completely desalinated. The rest of the water, what he called the concentrate, would stay on the outside. And be sent out into the ocean again.

It was an eighty-to-twenty ratio. Twenty liters of clean water for every eighty liters of concentrate.

He had shown me the cylinder. Inside was a pipe with holes. It should be possible to build one. Between the layers in the pipe lay the feed spacer. It resembled chicken wire. That shouldn't be so hard to find.

But the membrane ... my pencil stopped drawing on the paper.

I needed something that was almost impervious. A fabric. With a weave so dense that it seemed watertight. But nonetheless, the finest water molecules should be able to pass through it.

I stood up. Hurriedly, I climbed down off the boat.

I rushed through the forest and up to the house.

I went into the bedrooms, opening cupboards and drawers, but I didn't find anything I could use.

Sweaters, socks, T-shirts. Everything smelled old, like it had been in storage for a long time.

I walked down the hallway. Along the wall hung a row of outdoor garments.

I lifted the jackets. In the back I found a yellow raincoat.

An oilskin, the old kind.

Rain gear. There had been a time when we needed rain gear.

I tugged at the material. It was solid. Completely waterproof. Maybe it could...

"Hi."

I turned around.

It was Lou. I hadn't heard her coming. She was holding my drawing in her hands.

"What is it?" she asked.

Not a word about my restraining her by force. About everything she'd screamed at me.

She looked up. Looked at me. And waited.

I waited too. Were we testing each other's resolve?

No. We were starting over, my child and I.

I drew a breath.

"We're going to build a tank," I said. "A water tank."

She nodded slowly.

"For what water?"

"Salt water. From the ocean. We'll fill it up completely." I pointed at the tank I had drawn. "The water will be pushed through the pipe. Through this material."

I held up the raincoat.

"And then it will be fresh water?" she asked.

"Then it will be fresh water," I said.

My clever little girl. She knew about this.

"And we can drink it?"

"Yes."

"When we're on the ocean."

"When we're on the ocean."

She nodded.

"Then we won't need water. We just need the ocean."

She smiled faintly. The pressure in my chest relented.

"And then we can stay out there for weeks," I said. "For months. As long as we want. We can eat fish and make our own water. We can live on the ocean for the rest of our lives."

"I want to," Lou said. "I want to go all the way to the end of the ocean."

"Me too," I said.

For a moment she was silent. Her smile disappeared.

"But first we have to get there," she murmured. "To where the ocean starts."

I took a step towards her.

I wanted to hug her but felt that it was too soon. Instead, I smiled as broadly as I could.

"If only the rain would come," I said. "If only the rain would fill up the canal."

"Yes," she said. "If only the rain would come."

"Sooner or later, it has to start raining again."

"Do you think so?"

"I know so. Sooner or later the rain will come."

In the days that followed, Lou didn't ask any questions, not a single one.

She just worked by my side. She went with me to the neighboring farms where we searched for food and materials. Carried as much as she could manage, more than I thought she could.

She ate what little I fed her, without grumbling.

No complaints when it tasted bad. When there wasn't enough.

On the whole, she said very little.

But she was there, with me, beside me.

She didn't even ask questions in the evenings.

We sat on deck and watched the light over the trees, the lights from the camp. Sometimes we heard sounds from there. They reached us from across the silent landscape.

Shots.

Screams.

I shouldn't have allowed her to see the lights, hear the noises. But initially during the evenings I sat watching as if transfixed.

Then I started putting her to bed earlier. Lying down beside her. Slipping out when I thought she'd fallen asleep.

But she got up again. Every single night. And sat down beside me, just as captivated by the sight of the light above the trees as I was. Just as alert to the sounds of the people we had known.

She only asked me once.

"Caleb, Christian, Martin, where are they now?"

I was unable to respond immediately. I didn't know what I should say. Then I came up with something.

"They've taken the tractor," I said. "We said they could have it, remember?"

"Yes."

"They've taken it and driven away."

"That was smart."

"Yes. That was very smart."

With each passing night, there were fewer lights. The screams and shots diminished.

And then one evening there was only darkness above the trees. Silence from the camp. As if it had never existed.

She didn't ask any questions then either.

She never asked about Francis. And never asked about Marguerite.

SIGNE

The last time I saw you, Magnus ... the last time we spoke ... that was right after London.

I left without saying anything to anyone. I just left, went straight from Eidesdalen to Bergen, took out all the money I had in my bank account and bought a ticket for the ferry to England that was leaving that very evening. I remember the smell on board, stale cigarette smoke, beer and the odor of deep-fried food, the smell of decaying leather seat cushions and sticky linoleum, of diesel from the engine room.

There were towering waves on the crossing, heavy gales, a sea that turned white, choppy breakers crashing against one another, the surface as chaotic and wild as only the North Sea can be.

As if I wasn't feeling nauseous enough already.

London welcomed me with its narrow streets and smoke-filled pubs, but I didn't embrace this city, didn't want to make it mine. I had no address, no medical referral. The only thing I'd heard was that you had to find a doctor and then the rest would take care of itself.

Perhaps I hadn't needed to leave—most women submitted

an application to the Medical Committee, and some applications were approved, but was I supposed to stand there and beg? Cry? I was furious, I remember, about how they made it so difficult, this choice that after all was mine alone.

I checked into a hotel right beside a large railway station, received the key from the receptionist, and when I stood there, with the key in my hand and the knapsack in which I had packed a few things leaning against my leg, in my colorful traditional *lusekofte* sweater and my blonde hair in a single, practical braid, I must have looked both Norwegian and naïve, and those two things were often connected, braids or no braids.

"Was there something else?" the receptionist asked, warmly and jovially, when I showed no sign of moving. "Anything more I can do for you, love?"

He leaned over the counter, gave me a fatherly look, or perhaps he was trying to hit on me—he was at the age when both were possible—maybe he wasn't sure about it himself. But then I had to ask him, otherwise I wouldn't know how to proceed.

"I'm looking for a doctor," I said. "A doctor. A ... women's doctor?"

He drew away from me suddenly, distancing himself, and the smile disappeared. "Right..." he said. "I see."

At first he didn't say any more, but then he didn't need to, because I could see that I wasn't the first, that he had checked in many girls from abroad like me, that we constituted a not insignificant segment of the city's tourist industry at that time. We came alone, we weren't going to visit Big Ben or Covent Garden, all we needed was a packet of painkillers, a hot water bottle and a quiet room with good sound-proofing so we could cry in peace.

"So you need a gynecologist," he said finally.

His tone of voice was neutral, but he didn't meet my gaze. He stood there for a moment as if he couldn't make up his mind: was that a no?

But then he scribbled something down on a notepad, tore off the page and handed it to me; I accepted it, careless male handwriting, the letters slanting to the left. A name and an address.

I looked up, mumbled *thank you.*

"You should be married," he said. "You shouldn't be forced to do this."

I couldn't reply, because I couldn't admit that I wasn't *forced* to do this, not the way he meant, that there was still somebody who would probably marry me, if I were willing to become the person he desired, but that I didn't want him and absolutely didn't want his child, that the world didn't need this child, not another child and at least not our child, and if the receptionist had asked me why, I would have said that there was nothing more to explain, it was so obvious, it was the ones who *wanted* children who should explain themselves, not the rest of us, and I had maybe believed otherwise for a while, Magnus had tried to get me to believe otherwise, but after Eidesdalen I knew better than ever before that I was the one who was right.

I just thanked him again and lifted up my knapsack, struggled a bit getting it on my back, but the receptionist didn't lend me a hand.

"Hope you enjoy London," he said and turned away.

I pushed the elevator button and stood there waiting, but it didn't come.

The receptionist had sat down. He must have seen that I was standing there waiting, but he made no attempt to explain, to say that the elevator was slow or maybe out of order, he just sat behind the desk, completely indifferent.

Finally, I ended up taking the stairs.

I was sweating when I reached the fifth floor.

At the gynecologist's I had to wait for an appointment, but when I finally got in, everything went quickly; he called a clinic and scheduled the procedure for the next morning—just one night, I thought, just one night, then it will be over.

That night I walked the streets. I passed the Royal Opera House, the National Gallery, walked across Trafalgar Square, but nothing made any impression on me; I continued walking past imposing buildings, all of them reminders of the Brits' former glory, their ability to conquer the world. It's just stone, I thought, the entire city is stone and red brick; it made me sick, this burned clay, this man-made material, precisely cut and stacked into houses wherever I turned.

I found my way to the River Thames where the air was rawer, damper. I inhaled it with an open mouth, as if I were drinking it, and stood for a long time on a bridge watching the river flow by under my feet.

Then a boat appeared. I turned and watched it as it disappeared under the bridge and popped out again on the other side—it was going east, maybe headed for the ocean.

The river connected the city to the ocean, the ocean connected the country to the world. All big cities have a river, Daddy had once told me, it's rivers that create big cities, rivers are the world's most important highways. Daddy, I thought suddenly, Daddy, what would he say if he knew, what would he say if he were here now? Maybe I should have told him before leaving, maybe he was the only one I should have said something to. I could have brought him with me, or let him bring me, we should have been standing together on this bridge, we could have talked about rivers, about the man-made nature that develops around all the waterways of the world, as it has been doing for thousands of years. He could have talked about the Euphrates, about the Tigris, created by the Sumerian Enki, the god of the seas, of the ocean, of creativity and creative power, who filled the landscape with running water ... all Daddy's anecdotes, all his words, no, I didn't want them, wouldn't be able to disappear into them. And Mommy, what would Mommy have done if she were here now? Taken me away, given me a bath? Would she have tried to talk me out of my decision?

Garbage floated past, more slowly than the boat, at the river's own pace. I tried to make out the contents: a coil of rope, wound up into a large tangle, and inside it a semi-decomposed cigarette package, a whisky bottle with the cap still on. It imprinted itself into me, like a stamp in my consciousness, this image of the coil of rope, the tangle, the decomposing cigarette package, the whisky bottle, traveling past in that which had once been clean water. And me on the bridge alone. The only way it could be.

I stood there until my teeth were chattering, till the cold rawness of the Thames had settled into every fiber of my body. Only then did I go back and let myself be surrounded by brick, walking as fast as I could to get warm, until it was as if the heat of fired clay filled my body.

Also the next morning, within the white walls of the clinic, I could sense the red brick, as if I could taste it, chew the dust of it between my teeth, as if it were the brick that was making me feel nauseated. It was the last sensation I had before I fell asleep and the first when I woke up afterwards, and it was still there when I came home. I could feel the dust between my teeth while I told Magnus what I had done, I could still feel the nausea when he was yelling at me, when he was crying, sobbing, telling me how much he had wanted that child, our child, telling me he could never forgive me, telling me it was his child too. And also afterwards it was there when I lay curled up in bed in my room, as burning sobs pushed their way out, tearing at my body, and I tried to cry more quietly, softly, muffle my sobs, so I would hear if he knocked on the door, if he came back. Because I remember that I wanted him to come back, even though I didn't regret it, even though I was furious. I just couldn't believe that it would end this way.

But he never came. Or maybe I didn't cry quietly enough.

DAVID

It was morning. I was sitting in the cockpit, in the shade of the awning we'd hung over the boom.

I was so tired. So tired all the time. I didn't sleep well, listening all the time for the sound of raindrops. The sound of rain.

I could feel beads of sweat forming on my forehead, even though it was still early. I would have to get to work soon. But I was unable to move.

Lou made up our beds in the saloon and sang in a high voice, *Frère Jacques, Frère Jacques, dormez-vous, dormez-vous?*

Anna used to sing this song at her bedside.

I was hungry, even though we had just eaten.

I had raided all the farms in the vicinity. Found some food, a little flour, some canned goods, a bag of rice. Enough to last for nine weeks, by my calculations. If we didn't eat much.

But half a cup of boiled rice wasn't enough.

And I was thirsty. I took a sip from my bottle, even though I knew that I shouldn't. The water was from the tank in the garden. I had taken all the water that was in it. Boiled it. Filtered it. Tested it on myself before giving it to Lou. It tasted of soil and of something bitter that I couldn't identify. The aftertaste lingered in the mouth. But I didn't get sick.

Don't think about it. Don't think. Just work. One day at a time, new tasks every day. Slowly on our way to finishing the boat. To finishing the desalination machine.

And when it finally began to rain, then we would be ready.

I was certain that it would start raining.

When the rain came, we would use the final remnants of diesel I had discovered in the tank to make our way west through the canal.

To the coast.

When the rain came.

And then, finally, out onto the Atlantic Ocean.

The security of the ocean, where you could see everyone who approached, everything approaching, for miles around.

It would be only Lou and me there, on the boat.

We would sail for weeks, maybe it would take months, to the west. Maybe we would just remain at sea forever. Or maybe we would sail all the way to South America.

Lou talked about it. That under the ground in South America there was water. That if we grew tired of the ocean, we could go there.

We just had to wait.

Wait and work. While we rationed the water and our strength sensibly.

Around us everything was drying up. Even the mud in the canal had turned to dust.

Lou had stopped singing. The world was silent. Almost no insects buzzing; I couldn't even hear the crickets. Had they also disappeared?

I took another sip. Had to stop now. No more water for one hour. We had enough to manage for twenty days. Only twenty days. And after that, what would we do? Would I watch Lou become dehydrated, get cramps, overpowering headaches? Or would I put her out of her misery? Hold a pillow over her face while she was asleep?

Suddenly there was something drumming lightly on the awning. I stood up.

Drops. Wasn't it the sound of raindrops?

I remained standing. Listening.

It must have been drops.

I peeked out from beneath the awning. Up at the sky.

Blue. An intense blue. The color made me dizzy.

But there had to be a cloud, somewhere or other.

I went out on deck. From there I could see the entire sky. My eyes stung. The sun burned. It was as if it had grown. As if it grew every day, threatening to swallow the world.

I turned around. And discovered that somebody was standing on the bank of the canal.

Marguerite.

Maybe she'd been there for a long time. Looking at the boat, looking at me. Waiting.

There was a suitcase on wheels on the dry grass behind her. It had probably been expensive once upon a time. But now it was dusty and dirty.

A suitcase? Had she managed to hang on to it, in the midst of everything? Had she dragged it with her the whole way? The whole way here, but also all the way from her previous life?

"Can I come up?" she asked me.

Her voice was almost casual.

I didn't reply.

Lou crawled out of the saloon and smiled.

"Hi, Marguerite."

"Hi, Lou," Marguerite said. "Is it OK if I come up?"

"Yes!"

"No," I said. "I'll come down."

"Me too," Lou said.

"You stay here," I said.

"No."

"Yes."

Fortunately, she did as she was told.

As I climbed down, I noticed that I was shaking. Because Marguerite was alive, thank God, she was alive.

"Come," I said.

I walked towards the forest without looking back. But I could hear her following me.

When we'd reached a spot where Lou couldn't see us, we stood facing each other. Only one meter between us. I wished the distance had been greater.

Her face, her eyes; she stood there and still *was*.

Even thinner, emaciated now. And so dirty, traces of filth on her cheeks.

"I don't know what to do," she said softly.

I was unable to reply.

"I don't know what to do, David."

"..."

"I have nowhere to go."

"..."

"Almost no food."

"..."

"David ... David ... The camp no longer exists."

And then she collapsed, right in front of me.

Her knees suddenly buckled, her entire body, that erect silhouette dropped to its knees abruptly in front of me. And begged.

"Water. Please."

Her eyes were shiny. She was on the verge of tears. That thought, those words, on the verge of tears, of crying. No. On the verge of weeping. Women like her don't cry, they weep.

It was like looking at a picture. A photograph. As if she were a photograph.

Don't cry, Marguerite, I thought. Don't waste any more fluids than you have to. We have nothing, we can't share. I have Lou, I have only her and I can't give water to anyone else.

"You must leave," I just said. "You must leave."

But she didn't get to her feet.

"You must leave."

I turned away.

"David, wait," she said.

I stopped in spite of myself. Couldn't help looking at her.

"What are you going to do?" she asked. "How—"

"Lou and I are getting out of here."

"But how?"

Her eyes brimmed over now. I had to look away.

"With the boat," I said. "We're going to the ocean. When the rain comes. When the canal fills up."

Then she laughed. She sat down, right there on the ground, so much smaller than me. It seemed as if she might disappear at any moment. But her laughter was strong and loud.

The tears vanished. Only her laughter was there. A laughter without warmth. Maybe that was how she laughed before, on vacation in Provence, wearing her silk dresses, at people like me.

And I knew why she was laughing.

A helpless young whippersnapper with a child in tow, a boat on land. I was lacking everything, even a plan.

Just as suddenly as she'd begun laughing she stopped.

She stood up. It was an effort, because she was so frail, but she tried to conceal it.

Then, without saying another word, she turned her back on me and walked back to the suitcase on the bank of the canal. But she didn't pick it up. Just climbed down into the canal. Passed the boat and kept walking.

"Marguerite?" Lou called.

She didn't answer.

"Where are you going?"

Then Marguerite turned to face me.

"To the ocean. I'm walking to the ocean."

And then she kept going. Her back was so small and narrow between the concrete walls. But she held her head high.

She staggered slightly.

The dried sludge whirled up around her feet as she walked.

Soon she would be gone and the dust would settle.

But her suitcase remained where it was on the bank. Her suitcase, the only thing she had.

I grabbed it and ran after her.

She turned around, her face quizzical, a tiny glimmer of hope in her eyes.

"Here," I said.

But the hope was extinguished immediately. "What shall I do with it?"

All the same, she took hold of the handle of the suitcase and started pulling it behind her.

The small wheels dug down into the dry ground, but she kept dragging it anyway. Pulled and pulled, filling the air behind her with dust.

It will nonetheless be the last I will see, I thought, the last I will see of her, her back in the canal, the dust, the suitcase. The last sound will be that of suitcase wheels against desiccated mud. This is what she looks like when she walks. And just this sound, nothing else. No words, screams, tears.

But I had forgotten about Lou. She was there, because she had come down from the boat without my noticing it and had seen the same thing that I'd seen.

Now she filled the air with *her* sounds, her words, her screams, her tears. Yet again she howled in my arms, yet again she protested against my decisions. And this time there was no stopping her.

"You can't leave, Marguerite! She can't leave, Daddy! She has to stay here with us!"

Everything inside me came to a halt and everything began. At long last, I listened to my child.

And then I ran. Towards the dust whirling upwards. Towards the suitcase. Towards Marguerite.

SIGNE

I go to the bow to loosen the mooring but end up sitting on deck for a little while, listening. There's a silence inland here, the likes of which I have seldom heard. The canal is silent beneath me—there's no wind, old trees lean over the water, their leaves motionless—and neither are there any birds or insects to be heard.

The feeling of being cramped, confined, it's not just the sluices that give me that feeling, it's all the wildlife around me, the monitored canal, the trees planted in straight lines, the flat farming landscape surrounding the narrow strip of water. Even when the canal passed through woods, I felt the same thing, as if the woods down here are also under control, a cowardly nature without claws, boring through and through, planned by humans. Imagine living here, imagine being able to live by the mountains, near the gorges, the ruggedness, the plunging drama, and then choosing this instead?

I stand up, take hold of the mooring line, loosen it quickly. I am on the outskirts of Timbaut now, today I will find his house, find him.

Today I will throw the ice out in front of him.

"Here's the rest of the ice," I'll say. "What little is left. I thought you'd like to have it in your drink."

And he will stare at the ice with big eyes.

"The rest of it, as you have no doubt heard, has been dumped into the ocean," I will add. "And melted. Just as well, don't you think, that it melts, sooner rather than later? That's how you want it." I will speak these words like a declaration, not a question.

Maybe the plump Trine will come out, she will stand there, gaping a little, her appearance every bit as indifferent as she is.

Both of them are clutching wine glasses and I toss a few lumps of ice into them, *vintage ice*, maybe I'll say, while the rest lies melting on the ground, and if there are any grandchildren there, they'll come out as well ... no, to hell with the grandchildren, they don't care anyway, they just want to play computer games, but Magnus will stand there with his mouth wide open, so I can see his uvula, deep in the back of his red-wine-stained gullet, and he will scratch his padded stomach in confusion under the expensive but loose-fitting linen shirt and then I will turn around and leave, but before I do that, I will make the very last statement:

"I'll be keeping an eye on you, Magnus. If you take more ice, I will dump that as well. As long as you keep this up, you can be sure that I will also continue doing my part."

Doing my part ...

No ...

I can't say that, can't say it like that.

I'll be keeping an eye on you…

Good Lord.

They will look up, the two of them, from the ice, from the red wine, look at each other, their eyes will meet above their glasses, telling gazes, *what has she done now?* Then Magnus will turn towards me with a mild, puzzled smile—Signe, what are you doing, he will say, he will think.

And then they will clean up after me, put the plastic containers in the two-car garage, pour another glass of expensive red wine and talk about how happy they are that they have one another, about the life they have lived, the harmony they feel, all the lovely, small experiences they are accumulating, how nice to be able to approach old age with such peace of mind, such a house, such a garden, such a spouse, such joy, so good to be able to approach old age knowing that one has made the right choices.

And I … I will go back to *Blue*, sit down in the saloon, it is empty now, the containers are gone, I will miss them, because it was all I had, my rage in these containers.

I'm doing my part.

Or I can turn around, go back, navigate through all the sluices I have forced my way through, put up the mast, get rid of the tires, refuel, head out to sea, to the west, disappear in the Atlantic Ocean and dump the containers out there somewhere, not just the ice but the containers too, there's so much plastic in the ocean, such an endless amount of plastic, eight million tons are dumped in the ocean every single year, nobody will notice the difference, these containers can float around out there, along with all the rest of the plastic, in a way they belong there, and the ice, the water, will disappear in the ocean, become salt, undrinkable, useless, become a part of the salty desert our oceans are, a desert that is constantly growing.

"No," I say loudly and suddenly, the sound of my voice strident as it breaks the silence. Because you've traveled all the way here, come all this way, you have covered so much ground, you are here, you, this boat ... this is a choice you have already made and, strictly speaking, Signe, strictly speaking, you have very little to lose.

The boat glides through the water, closer and closer to his house. I have plotted in the address on the GPS. The landscape is as flat as a pancake: there is only a single wooded hill a short distance away on which to focus. Maybe they call that a mountain, the people who live here, but it's actually only a misplaced bulge.

Five hundred meters, one hundred meters and then I'm there. The house must be located behind a dense grove right beside the bank of the canal.

But there's no place to dock, not a single mooring point along the canal and, besides, I will obstruct boat traffic if I dock here.

I have to start up again and keep going.

It is hot and quiet, the sweat is pouring off me, my hair is greasy, I probably look a fright, no doubt I smell of boat—a mixture of old seawater, wet clothes, plastic, septic sludge and diesel—but it doesn't matter, now I just have to do what I've come here to do.

Finally a guest harbor, in the center of Timbaut. I moor the boat quickly, but when I jump to shore, my heart is pounding as I realize that I can't take the ice with me. I will have to leave it here while I find my way to his house empty-handed, alone.

I rent a bike, a modern, men's bicycle with off-road tires. My feet barely reach the pedals and the screw connecting the seat to the pole is loose, so it keeps tipping backwards. I have to straighten it out by force, using my own balance, and this produces an odd, awkward bike-riding technique.

The city is exactly as I expected: sweet, charming, well-tended gardens, small tilting houses in mismatching colors, a *boulangerie*, a butcher, a bountiful florist's. I cross the historic city center, where there's a cobblestone square surrounded by trelliswork, and the overwhelming scent of hollyhock, lavender and freshly painted wrought-iron gates makes it difficult to breathe.

I slip forward on the bike seat, struggle to adjust my position, wobble a bit, lurch through a dip in the road, the front tire hits a cobblestone a bit more crooked than the others and I almost fall, but pull the bicycle upright just in time and keep going, away from the square, put the city center behind me, come out on the other side, pass an awning factory, turn a corner, keep riding down a hill, searching for a road sign, but can't find any.

Then, on the next corner, a sign finally appears, but it's wrong. I can see that as I get closer—I'm on the wrong street, I've missed my turn-off.

I have to turn around and ride back, sweating heavily. Finally, I stop at an intersection where one of the signs has the right name. Here it is, his street. It is lined with trees; the sun breaks through the treetops in patches, the leaves creating shadows in constant movement, even though today there is no wind.

I'm shaking as I concentrate on keeping the bike upright—I must not fall, must not lose my balance. I want to ride slowly but I can't; due to the instability of the bicycle I have to maintain a certain speed.

Then it appears and at first I don't believe that I'm here, that I have in fact made it, but a number on the wall indicates that this must be it and at first that's all I see, the number, and then I see the house. It's lovely, typically French, thick stone walls, green window shutters and a wrought-iron fence. The way I had imagined it.

But not exactly. Because it's smaller, quite a simple house, the paint is flaking off the walls, the flower beds are untended, the shutters broken and the fence hasn't had a fresh coat of paint for many years.

I stop outside and lower the bike to the ground.

He has a door knocker, not a doorbell—a copper dog's head. I lift my hand, knock once, twice, before releasing it. My hand dangles at my side, my fingers stroking the fabric of my trousers. I wish I could hold on to something, my hand feels so empty, both hands so empty; now is the moment when I should have had the ice.

I listen for footsteps, but hear only insects, birds and the drone of farm machinery in the distance.

I lift my hand again, take hold of the copper dog's head and knock again, harder this time.

Still nothing.

He's not home. Nobody's home.

I collapse on the stoop, suddenly parched. I didn't bring any water. I should have had the ice, a cold lump on my tongue that would melt in my mouth, until my tongue was frozen and numb. I should have had the ice now.

I just sit there like that, completely still, but drifting all the same. A stoop, a closed door, I'm here and nothing has changed. This is it.

But then he comes.

Quick footsteps against the asphalt, that's the first thing I hear—quick, light footsteps. I look up, he's approaching me at a sprint, has already seen me; he's sweating too, he's out running, wearing shorts, a ragged T-shirt and well-worn running shoes that once upon a time were white.

How thin he is, sunken, his face has sharp edges and maybe it's not him after all, maybe I'm not seeing clearly. It can't be him; this wasn't how he was supposed to be. And he's running. I haven't seen him run since he was a child, but now he's running, with a surprising lightness, his feet hitting the ground rhythmically.

It's him and he doesn't stop running, he runs all the way up to me, through the gate. I've stood up without being aware of it, he runs all the way up to me, he's sweating, I can smell it, but it's not a bad odor, just fresh sweat, and I step down off the stoop and stand there facing him.

And then he throws his arms around me.

He throws his arms around me and laughs.

DAVID

We moved into the house that very evening. It was only once we were there, inside the cool stone building, designed to absorb the heat, that I realized how confined and hot the boat had been.

The airiness was a relief. Lou ran through the rooms. So much space, she'd never had so much space before.

She changed her mind three times before she decided where she wanted to sleep. In a floral-patterned attic room begging to be inhabited by a little girl. With lace curtains and soft pillows on the bed.

For a few days ... she would live there. For now.

I poured all the water we had into a transparent plastic container in the kitchen.

We would run out of water sooner now that there were three of us. Much sooner. It wouldn't be enough, it wouldn't last until the rain came.

But we weren't going to live long anyway, and right now, right here, this was the life we had.

Dogs experience time differently from humans. For them, each day is like several weeks, for an ant the days are even longer. That's how I thought, that's how we thought, that was the kind of thing we said to each other, Marguerite and I.

We didn't have the strength to fight any longer, to struggle. We just wanted to be here, together.

The few days that were ours would become a life.

When Lou had gone to bed beneath the flowery sky in the attic, when she had curled up, reveling in the clean sheets, then Marguerite and I came to life.

The energy we had formerly spent on struggling, fighting for our lives, we now applied to one another.

I invested all my strength in her and she invested hers in me. And the heat intensified everything.

We made our way around the house.

We were everywhere. First in the beds. Then on the couch. Against the kitchen counter. In the bathroom, in the dry shower. On the coffee table.

But then an evening came when the heat was intolerable, when it felt impossible to move inside the house.

So we took the blanket outside, lay down on the dry grass, on the ground under the trees, beside the trace of what had once been a brook, while the day slowly faded away.

There we had sex again. Quickly. It was too hot to continue for long.

Afterwards we lay beside each other, breathing hard.

My gaze slid across the darkening landscape. Across trees

releasing dry leaves to the ground. The soon-to-be empty branches, where no birds were singing any longer.

My gaze slid onward, into the darkness between the trunks.

I jumped. Because there she stood. A little, white face. An astonished child's face, which slowly changed as she gradually realized what she had just witnessed.

All at once there were tears in her eyes and she turned around and ran.

Dammit!

"Lou!"

Everything was ruined now, I thought. The last days would be painful. What little time we had left would be turned into something ugly.

I ran behind her through the forest.

I was naked, barefoot. I stepped on something. A stone, it hurt like hell!

I had to stop, bend over to catch my breath.

And when I straightened up again, she was gone.

"Lou? Lou!"

Marguerite came after me. She had pulled on a sweat-shirt and shorts. She handed me the blanket. I wrapped my-self up in it.

"Lou?" Marguerite called.

Again I was thirsty, so thirsty, my mouth so dry. Sweaty, my body was losing fluids with every passing minute.

Then we found her. She was standing completely still a

short distance up the slope leading to the only knoll in the landscape.

I rushed towards her.

"Lou! Wait!"

But when she saw me, she started running again.

"Lou!"

She kept running up the hill.

I was breathing hard, the soles of my feet were already scratched, but I kept my eyes glued to her back as I ran after her.

I didn't catch up with her until we had reached the top. The highest point in the landscape, a bump amidst all the flatness.

It was brighter here. The trees didn't block out the pale evening sky.

I thought she was crying, because she was leaning forward. I thought she was doubled over and sobbing.

But then I discovered that she was busy investigating something on the ground. She knocked one hand against something. It sounded odd. Hollow.

I approached her cautiously.

Leaned down to see what she was looking at.

Large plastic containers. Two rows of them, half buried underground, almost hidden by dried vegetation.

She tried lifting one, but it slipped out of her hands.

I tried helping her and it was heavy. Slippery, solid, hard blue plastic between my hands.

Now Marguerite also joined us. She looked searchingly at Lou, and then at me.

"We've found something," I said. "Lou found something."

Marguerite took hold of another container. She was also startled by how heavy it was.

"Is there something in them?"

"Yes," I said.

Because now we could hear the sound. A sloshing sound from within.

I put the container down on the ground and tried to remove the lid, but it wouldn't budge. My hands were shaking. I found a stick, gave it a try, but it was too thick.

I found another one. It fit. I wriggled it down into the crack between the lid and the container.

Finally it opened.

We leaned over the container, all three of us.

The contents were packed in plastic. I pierced a hole in the packaging with the stick.

Lou poked one finger inside. Lifted it up. Tasted it.

I did the same thing, stuck my hand in, just the way I used to do in the ocean at home. But this time I tasted it.

Water. It was water.

SIGNE

The house is run-down, he is run-down, the grandchildren have only been here on one single occasion, there is no swimming pool and Trine has left for good. I don't ask why.

We go out into the garden. He serves instant coffee, stirring with an unpolished silver spoon until the powder has dissolved.

I sit holding the mug, watching the steam form droplets along the inside of the rim. I hold the other hand over the top and feel how my palm becomes damp from the rising warmth.

"I thought it was you. There's nobody else who could do something like that," he says. "And then I heard you'd been home, that someone had seen *Blue* in the harbor, so then I knew for sure."

"I know of a lot of other people who could have done something like that," I say.

"In your world, sure. You live in another world."

"We live in the same world."

"Do we?"

He smiles.

"Do you think it's ridiculous?" I ask. "That I dumped the ice?"

"No ... I don't think so. I don't think anything you've ever done has been ridiculous."

"But it hasn't done any good," I say.

"You don't know how the world would have been if you hadn't tried," he says.

Neither of us speaks; we drink the coffee. Slowly it cools off and becomes lukewarm.

"You're running," I say.

"Every day," he says. "Had to find something to do."

"What about the garden? The house?"

"What about it?"

"That's the kind of thing retired folk like to do."

"I don't like carpentry. Or gardening."

He studies me over his cup. Again there's laughter in him; his eyes are shining even though he is serious.

"You still want to laugh at me," I say. "You can't stop. People laugh at what they don't understand."

"No," he says. "No, I don't want to laugh at you."

"Well, what is it, then?"

"Signe, don't you understand anything?"

I look at him, don't know what to say, because no, I really don't understand a thing.

"Don't you understand that ... every time I went out running, ever since I started running, no, long before that, for my entire life ... every time I left the house, all the houses I've lived in, all the hotel rooms, every time I left them ... I wished, not always strongly, sometimes it's only been a flicker, but lately stronger and stronger ... every time I wished that when I came back from my trip or from work or from a run, that when I came back ... you would be sitting on the front stoop?"

And then he hugs me again, leans forward and throws his arms around me. I am still holding the coffee cup in my hand, it comes between us—a warm, hard lump of pottery in the middle of the hug—I try to pull it out, we are both clumsy, two thirteen-year-olds.

But when we let go of each other, he keeps his hand on my arm, just leaves it there, as if to confirm that I'm real, and I don't pull away.

"Why did you do it?" I ask.

"What?"

"Why did you approve the ice excavation?"

He draws a breath but doesn't reply.

"Was it so I would come?" I continue. "Was it to provoke me? So I'd come looking for you? Because you knew that I wouldn't be able to resist?"

He hesitates.

"No, Signe, no. I wish that was why. I would like to lie and say that was why. I wish I'd had that idea. You ... you're capable of doing something like that. Not me."

"But why?"

"Because ... I'm the same person I've always been. Because the price of electricity has gone down. Because it was a chance to increase revenues. A chance for continued security. And it probably doesn't make any difference when I say that I've stopped the excavation now. Because the damage is already done."

"Yes," I say. "The damage is already done." But the wind has gone out of my sails.

"And it doesn't help that I've stopped the excavation?"

"I don't know," I say. "I don't know yet."

"… I'm sorry," he says.

"Yes," I say. "You're sorry, but you're still the same person you've always been."

"I guess." He nods. "Just older."

"Me too," I say.

We sit in silence for a while.

"But you're aging well," he says.

He startles me into a near-smile. "Was that a compliment?"

"No. A relevant piece of information."

"Given the circumstances, I would say that it could be interpreted as a compliment."

"So we'll leave room for interpretation."

"Interpretation?"

"Yes."

"I'll think about it."

"Do."

Again we fall silent.

"I brought ice," I say then. "Twelve containers."

We retrieve the ice and stack the containers outside his house.

"What should we do with it?" he asks.

"I don't know," I say.

He places a hand on one of them.

"The containers are nice. Hard, solid plastic."

"Petroleum," I say.

"What?"

"They're made of petroleum."

"And petroleum is made of plants."

"The plastic isn't biodegradable."

"It won't break down."

"For thousands of years."

We leave the containers outside, beside the wall of the house. We don't open them.

I often go to check on *Blue* after breakfast, to take care of her; there's always something, a mooring line that needs replacing, a fender that has slipped out of place, a boat beside her that's too close and banging against the hull.

One day when I get back to the house, the containers are gone. I run out into the garden, but he's not there, I spin around in circles, search everywhere and finally I spot him, far away, on top of a hill he calls a mountain, the highest point in the landscape.

I run into the densely wooded forest, making my way through the trees and the tall grass. Then I reach a path leading upwards. I am out of breath when I finally reach the top.

He is bent over the containers, but when I approach he turns around and smiles. "Here you go."

He has stacked the containers on top of each other—two containers high, two wide, three long—and buried them halfway underground.

He thumps his hand on the container beside him, a slightly hollow sound, and at the same time I can hear the sound of the water inside.

"Don't you want to sit down?" he says.

We can see far into the distance and the landscape is peaceful and well-tended, fields in all directions; nothing is out of place here, there are no aberrations, the house is down below, half hidden amidst the trees. We can see only parts of the red roof, the yard, the brook, we can glimpse the canal amidst all the greenery, a ribbon running through the landscape.

And we just sit there.

Two old people on a bench.

DAVID

I pulled the sheet over Lou, even though it was so hot that she didn't need it.

Then I walked to the door.

"Good night, Lou."

"'Night."

She lay in silence, staring out into the darkness, into herself. And then, without looking at me, she asked:

"Daddy, are you going to do that ... that thing ... again tonight?"

"No," I said. "No. We're not."

And I meant it. This evening we were just going to sit together, Marguerite and I. Because finally we had time.

Lou drew a breath, was about to ask about something, but seemed unable to find the words. I should talk to her about this, I thought. Should say something to help her to understand that it isn't ugly. That it didn't tear us apart, but instead united us.

But I couldn't do this now. Because my mind was full of other thoughts. As was hers.

We'd carried the containers to the house. Twelve containers in all, of clean, clear water, vacuum-packed in plastic, sometime long ago. It took us twelve sweaty trips. Five for Marguerite, seven for me. While Lou ran back and forth between us, chattering excitedly.

The containers were in the middle of the living room.

We had locked the door this evening, for the first time since we moved in. We owned a treasure, twelve treasure chests. Enough water to enable us to survive for a long time. We would have to find food, but that we would manage. As long as we had water, everything was possible.

"Imagine if I wake up in the morning and they're gone," Lou said.

"They won't be," I said.

"But imagine?"

"We locked the door."

"Are you sure?"

"Yes."

"Did you check?"

"Yes."

"Can you double-check, afterwards?"

"... Yes ... fine."

"Promise?"

"I promise."

"Good."

"Good night, Lou."

"Daddy?"

"Yes?"

"I love water."

"Me too."

"Daddy?"

"Yes."

"Can we play it one more time?"

"The rain game?"

"Yes, yes! The rain game."

"Lou, it's late."

"Please?"

And it wasn't hard to convince me. Because I loved this game too.

I went back into her room and sat on the edge of the bed. She lay quietly waiting, but I could see how tense her body was. Her eyes were wide open; she didn't look the least bit tired.

"Start, then," she said.

"Yes," I said. "Close your eyes."

She closed them.

"It's morning and you're in bed and asleep," I said.

"I'm sleeping," she said and snored loudly.

"It's completely silent," I said. "But then you hear sounds on the roof. It's the sounds that wake you up."

"No," she said and opened her eyes. "There aren't any sounds yet. Because it doesn't start with real rain."

"No, you're right," I said. "That's how it was. It starts with drizzle."

"And drizzle isn't proper rain."

"Drizzle just hangs in the air. Almost like fog."

"And I wake up," she said.

"You wake up all on your own," I said. "Then you go downstairs to see me."

"Because now you're awake, too."

She sat up in the bed.

"We go outside together. And Marguerite comes too," Lou said.

"Outside we can feel how there is a drizzle in the air," I said. "Almost like fog."

"We see how droplets of moisture form on the leaves."

Lou turned her head towards the ceiling. "I think it's raining, I say."

"Yes, I say."

"Then we sit down and wait."

We sat side by side on the bed, both of us staring at the ceiling.

"Gradually it rains harder," I said. "It gets stronger. The drops get bigger. And we can hear them."

"We hear them," Lou said.

"Do you remember the sound of rain?" I asked.

"Yes," she said. She thought about it some more. "... No."

I drummed my fingertips against the night table, a gentle tapping. "Like this."

She nodded. "That's how it was." She lay her little hand down beside my own and drummed as well.

"A heavy downpour," I said and made my fingertips hit the

wooden tabletop harder. "The rain pours down harder and harder. The drops become larger and heavier."

"They're huge," Lou said.

"It's never quiet. It splashes. Gushes. Drips. Pours. The days pass. We fall asleep and wake up to the sound of rain on the rooftop. We have to raise our voices when we talk to drown out the noise of millions of drops constantly hitting the house, the ground, the trees."

She curls up beside me.

"It's pouring down," I continue. "The rain connects everything. The air is full of water. And the canal changes. The drops hit the bottom, penetrating dry leaves, breaking up the hard soil."

"And what are we going to do every morning?" she asked. "Say what we're going to do every morning."

"Every morning," I say, "we run down to the canal. We stand on the bank and look at how much the water has risen in the course of the night. And we see what happens to the boat."

"Yes?"

"Soon the water level reaches the hull. The keel is submerged. The water keeps rising. Until the boat is no longer aground. Till we have to moor it to the canal bank."

"And I, like, catch hold of the line."

"You catch the mooring line when I throw it and you tie it tightly to a big tree."

"With a lot of knots."

"Yes."

"So the boat doesn't sail away."

"And then, one morning we find the cradle floating on the surface of the water. Gravity no longer holds the boat in place."

"Gravity?"

"The force that keeps us on the ground. That makes things fall down. Not up. And when that happens, when the boat is floating, then it's ready for us."

"Then we get on board."

"We pack our things and get on board."

"All three of us."

"And I start the engine."

"No, I start the engine."

"You start the engine."

"Then we sail away."

"The boat glides slowly through the canals. We pass through the sluices. Towards Bordeaux. Towards the coast."

"And I get to steer."

"You get to steer."

"We're not in a hurry. We watch the landscape around us. How it changes. How everything has turned green. The water has infused all the grayness with color. The ground is no longer dusty, but safe, solid. The trees are no longer black, they are sprouting leaves. And then we notice something new in the air. You're sitting on deck when I first become sure. I walk over to you and Marguerite takes the tiller. I sit down with you. Pull you towards me."

I put my arm around her, felt her body against mine, fragile, but still alive, heard her breathing, a child's eager and slightly irregular breathing.

"Keep going," she whispered.

"Then you notice it too," I said. "That something is about to happen. At first we think we're just imagining it. But the longer we sit there, the more certain we become. And you look up at me, sort of to ask me if I am feeling the same thing as you are. And I nod."

"Yes?"

"There's something different in the air. The dry, dusty air that always makes your throat scratchy clears up. It's easy to breathe. We move into something else. We're on our way. We will get there. Everything is fresh. Everything is clear. Everything is new. But all the same, familiar. Because we recognize this smell. This air, this dampness, the openness. It's what we came from. That's how the air was at home."

"Home."

"Do you feel it? I will ask you. Can you smell the air? Do you smell the scent of salt?"

ACKNOWLEDGMENTS

A big thank-you to the people who contributed their expertise to the novel: hydrologist Lena Merete Tallaksen, former construction manager and spreader base Ole Bjørn Helberg, Communications leader Anne Gravdahl and professional consultant Dag Endre Opedal at the Norwegian Vasskraft- og Industristad museum, production manager at Istad Kraft AS Geir Blakstad, Carl Erick Fuglesang in Profinor, Geir Blakstad, zoologist Petter Bøckman, technical advisor Christian Børs Lind and former General Secretary Per Flatberg of Friends of the Earth Norway, firefighter Jørund Lothe Salvesen, general manager Jonas Ådnøy Holmqvist in Fivas, senior advisor Ellen Hofsvang in the Rainforest Foundation, and author Erik Martiniussen. Thanks also to my wise editors Nora Campbell and Hilde Rød-Larsen, as well as the entire staff at Aschehoug and Oslo Literary Agency who work with professionalism and enthusiasm for my books every single day.

Special thanks to the organization A Drop in the Ocean, which made it possible to visit the refugee camp Skaramangás in Athens; to volunteer Anne-Lene Bjørklund for her invaluable help, and to all who showed me around and welcomed me with open arms: Nanci Vogel Clifton, Hesham Jreeda, Fahimzia Ahmadi, Halitim Mohamed Rafik, Sam Aloso, and Sayed Hashimi. And especially thanks to Jack, who invited me to his 12th birthday.

Last, and most importantly, a big thank-you to Kari Ronge, Stein Lunde, and Gunn Østgård, who have shared their lives and their knowledge, both on land and at sea, and to Steinar Storløkken, Jesper, Jens, and Linus for being my life.

Loved *The End of the Ocean*?

Read on for an extract from Maja Lunde's
international bestseller

THE
HISTORY
OF
BEES

TAO

District 242, Shirong, Sichuan, 2098

Like oversize birds, we balanced on our respective branches, each of us with a plastic container in one hand and a feather brush in the other.

I climbed upwards, very slowly, as carefully as I could. I was not cut out for this, wasn't like many of the other women on the crew, my movements were often too heavy-handed. I lacked the subtle motor skills and precision required. This wasn't what I was made for, but all the same I had to be here, every single day, twelve hours a day.

The trees were as old as a lifetime. The branches were as fragile as thin glass, they cracked beneath our weight. I twisted myself carefully, mustn't damage the tree. I placed my right foot on a branch even further up, and carefully pulled the left up behind it. And finally I found a secure working position, uncomfortable but stable. From here I could reach the uppermost flowers.

The little plastic container was full of the gossamer gold, carefully weighed out. I tried to transfer invisible portions lightly out of the container and over into the trees. Each individual blossom was to be dusted with the tiny brush of hen feathers, from hens scientifically cultivated for precisely this purpose. No feathers of artificial fibers had proven nearly as effective. It had been tested, and then tested again, because we had had plenty of time—in my district the tradition of hand pollination was more than a hundred years old. The bees here had disappeared back in the 1980s, long before The Collapse; pesticides had done away with them. A few years later, when the pesticides were no longer in use, the bees returned, but by then hand pollination had already been implemented. The results were better, even though an incredible number of people, an incredible number of hands were required. And so, when The Collapse came, my district had a competitive edge. It had paid off to be the ones who polluted the most. We were a pioneer nation in pollution and so we became a pioneer nation in pollination. A paradox had saved us.

I stretched as far as I could, but couldn't quite reach the blossom at the very top. I was about to give up, but knew I might be punished, so I tried once more. Our pay was docked if we used up the pollen too quickly. And our pay was docked if we used too little. The work was invisible. When at the end of the day we climbed down from the trees, there was no evidence of our work except for the red chalk *X*'s on the tree trunks, ideally up to forty trees each day. It wasn't until autumn came and the trees were laden with fruit that we would know who among us had actually succeeded in their work. And by then we had usually forgotten which trees had been dusted by whom.

I was assigned to Field 748 today. Out of how many? I didn't know. My group was one of hundreds. In our beige work uniforms we were just as anonymous as the trees. And just as close together as the flowers. Never alone, always together in a flock, up here in the trees, or wandering down the tire ruts from one field to the next. Only behind the walls of our own small flats could we be alone, a few short hours a day. Our whole lives were out here.

It was quiet. We weren't allowed to speak while we worked. The only sound to be heard was that of our careful movements in the trees, a faint clearing of the throat, some yawns and the material of our uniforms against the tree trunks. And sometimes the sound we had all learned to dislike—a branch creaking and in the worst case breaking. A broken branch meant less fruit, and yet another reason to dock our pay.

Otherwise only the wind was audible, passing through branches, brushing across the blossoms, slipping through the grass on the ground.

A fly buzzed through the air, a rare sight. It had been several days since I had seen a bird, there were fewer of them as well. They hunted the few insects to be found, and starved, like the rest of the world.

But then an earsplitting sound broke the silence. It was the whistle from the management's barracks, the signal for the second and final break of the day. I noticed immediately how parched my tongue was.

I climbed down with awkward caution. My workmates and I crept down from the trees to the ground. The other women had already begun chatting, as if their cacophonic prattle was flipped on like a switch the split second they knew that they could.

I said nothing, concentrating on getting down without breaking a branch. I managed it. Pure luck. I was infinitely clumsy, had been working out here long enough to know that I would never be really good at the job.

On the ground beside the tree was a beat-up metal water bottle. I grabbed it and drank quickly. The water was lukewarm and tasted of aluminum, the taste made me drink less than I needed.

Two young boys dressed in white from the Trade Commission rapidly distributed the reusable tin boxes containing the second meal of the day. I sat down by myself with my back against the tree trunk and opened mine. The rice was mixed with corn today. I ate quickly. As usual, a bit too salty, and seasoned with artificially manufactured chili pepper and soy. It had been a long time since I had tasted meat. Animal feed required too much arable land. And a lot of the traditional animal feed required pollination. The animals weren't worth our painstaking handiwork.

The tin box was empty before I was full. I stood up and put it back in the return basket from the Trade Commission. Then I jogged in place. My legs were tired, but nonetheless stiff from standing still in locked positions up there in the trees. My blood tingled; I couldn't stand still.

But it didn't help. I took a quick look around me. Nobody from management was paying attention. I quickly lay down on the ground, just to stretch out my back. It was aching after having been bent over in the same position for a long time.

I closed my eyes for a moment, tried to shut out the conversation of the other women of the crew, instead listening to how the chatter rose and fell in volume. This need to talk, all of them at the same time, where did it come from? The other women had started when they were little girls. Hour after hour of group conversations where the subject was always of the lowest common denominator and one could never really go into depth about anything. Perhaps with the exception of when the one being talked about wasn't there.

Personally I preferred one-on-one conversations. Or my own company, for that matter. At work, often the latter. At home I had Kuan, my husband. Not that we had the longest conversations, either, conversation wasn't what held us together. Kuan's references were here and now, he was concrete, didn't crave knowledge, something more. But in his arms I found peace. And then we had Wei-Wen, our three-year-old. *Him* we could talk about.

Just as the cacophony had almost sung me to sleep, it suddenly fell silent. Everyone was quiet.

I sat up. The others on the crew were facing the road.

The entourage was walking down the tire ruts and towards us.

They were no more than eight or nine years old. I recognized several of them from Wei-Wen's school. All of them had been given identical work clothes, the same synthetic beige uniforms that we were wearing, and they walked towards us as quickly as their short legs could carry them. Two adult leaders kept them in line. One in front, one behind. Both of them were equipped with powerful voices that corrected the children without cease, but they did not reprimand them, giving instructions with warmth and compassion, because even though the children had not yet fully taken in where they were headed, the adults knew.

The children walked hand in hand, in mismatched pairs, the tallest with the shortest, the older children taking care of the younger. An uneven gait, disorganized, but the hands held on tight as if they were glued together. Perhaps they had been given strict instructions not to let go.

Their eyes were on us, on the trees. Curious, wrinkling their noses a bit, cocking their heads. As if they were here for the first time, even though all of them had grown up in the district and didn't know of any kind of nature other than the endless rows of fruit trees, against the shadow of the overgrown forest in the south. A short girl looked at me for a long time, with big, slightly close-set eyes. She blinked a few times, then sniffed loudly. She held a skinny boy by the hand. He yawned loudly and unabashedly, didn't lift his free hand to his mouth, wasn't even aware that his face stretched open into a gaping hole. He wasn't yawning as an expression of boredom; he was too young for that. It was the shortage of food that caused his fatigue. A tall, frail girl held a little boy by the hand. He was breathing heavily through a stuffed-up nose, with his mouth open, missing both front teeth. The tall girl pulled him behind her while she turned her face towards the sun, squinted and wrinkled her nose, but kept her head in the same position, as if to get some color, or perhaps glean strength.

They arrived every spring, the new children. But were they usually so small? Were they younger this time?

No. They were eight. As they always were. Finished with their schooling. Or . . . well, they learned numbers and some characters, but beyond that school was only a kind of regulated storage system. Storage and preparation for life out here. Exercises in sitting quietly for a long time. *Sit still. Completely still, that's right.* And exercises to develop fine motor skills. They wove carpets from the age of three. Their small fingers were ideally suited for work with complex patterns. Just as they were perfect for the work out here.

The children passed us, turned their faces to the front, towards other trees. Then they walked on, towards another field. The boy without teeth stumbled a bit, but the tall girl held his hand tightly, so he didn't fall. The parents were not here, but they took care of one another.

The children disappeared down along the tire rut, drowned between the trees.

"Where are they going?" a woman from my crew asked.

"I don't know," another replied.

"Probably towards forty-nine or fifty," a third said. "Nobody has started there yet."

My stomach twisted into a knot. Where they were going, which field they were headed for, made no difference. It was *what* they were going to do that—

The whistle sounded from the barracks. We climbed up again. My heart pounded, even though I wasn't out of breath. For the children had not grown smaller. It was Wei-Wen . . . In five years he would be eight. In just five years. Then it would be his turn. The hardworking hands were worth more out here than anywhere else. The small fingers, already accustomed to weaving carpets, trained in fine motor skills every single day at school, already fine-tuned for this type of work.

Eight-year-olds out here, day in and day out, stiffened small bodies in the trees. Not even an excuse for a childhood, as my peers and I had had. We had gone to school until we were fifteen.

A non-life.

My hands shook as I lifted the hand holding the precious dust. We all had to work to acquire food, it was said, to make the food we would eat ourselves. Everyone had to contribute, even the children. Because who needs an education when the wheat stores are diminishing? When the rations become smaller and smaller with each passing month? When one must go to bed hungry in the evenings?

I turned around to reach the blossoms behind me, but this time my movements were too abrupt. I hit a branch that I had not noticed, suddenly lost my balance and leaned heavily over to the other side.

And that did it. The cracking sound we had come to hate. The sound of a branch breaking.

The supervisor came quickly towards me. She looked up into the tree and assessed the damage without saying anything. Quickly she wrote something down on a pad of paper before leaving again.

The branch was neither large nor strong, but I knew all the same that my entire surplus for this month would vanish. The money that was supposed to go into the tin box in the kitchen cupboard where we saved every single yuan we could spare.

I drew a breath. I couldn't think about it. I couldn't do anything but keep going. Lift my hand, dip the brush into the pollen, move it carefully towards the blossoms, brush across them as if I were a bee.

I avoided looking at my watch. Knew it wouldn't help. I only knew that with each flower I moved the brush across, the evening came a bit closer. And the one hour I had every day with my child. That tiny hour was all we had, and in that tiny hour perhaps I could make a difference. Sow a seed that would give him the opportunity that I myself never had.

WILLIAM

Maryville, Hertfordshire, England, 1851

Everything around me was yellow. Endlessly yellow. It was over me, under me, around me. Blinding me. The yellow color was completely real, nothing I was imagining. It came from the brocade tapestry my wife, Thilda, had stuck up on the walls when we moved in a few years ago. We'd had a lot of space at that time. My little seed shop on Maryville's main street was thriving. I was still inspired, still thought I would manage to combine the business with that which really meant something, my natural science research. But that was a long time ago. Long before we became the parents of an inordinate number of daughters. And a very long time before the final conversation with Professor Rahm.

Had I known the kind of anguish the yellow tapestry would cause, I would never have gone along with it. The yellow color did not settle for remaining on the tapestry. If I closed my eyes, or kept them open, it was there, every bit as furious. It followed me into my sleep and never let me get away, it was like the sun's highlights from foliage in the forest. The color kept forcing me to return there, to the forest of my childhood. In there I became blind to the rest of the world.

I forced my eyes open, did not want to go in there again. Compelled myself to be present. To listen.

It was late afternoon; from the kitchen the sound of the rattling of pots and the burner rings being moved about on the stove could be heard. Perhaps it was the sound of food being prepared that awakened my stomach, twisting it into knots. I collapsed into a fetal position.

I looked around. An untouched piece of bread and a dried slice of cured ham lay on a plate beside the half-empty water glass. When had I last eaten?

I sat up halfway, grabbed the glass of water. Let it run through my mouth and down my throat, washing away the taste of old age.

The saltiness of the ham was rancid on my tongue; the bread dark and heavy. The food found its way to my stomach, which settled.

But I still could not find a comfortable position in bed. My back was one large blister, my hips worn to the bone from lying on my side.

An agitation in my legs, a prickling.

The house was all of a sudden silent. Had they all left? Nothing but the crackling of coke burning in the hearth. But then, suddenly, singing. Clear voices from the garden.

Hark! the herald angels sing

Glory to the newborn King

Would it be Christmas soon?

In recent years, the region's different choirs had begun singing at people's doors during Advent, not for money or gifts, but in the spirit of Christmas, solely to bring joy to others. There was a time when I'd found it beautiful, when these small performances could ignite a light in me that I was no longer certain existed. It felt ever so long ago.

The bright voices flowed towards me like meltwater:

Peace on earth and mercy mild

God and sinners reconciled

I placed my feet on the floor. Beneath the soles of my feet it felt unusually hard. I myself was the infant, the newborn, whose feet were not yet accustomed to the ground, but instead still shaped for dancing on my toes. That's how I remembered Edmund's feet, with a high instep and just as soft and arched underneath as on top. I could stand with them in my hands, just look and feel, as one did with one's firstborn. I thought that I would become something else for him, *be something else for you*, something else entirely, than my father had been for me. That's how I stood with him until Thilda snatched him away from me under the pretext of a feeding or diaper change. The infant feet moved slowly towards the window. Every step hurt. The window grew before me, huge and white.

Then I saw them.

All seven of them. For it wasn't a choir of strangers from the village. It was my own daughters.

The four tallest in the back, the three shorter ones in the front. Dressed in their dark winter clothes. Wool coats, too tight and too short, or too big and with ever more patches, the threadbare quality disguised behind cheap ribbons and pockets in odd places. Brown, dark blue or black wool bonnets with white lace trim framed narrow, winter-pale faces. The song became frost in the air before them.

How thin they had grown, all of them.

A path showed where they had walked, footsteps through deep snow. They must have waded through it far above the knees and had certainly gotten wet. I could feel the sensation of damp wool stockings against bare skin, and the frost penetrating up from the ground through the thin soles of their shoes—none of them had more than this one pair of boots. I walked closer to the window. I half expected to see others in the garden, an audience for the choir, Thilda, or perhaps some of the neighbors. But the garden was empty. They weren't singing for anyone. They were singing for me.

Light and life to all He brings
Risen with healing in His wings

All of their gazes were focused intently on my window, but they had not yet discovered me. I stood in the shadows, at the back of the room, and the sun shone on the windowpane. They probably could only see the reflection of the sky and the trees.

Born to raise the sons of earth
Born to give them second birth

I took one step closer.

Fourteen-year-old Charlotte, my eldest daughter, was standing at the far end. Her eyes were on the window, but she was singing with all of her body. Her chest rose and fell in time with the melody. Perhaps it was her idea, all of it. She had always sung, hummed her way through childhood, with her head in her schoolwork or bent over the dishes, a melodious murmuring, as if the soft notes were a part of her movements.

She was the one who discovered me first. A light slid across her face.

She nudged Dorothea, the precocious twelve-year-old. She quickly nodded to eleven-year-old Olivia, who turned her wide-open eyes towards her twin sister, Elizabeth. The two did not in any sense resemble each other in appearance, only in temperament. Both gentle and kind, and dumb as posts—they couldn't understand arithmetic even if you were to nail the numbers onto their foreheads. In front of them a restlessness had begun in the ranks. The young ones were also about to discover me. Nine-year-old Martha squeezed seven-year-old Caroline's arm. And Caroline, who always sulked because she really wanted to be the youngest, gave little Georgiana, who would have liked to have escaped being the youngest, a hard shove. No great cheer to the heavens above, they didn't allow themselves that, not yet. Only the slightest irregularity in the singing betrayed that they had seen me. That, and weak smiles, to the extent that their singing, O-shaped mouths would allow.

A childish lump pushed forward in my chest. They did not sing badly. Not at all. Their narrow faces glowed, their eyes shone. They had arranged it all just for me. And now they thought that they had succeeded. That they had pulled it off—they had gotten father out of bed. When the song was over they would release the cheer. They would run jubilantly light-footed through the freshly fallen snow into the house and tell me about their own homespun miracle. We sang him well again, they would crow. We sang father well!

A cacophony of enthusiastic girls' voices would echo in the hallways, bouncing back at them from the walls: *Soon he will return. Soon he will be with us again. We showed him God, Jesus—the born-again. Hark, the herald angels sing, glory to the newborn king. What a brilliant, yes, truly dazzling idea it was to sing for him, to remind him of beauty, of the message of Christmas, of everything he had forgotten while bedridden, with the thing we call illness, but which everyone knows is something else entirely, although mother forbids us to speak about it. Poor Father, he is not well, he is as thin as a ghost, we have seen it, through the cracked-open door as we have crept past, yes, like a ghost, just skin and bones, and the beard he has let grow, like the crucified Jesus. He is beyond recognition. But now he will soon be among us once more, soon he will be able to work again. And we will once more have butter on our bread and new winter coats. That is in truth a real Christmas present. Christ is born in Bethlehem!* But it was a lie. I couldn't give them that gift. I did not deserve their cheers. The bed drew me towards it. My legs trembled, my new-born legs were unable to hold me upright any longer. My stomach knotted again. I gritted my teeth, wanted to crush the pressure in my throat. So I slowly pulled away from the window.

And outside the singing subsided. There would be no miracle today.

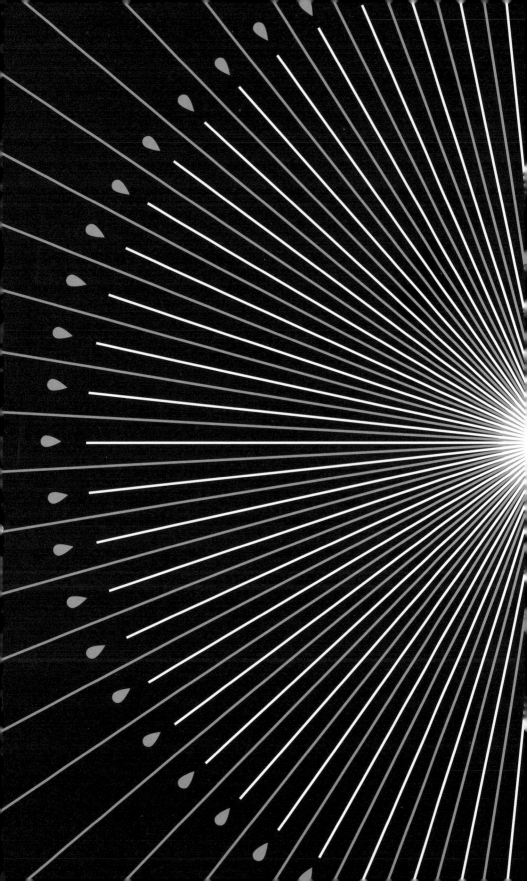